HOME
for
CHRISTMAS

Also by Courtney Cole

The Christmas Dress

HOME
for
CHRISTMAS
A Novel

COURTNEY COLE

AVON
An Imprint of HarperCollinsPublishers

HOME FOR CHRISTMAS. Copyright © 2022 by Courtney Cole. All rights reserved. Printed in the United States of America. No part of this book may be used or reproduced in any manner whatsoever without written permission except in the case of brief quotations embodied in critical articles and reviews. For information, address HarperCollins Publishers, 195 Broadway, New York, NY 10007.

FIRST EDITION

Designed by Diahann Sturge

Garland image throughout © Yellowj / Shutterstock

Library of Congress Cataloging-in-Publication Data has been applied for.

ISBN: 978-0-06-321689-1

22 23 24 25 26 LSC 10 9 8 7 6 5 4 3 2 1

To my family. You are my legacy,
my everything, my home.

HOME
for
CHRISTMAS

CHAPTER ONE

From the air, my family's lodge and the surrounding property sprawls amid snow-covered evergreen trees and mountainous rock.

On any given day, you can see bear, elk, moose, deer, coyotes, snowshoe rabbits, or cougars roaming the mountain. On any given night, you can hear mountain lions screaming or snow owls screeching. To someone who isn't used to it, it can be terrifying.

To those of us who live in Alaska, it's home.

But either way, it's breathtaking.

Especially now, with the Christmas lights aglow on every surface of the house and holly boughs hanging from the wraparound log porch. It's a welcome retreat, one that wealthy hunters pay us big bucks to fly them into.

I grab the radio and punch the button, high on the joy of flight, because it never gets old. Not ever.

"Shelly, tell the Norton party that we'll be landing in two minutes. It's time for seat belts."

"Already done, Cap!" she chirps.

Our plane, a fully loaded Cessna Citation Latitude, descends smoothly to the strip below. I guide us in for a landing with the hands of a master. There's nary a bump as we touch down.

I smile. *Skills. I haz 'em.*

Shelly joins me as we lower the steps and wait to greet our passengers.

"Welcome to Great Expectations Lodge," I tell the group as they descend the stairs. The four of them look alike, all wearing expensive jeans and parkas, top-of-the-line boots . . . all of which match their outrageously priced equipment that is currently stowed in the belly of the plane. "We hope you'll enjoy your stay."

Hank Norton, the CEO of a multibillion-dollar company, and the leader of this team of powerful C-suite executives, pulls me along by the elbow as we head for the lodge.

One of his men quickens his pace to keep up.

"This is your family home, correct?" he asks, his nose red from the cold. "Isn't that what you said, Hank?"

Hank nods. "That's exactly what I said." He turns to me. "I was telling Paul a bit of the story of this place earlier. Paul is my CFO, and he's easily intrigued by corporations that have outlasted time."

I smile. "Well, I don't know that I'd refer to it as a corporation, but Great Expectations has certainly been in my family for generations. My great-great-great-grandfather built it in the eighteen hundreds. At first it was a home, and when the Depression hit, my family used it to rent out rooms. It's been a bed-and-breakfast, a hotel, a home, and most currently, it's a host to amazing folks like you as you hunt for your next prized game trophy."

He winks at me. "Oh, I'm gonna do my best, I can tell you that, young lady. I'm looking for an Imperial bull this year. The elk I got last year was good, but it was only a six-point Royal. Jenkins over there says that he got an eight-point Monarch last year in Alaska. I'm gonna beat that."

I hide my flinch, as I think about the stunning Imperial I had seen standing on the snow-covered mountain just yesterday. It was so majestic, so beautiful . . . It makes me sick to think of it being hunted for sport. But as my gran always said, *Buck up, Piper. This is our family business.*

"I'm sure you'll find one," I tell him, swallowing my dismay as we stroll up the wide stone steps and onto the wraparound porch. "I saw one myself just yesterday."

Mr. Norton crows and yells back at his friends, "I call dibs, fellas!"

They laugh, and Mr. Norton hums "Rockin' Around the Christmas Tree" as they tumble into the foyer of the lodge.

Hank holds the door open for me, confident in the way that the ultra-wealthy are, although every once in a while, there are hints that he might not have always been rich. He'd grabbed his own carry-on bag, for instance, instead of leaving it for someone else.

He also easily chats with my staff, something that few powerful men seem to do.

Ellen, our housekeeper/hostess, takes their coats and offers them drinks. White Christmas lights twinkle from high above, hanging lazily from the cathedral ceilings and exposed beams. A massive blue spruce stands in the corner, lit up for the holidays, a golden gleaming star on top, but no presents beneath.

Not this year. I swallow hard.

I try to slip away, handing the men off to Ellen's capable hands, but Mr. Norton catches me.

"Wait, young lady," he calls. "Where's your gran? I was expecting her when we landed. She always waits for us out front with hot brandy."

I nod to Ellen, a signal to go fetch that particular drink, then I clear my throat, trying to swallow the lump that lingers there.

"Um. I'm so sorry. Gran passed away a few weeks ago, I'm afraid. But I assure you, your experience here will be just as good as it's always been. I've been working here since I was a kid. I know all the ropes."

"Oh, I know you," he tells me. "I've watched you grow up over the years, although in my head you still have knobby knees and pigtails. Time can be cruel. In my head, *I'm* still twenty-five." He looks at me, sympathy gleaming in his cloudy eyes. "I'm sorry about Marina. She was one hell of a woman."

"That she was," I agree.

"One year, when I was here, she and I sat out in the barn to see who could drink the most tequila without passing out."

I grin, a real one, which is odd, since my grief has prevented genuine joy lately. "That definitely sounds like her," I tell him. "Who won?"

He wrinkles his head. "It's the damndest thing . . . After drinking a fifth and a half, I don't remember!"

He roars with laughter and I chuckle.

"Well, to be fair, Gran weighed ninety pounds soaking wet. So I think you might've had a little bit of an advantage, Mr. Norton."

He laughs again, and his group heckles him for trying to outdrink such a lightweight.

"Now, now, none of that," he tells them. "She was no ordinary woman. That Marina was . . . well, she was . . ."

"Something else," I finish for him, nodding my head. "It's been said. And it's true."

Everyone laughs.

"Well, you've certainly done her proud. I've never seen a better pilot," he tells me. "And I don't hand out compliments often."

"No, he doesn't," the younger man to his left interjects. "My dad rarely, if ever, offers praise." There's a bit of bitterness in his eyes, and I wonder if he's ever been the recipient of his father's praise.

"Oh, pish," Mr. Norton answers dismissively. "I praise someone when they earn it, Josh."

Josh's cheeks flare a dramatic shade of red, and I try once again to slip away.

"Marina was so proud of you," Hank continues, and he's got ahold of my arm again. "There were a few years when I'd come here and you were gone for pilot's training. She talked about you nonstop and almost glowed from pride."

"Really?" I ask. "She didn't dole out compliments often either."

"She did when they were warranted," he corrects me with a grin. "Just like me." He winks now, and I blush.

"Well, thank you. Sometimes . . . I feel that I disappointed her by choosing to fly."

"She knew why you wanted that, my dear," he says, more

quietly now. "When your parents died, it hit her hard, but I'm sure you knew that. She didn't talk about it much, but when you chose to become a pilot to honor them . . . well, she could not have been more proud."

I'd like to think that was true. But I know, deep down, that it pained her. A plane crash took my parents, and Gran hated the idea that the same thing could happen to me.

"Ellen will take care of anything you need," I tell them, steering the subject away from memories. "A hearty breakfast will be served at six A.M., to get you off to a good start for your first day of hunting."

"Thanks, Captain," he tells me with a wink. He presses a handful of cash into my hand. "Have yourself a merry Christmas."

"Sir, you don't need to tip," I tell him. "It's my pleasure, really."

"Call me Hank," he answers. "And buy yourself something nice. You deserve it. And don't try telling me your grandmother wouldn't take it. It's how she bought that Bobcat out back. It's a long story, but let's just say . . . I lost a bet."

He winks and follows the rest of his party to the lounge bar with Ellen, and I head back out into the snow to help Shelly with the luggage. As I do, I eye the faded edge of that old Bobcat poking around the corner of the lodge.

Hank had supplied the money for that?

Gran was full of surprises . . . and I doubt I'll ever learn them all.

Judging from the heft of the money in my pocket, I'm sure I'll be having a *very* happy holiday. Perhaps even a Louis Vuitton–sized holiday. My smile widens as I join Shelly.

She instantly narrows her eyes, pausing as she loads luggage onto the trolley.

"Why are you smiling? If you think you get Josh for the week, you're wrong. I already called him."

I don't want Josh. He likely has too big of a chip on his shoulder for my taste, but I don't tell her that. Instead, I play along.

"You can't call someone unless I can hear it," I tell her, feigning indignance. "Otherwise, it doesn't count."

"Piper Millicent McCauley," she says seriously, full-naming me. "*I called him.* Did you see the cheekbones on that guy?"

I shake my head. "No. I guess I missed them while he was sticking his nose in the air to pout."

"He's a bit spoiled," Shelly acknowledges. "But that's to be expected with someone that rich. He can hardly help it."

"I've known lots of rich people who aren't like that," I tell her. "You can do better."

"I'm not marrying the guy. I just want him this week. Do you concede?" Shelly's red eyebrow raises as she waits. I nod.

"Shelly, when have you ever known me to hook up with a guest? Go ahead, I'll wait while you think."

She rolls her eyes.

"Shel, when we say we're full-service, we don't want there to be misunderstandings." She laughs, and I can see my breath in the air as we push the heavy trolley up to the four-car garage. I tap in the code and wait as a door opens. The warmth hits my face immediately.

"Lord, it's cold this weekend," I say absently, as we cross through to the back entrance to unload.

"It's gonna get down into the negatives," Shelly answers. "I already warned the Nortons."

"Good. They've got to be prepared. Hypothermia could set in in a matter of minutes if they don't pay attention to what we tell them. Make sure they pack provisions . . . heated pads for gloves and feet, flares, et cetera. Who's taking them out?"

"Pete was going to," she answers. "But they changed their mind and want to be self-led. Mr. Norton has been here so many times, your gran would've said it's okay."

She's right. Gran had faith in the regulars, the ones who returned year after year. But even still, something feels wrong in the air tonight. Whether it's the enormous yellow moon that hangs close to the horizon or the nearly starless sky . . . something feels amiss, almost eerie.

"Can't you feel that?" I ask her. "It's like . . . electricity in the air. Something feels off. I don't know . . . I think maybe Pete should take them."

She shakes her head. "It's just the full moon, weirdo. The pull of gravity or some crap. More babies get born during full moons. And more crazies get taken to the emergency room."

"Exactly," I tell her. "We don't want anyone having to get medevaced. That would *not* help us solidify our reputation without Gran."

Shelly turns to me and squeezes my arms lightly. "Piper, I know you're worried. But Great Expectations has a sterling reputation. The clients here have seen you every year for a long time. They trust you . . . even without Marina." Her normally sharp eyes soften. "You're doing great, babe. Truly."

"Thank you," I murmur. "Some days, I still feel like I'm in

shock and I'm just stumbling through. I worry that people will notice I'm just phoning it in."

"You're not phoning it in," she argues. "You just feel like you are. You're amazing at your job, and everyone knows it."

"I don't know," I say. "I heard Dan tell Pete the other day that he thinks I should've taken more time off to grieve."

Shelly roll her eyes. "Dan always has great advice for everyone else. Yet you notice that he's a lifelong grumpy bachelor who lives in a one-room cabin in the woods like the Unabomber."

I have to laugh. "He even kinda looks like that guy," I tell her. We giggle together. "But, he's the best mechanic around, and he knows this area like the back of his hand. I'll put up with his . . . eccentricities."

"That's one word for it," Shelly mutters. We giggle again. "He's a million years old. I don't know why your gran kept him so long."

"He's got a good heart," I tell her. "Somewhere in there."

"*Deep* in there." She nods.

"And he's just always been so loyal to Gran. He took it hard when she died, so I know that he does have a heart in there."

"He was always good to your gran," Shel replies. "Do you think they ever hooked up?"

The thought is mortifying. "No," I say stiffly. "Ew."

Shelly shrugs. "I'm just saying. They were about the same age, I think, although it's hard to tell now." She shivers briefly. "And this is Alaska. Maybe at some point they just got lonely and—"

"Shut. It. I just threw up in my mouth."

She giggles.

"Besides. She only loved my grandfather her entire life. I think he was even her first love. She never stopped loving him. Even after he died."

Shelly's face softens. "They really did have an amazing love story. She adored him."

"So there were no *Dan hookups.*" We both pause to shiver. "Let's talk about more important things. Should we grab a bottle of Merlot and head out to the loft, or . . . should we grab the tequila and sit in the hot tub? I kinda feel like soaking this day off."

Shelly grins. "I'm always up for tequila," she tells me. "As you know. However, and I don't want to sound trampy here, Josh gave me *that look* earlier. I think I'll go see if he needs turn-down service."

"You're incorrigible," I answer. "Seriously."

She beams, as though it were a compliment. "Thank you!"

"He's a spoiled rich boy," I tell her. "And as a guest, he's off-limits. So . . . no."

She lifts an eyebrow. "No?"

I shake my head. "Absolutely not. I know that you've bent the rules in the past, but now that Gran is gone, I have to prove myself, Shel. We have to be serious about this. Do not do anything unprofessional. You're going to have to restrain yourself."

"Fine. I'll just go to bed early," she says, and she thinks she's sneaky.

"I'm onto you," I tell her. "You're not going to his room, Shel."

She groans. "Fine. I'll just go put a hair mask on my hair, then, Grinchy."

She disappears into the lodge, and I ponder whether I should just take a long hot bath with a cup of cocoa.

The fireplace beckons me, though, and I follow Shelly inside and grab a bottle of Merlot from behind the bar.

The tall wing-back chair welcomes me, and the fire toasts my cheeks as I soak up the warmth. Sometimes, after being outdoors in the snow, a person can feel frozen to their bones.

The wine will help that.

I uncork it with a pop, and fill my wineglass to the rim while I softly sing a Christmas carol.

As I sip, I focus on the liquid turning my chest warm and flushing my cheeks. Above the mantel, a picture hangs of my great-grandparents, Sophie and Eberdale, standing on the steps of this very lodge with my gran at their side. She's eighteen or so in the picture, and she's black-and-white and two-dimensional. She looks somber, as do her parents. Why do old-timey photos always look so serious? Surely they laughed, too, like we do. I'm sure times were harder, but still. Levity can be found anywhere.

Gran's eyes look past the photographer, like she's watching for something on the horizon.

"I miss you," I tell her grumpily. "I wasn't ready, Gran."

Her serious eyes look past me.

"Also, please never have hooked up with Dan."

I shiver and take another drink at the thought.

Please, God, no.

The grandfather clock ticks the minutes past, and I stretch my sock-covered feet out in front of me, closing my eyes.

I listen to the flames licking at the stone, and before I know it, I'm sliding into sleep.

CHAPTER TWO

I wake to the noise of the Norton party preparing to leave the lodge.

"Did you sleep in that chair?" Hank booms from the foyer. I try to turn in his direction, but my stiff neck protests. I rub it, hard, my thumbs digging deep into the rigid muscle.

"Not intentionally," I clarify, rolling my neck this way and that to loosen it. "Let me check the weather report before you go. I'm sorry. I normally would've had this all taken care of by now. I overslept in this dang chair."

"You're up now," Hank says, without concern. "Don't fret about it. The weather is fine, see?"

He gestures toward the large windows, and it's clear and bright. Frost had created intricate designs on the glass in the night, delicate artwork made from crystal.

"Just lemme check," I say as I spin through my phone. "It can change in a moment."

But my phone won't connect to the network.

"Dang it," I mutter, shaking it, as if that will help.

"Don't fret about it," Hank repeats as he drops another bag

onto their gear pile. "It's fine. We're only going out for a few hours today, anyway."

I fumble with my useless phone, trying another weather site. It still won't connect. I can't even text Shelly.

I get to my feet, straightening my shirt.

"Just give me a minute," I tell the group. Josh looks up from where he's lacing his boots.

"We're not going to be out long," he tells me. "Seriously. It's freezing out there."

"Alaska generally is in the winter," I tell him, with a wink. *Dang it, Piper. Control your tongue.*

"So I've heard," he replies, unoffended. He stands up and shakes his hair out before he puts on the stocking hat. "I'm ready. Let's do this!" he declares.

The group thumps their chests like Nordic warriors.

"Just wait a sec," I plead, but they don't. They continue suiting up and I sigh. "The sun sets around two forty-five right now," I tell them. "Please be back before then."

"We will be," Hank assures me, and then they're gone.

"Damn it," I mutter, searching for Shelly. I find her in the kitchen, leisurely making coffee.

"Internet is down," she tells me as I come in. "Good morning, by the way. You look like hell. Wait a second. . . ." She stares me up and down. "You're wearing the same clothes as yesterday. Did you . . . *Piper McCauley!*"

I stare at her. "No, I did not sleep with a guest. Lord, Shelly. Get it through your head—we can't sleep with guests."

She relaxes. "Good. Josh turned in early last night, so I didn't have a chance to work my magic on him."

"Again, *we can't sleep with guests,*" I tell her. "Fantasize all you want, but keep your paws off him."

"A girl can dream," she says stiffly. "You don't need to call me out."

I roll my eyes. "Did you have a chance to check the weather before we lost our signal?"

She shakes her head. "No. I checked it last night before bed, and it's supposed to be clear, with a high of negative seventeen." She glances at me. "I low-key checked their gear this morning. They've got all of the right stuff, Piper. They'll be fine."

"I don't know why I'm so unsettled," I admit.

"Because you're a perfectionist," Shelly tells me. "They're gone for the day, though. You can relax, let down your hair . . ." She eyes me. "You can relax and *comb* your hair," she amends.

I shove her arm playfully and she grins.

"Seriously, though. Go shower. I think you spilled wine on yourself. I mean, unless you committed murder in the night."

I glance down and indeed find a wide crimson stain on my shirt. "This morning just keeps getting better and better!"

Shelly laughs, but I honestly feel a bit deflated. She notices.

"What's wrong?" she asks, her tone turning serious.

I shake my head. "I . . . I don't think I can do this, Shel."

Her head snaps up.

"Are you being serious right now?" she asks. I nod.

"I'm not Gran," I tell her. "Gran wasn't afraid of a thing. She ran this place for so long by herself, and she was perfect. Me, on the other hand . . . I overslept in a chair in the great room and let my first tour group since Gran died leave without a weather report. I'm hopeless."

Shelly stares at me. "They'll be fine, Piper. You, I'm worried about. Why are you so hard on yourself? You know what to do. You were trained for this your entire life."

"I've never been alone before," I admit quietly. "I always had Gran."

"You're not alone," Shelly tells me, her eyes uncharacteristically somber. "You have us. You have *me*."

"Thanks, Shel."

"I mean it," she insists. "We're a family too. Not by blood but by choice. Do you think I stay working here for my health or for the outstanding salary? No. I stay here for you. For your gran. For everyone here. We're a family too. As you know, you're the only family I have."

"Gran always did have a soft spot for rescues." I smile and nudge her shoulder.

"I love you, Piper," Shelly says, still serious.

"You're freaking me out now," I tell her. "You never show your emotions."

"Well, your needy self needs to hear this right now." Shelly laughs. "We all respect you. We all love you. You are not alone, and you're doing great."

"I love you too," I tell her, and a lump forms in my throat as I hug her tightly. She smells like Chanel.

"You smell." She wrinkles her nose as we pull apart. "You really should shower."

I roll my eyes, but I know she's right, so I sigh. "Fine. I'll do it before I eat."

As if she's afraid I'll change my mind, Shelly pushes me lightly toward the stairs, and I climb them without looking back.

Floor-to-ceiling honeyed oak abounds here at the lodge.

Every room, every inch. Rough-hewn logs from this very property were used to build it, and while it appears rustic, the lodge has every modern convenience for travelers. They're accustomed to luxury, so that's what we give them.

En suite jetted tubs, granite double vanities, automatic faucets, TVs in the bathroom mirrors. We had to renovate a few years ago to keep up with their expectations. Wealthy travelers expect a certain level of amenities to be available, even when they want to pretend they're "roughing it."

"Listen," Gran had said. "Our name is Great Expectations. They won't come if we can't offer them the best in everything. We've got the wildlife and the scenery in spades. But we need to invest in the lodge."

She was right, of course, and we did. Even though we paid for it in ways far more expensive than money.

I glance at my parents' photo hanging on the wall in the hallway.

They were so happy, their eyes so bright. They were living their dream. Right up until they weren't.

I swallow and open my bedroom door. *Gran is with them now.*

As I cross the room to my bathroom, I eye my massive four-poster bed enviously. I could've slept in comfort last night, but no. I had to fall asleep in the least comfortable chair in the house. Gran insisted on keeping those ratty chairs. They should've been pitched during the renovation, but she had them refinished instead.

"There are some things you just can't throw out," she'd said. "My father sat in this chair, next to that fire, and in front of that grandfather clock. It's all staying, Piper."

So she'd had the chairs refinished, the clock refurbished, and the fireplace remained the same. If I change any of it, she literally might return to haunt me.

I change my clothes and head back down to the dining room, where Ellen saved me a plate. Perfectly cooked turkey sausage, broiled potato wedges drizzled with truffle oil and fresh rosemary, and a toasted croissant with garlic butter.

"It's not like you to miss breakfast," she says. "You okay?"

I nod. "I fell asleep in front of the fire last night. I didn't have my alarm set."

"Ohhhh. I've been there." She nods. "Drink a lot of water. Take two aspirin. Eat that sausage."

"I'm not hungover. I only had one glass," I tell her, but she's already handing me extra sausage.

"Eat all the grease," she advises. "It helps."

I don't even bother trying to tell her again. I just accept the extra breakfast meat as the gift it is.

Ellen leaves me to continue her breakfast cleanup, and I carry my plate to the dining room.

I try to ignore the emptiness of the lodge with Gran gone, but it screams from everywhere. The old bells I'd forgotten to hang on the tree, the mistletoe she insisted on hanging every year but I'd forgotten to have gathered, the lack of gifts beneath the tree.

With Gran gone, the spirit of this place seems deflated, a balloon that has lost its air.

I carry my breakfast up to Gran's study instead.

When I push the door open, the quiet of the room wraps around me. The wooden shelves filled with her favorite books and the mahogany desk all wait for my gran to return. She used to sit at that giant desk for hours doing the books, and she had looked so tiny in the big chair.

It had been her father's desk and his father's before him, like pretty much everything else in this lodge.

I sit in the chair now, pulling my knees to my chin.

This lodge is mine now, and suddenly, the weight of it, along with Gran's absence, sinks in hard. Every responsibility, every chore, every bill, everything on the to-do list . . . is mine. I'm the only one left to shoulder it.

My throat feels tight and dry, and I swallow hard.

I open her center desk drawer and rummage for some gum. I know she keeps a pack here. In my mind's eye, I can see her unwrapping a stick while she examines columns of numbers, rubbing her temple because she hates doing it.

As my fingers stumble over a marble, a pack of staples, and an old rubber band, they also brush an envelope.

I glance down to see my name scrawled on the front in Gran's writing.

My fingers shake as I pull it out and open it.

My dearest Piper,

I know that these last couple of years have seemed hard. You battled with wanting to move away and become your own person, while wanting to stay and help me with the business.

I'll forever be grateful that you stayed with me, but I never, ever, want to stand in your way of living life on your terms. My sweet girl, you've lost so many people close to you. Your parents, your granddad, and now me. I fear that you'll withdraw into yourself and never want to get close to anyone again.

The truth is, life is a cycle of living and dying and loving and losing. You'll love hard, and lose hard, and cry hard, and laugh hard. If you're lucky! IF you're willing to take the chance of living, of letting people know you . . . of making yourself vulnerable.

I can't tell you what to do, but I will say that this lodge has been in the family for generations. It will be your home forever, no matter how far you go. I hope you will someday raise a family here, and feel the love that I've felt my entire life.

You're not alone, baby girl. I know you might feel that way, but just look around. I'm here, your mom is here, your dad, your granddad. We're all here in different ways. You're never alone.

I'm giving you this compass. I'm sure you'll remember it from all of the stories over the years. I want you to have it, so you'll always know what direction home is.

I love you with all of my heart.
Gran

My eyes close as tears streak my cheeks. I press the letter to my chest, hoping to draw some of my gran's love inside. I see the box next to this letter, and sure enough, an antique brass compass gleams from inside. I pick it up. I, in fact, don't remember the stories. I hadn't paid enough attention when I was younger. I should have. She's no longer here to tell me her stories.

"I miss you," I whisper to my gran.

She always knew what to say, what to do. If something was wrong, she knew how to fix it.

"Um, Piper?"

A voice from the doorway brings me out of my tears. I look up to find Ellen shifting uncomfortably, and I slide the compass into my pocket.

"I'm so sorry to interrupt," she tells me. "Are you okay?"

She comes in and sits on the chair in front of the desk. I nod.

"Yeah. I'm just missing her, I guess."

"We all are," she answers. "I've been wondering when it would hit you."

"Today, I guess." I smile weakly. She reaches across the desk and pats my hand.

"We're all here for you," she tells me. She fidgets and shifts her gaze. I eye her.

"What?" I ask. "Is something wrong?"

"We were just wondering if you could pay us," she says, and her cheeks are flushed.

"The estate lawyer hasn't paid you?" She shakes her head, and I feel a bit light-headed. "I'm so sorry. I thought he was paying everything until things are settled."

"Isn't it settled?" Ellen asks.

"Well, yes. I mean . . . it is. I just told him that I didn't know if I want the responsibility of being the CEO of this company, and that I needed time to think about it, and I guess I just thought he'd take care of everything in the interim."

Ellen looks stricken. "Are you going to sell?"

"No," I assure her. "I won't. Probably not. I don't know if I want to be as hands-on as I've been and as Gran was. I might want to travel for a while. But no matter what, I'll make sure you're cared for. Don't worry about that."

"We weren't," she assures me, but I can tell it's not true.

"Don't worry at all," I repeat to her. "Even if I decide I don't want to live here, I'll bring in someone to fill my position. Nothing will change."

She seems relieved now.

"I wonder what else he hasn't done?" I ask aloud. "I hope he's paid the bills."

Ellen doesn't look relieved anymore and presses a hand to her chest.

"It's okay," I assure her again. "I'll figure it out right now and take care of everything."

Ellen must figure she should get out before she learns anything else terrifying and darts away, leaving me with stacks of correspondence and bills to sort through.

It takes a good deal longer than I thought it would. My breakfast plate is a congealed oily mess by midafternoon when I finally look up from the desk.

It'd taken a two-hour phone call with the attorney, hours of research, and a mini heart attack to figure out where we are on bills, to get all employees paid, and to get us settled into this moment.

I exhale long and slow.

That wasn't fun.

When I walk back downstairs, Ellen, Shelly, and Dan are congregated near the Keurig and break into applause when I approach.

"I see your checks have been deposited." I grin. "You guys should've told me they hadn't been."

"I did." Ellen shrugs. "It's not a big deal."

"Speak for yourself," Shelly tells her. "I was on fumes."

"Always speak up," I tell them. "Seriously. I'm just feeling my way around right now. I'm doing my best."

They all assure me that I am and then laugh when my stomach loudly growls.

"You need to eat," Ellen says, and she takes my cold breakfast plate from me.

"What are we serving the Nortons tonight?" I ask. *Please be steak. Please be steak.*

"Roasted grouper, asparagus, rolls, baked potatoes. They should be back any minute now, shouldn't they?"

I glance at the clock. It's two thirty.

"Um. They should've come in already." I gaze out the window, to where the sun is sinking fast.

"Piper, there's a blizzard coming tonight," Dan tells me. "You knew that, right?"

"What?" I ask stiltedly. "I couldn't get a signal this morning, so I couldn't check."

"Visibility is going to be zero," he tells me solemnly.

My heart starts to pound. "That's not good."

Dan's ashen face confirms it, and this is exactly what I was afraid of. I've endangered the tour group.

I spring into motion.

"Shelly, get me a radio. Ellen, call the ranger station, let them know to be on the lookout. Dan, we might have to go out searching for them."

He nods and is already walking to get his overcoat.

Shelly is in the process of turning everything upside down to find a radio.

She finds one in the butler's pantry and sends a call out to the Norton party.

As she does, I hear beeps coming from another area in the house and I follow the sounds.

I find the Nortons' two-way radios still on chargers in the utility room.

"Shel, I thought you checked their stuff?"

"I said I low-key checked," she reminds me. "I didn't want them to see me digging through it."

"That's part of our job," I tell her, through my teeth. "To make sure they've got all of their safety gear. They're out there with no radio and no cell signal."

Shelly stares at me, wide-eyed.

"I don't usually do the morning send-off, so I didn't think. I'm sorry," she tells me, her cheeks flushed.

"It's my fault," I tell her. "I should've been prepared. Dang it."

"Piper," Dan says from the doorway. He's already suited up for the cold. "We should go."

I nod and grab my parka off the hook by the back door.

"Shel, stay here in case they come back or there's word . . ."

She nods quickly and hands me gloves.

I slide them on one at a time and look up at Ellen. "Have hot toddies ready for later," I tell her. "We're going to need them."

I head out into the cold and sit behind Dan on the snow-mobile. I use his shoulders to block the icy wind from my face.

It's snowing pretty heavily already, and Dan noses us through the snow and toward the best hunting spots.

We pass several without seeing a soul.

My anxiety rachets up a few notches with every empty spot we find.

"Surely they wouldn't have ventured farther up the mountain," I mutter to myself. Dan seems to hear me, because he turns the snowmobile.

We ride until we come to the thick underbrush of the forest, where we climb off.

"We're on foot now," Dan tells me needlessly. The underbrush is far too thick for anything else. "It's negative twenty degrees," he adds. "We need to find them."

"I know," I agree. "Do you have flares?"

He nods.

"Me too. Whoever finds them first, send one up."

He nods.

I turn and suck in a breath.

A beautiful caribou doe stands nearby, her eyes wide and placid as she languidly paws at the snow. She lifts her head to stare at us calmly.

Animals typically feel a storm and instinctively look for shelter.

This doe is unconcerned.

"You're beautiful," I murmur to her, taking this one brief moment to appreciate her. This is the reason I don't like hunting parties. The pure trust in her eyes as she watches me. If the Nortons had encountered her . . . I swallow hard.

The wind picks up, and the compass in my pocket begins

rattling in a strange and noisy way. The doe startles, bounding away on the packed snow. I pull the compass out, and the arrow is spinning. It must be broken, because it won't stop spinning.

Great.

I shove it back in my pocket and follow in the direction the doe has taken, while Dan sets out the opposite way.

The snow quickly becomes a whiteout. The wind howls, and I can't remember the last time we let something like this happen.

It would never have happened when Gran was alive.

I trek through the snow, ignoring the cold tang on my lips. I layered Vaseline on them before I left, but thanks to the bone-chilling wind, they're already dry.

"Piper!" Dan yells. I scan the swirling snow, trying to find him. "Piper! You need to see this!"

"Dan?" I call. "Shout again. I'll follow your voice!"

He yells again, then again, but the snow has disoriented me. It's hard to see which way is up.

I take another step, then another, and suddenly, I'm falling.

CHAPTER THREE

I don't know how long I've been out when I open my eyes.

Long enough that my fingers and toes feel frozen.

"Dan!" I shout, pushing at the snow around me. I'm in a hollow snowbank, and it's a person's best chance of survival if they're out alone and lost. The snow insulates you, and actually makes you warmer.

But I know Dan is near and he needs to see where I am.

I tear at the snow, trying to climb to the top.

The cold burns my face, but I ignore it, scratching at the snow, pulling it down by the handful.

"Hello?" someone calls.

"Can you hear me?" I scream. "I'm in here!" I shove at the snow, hoping to break through so they can see my fingers.

"Hello!" they call again. "Keep shouting!"

So I do, and five minutes later, someone grabs my hand.

I'm hauled through the snow and to the top of the bank, surrounded by men in hunting gear.

The Nortons have rescued me? How embarrassing.

But they're not the Nortons. I realize this as they peer down at me, and I don't recognize one single face. They're bearded and rugged . . . nothing like the Norton party.

I look around, and the blizzard has died down. The snow is no longer swirling.

"My friend," I tell them. "Dan. He must be close. We were together."

The man in front eyes me oddly.

"Ma'am, you're the only one here. There's no one else out here now."

"Dan was with me," I tell them firmly. "A search party is on their way. I've got clients out in this."

They all glance at each other.

"Miss, you should come with us and warm up," the front guy says. "You could have frostbite. I'm Dale."

He offers me his hand. "Let us take you somewhere warm."

"I live nearby," I tell them. "I can call for a ride when we get there. Do you have a signal?"

"Signal?" Dale asks. "We've got a radio, if you need it. Short-wave only, of course."

"Why only shortwave?" I ask as we turn to hike.

"Because of the war," he says slowly. "Long-range radios are banned. We've really got to get you warmed up; you're not thinking clearly. You'll have to tell us what you're doing out here alone. It's not safe."

"I know," I insist. "I live here. Great Expectations Lodge. Do you know it?"

They're silent, all four of them, as they eye me.

"She needs to be looked at," Dale tells them, and they all nod. They pull me along as we climb down the mountain. I take in their bulky canvas overcoats and wonder where they're from.

"Why are y'all out here?" I ask, trying to ignore the cold nipping my face.

"Hunting," one of them tells me.

"This is private property," I tell them. "I mean, thank you for pulling me out of the snow. But most of this mountain belongs to Great Expectations."

"Well, you're lucky we heard you," Dale says to me, unconcerned. "Or you'd be in a spot of trouble right about now."

I scan the area and don't see a trace of Dan. "I can't imagine where Dan went," I mutter. "He wouldn't have just left me."

"Ma'am, we didn't see anyone else, and we've been out for hours. The nearest town is five miles away, and this time of year, no one can easily travel to Wander. If someone were out here, we'd have noticed."

"This doesn't make any sense," I mumble.

"No, ma'am, it sure doesn't," one man agrees. I glance at him and the others, and they all just seem bewildered.

"Haven't you ever seen a woman alone out in the snow before?" I joke. But they all shake their heads, expressions serious.

"No," they all answer.

"You gentlemen should get out more," I advise.

We continue walking, and it's not long before we reach the clearing to the lodge. They all walk toward the doors, and as we get closer, I realize that it looks like the lodge . . . but it's different.

I stop. The logs seem so much newer, the wraparound porch

isn't here, and the Bobcat isn't poking around the corner. Also . . . the sign.

The big wooden sign looms in front, painted in bright blue. GREAT EXPECTATIONS. ROOMS FOR RENT.

Rooms for rent?

I'd think I was in the wrong place, but this *is* the lodge, it's just . . . different.

"I don't understand," I whisper, staring at the carved wooden doors. Those are custom to Great Expectations, and we've had them for over a hundred years. They look brand-new now.

"You must've hit your head pretty hard," Dale says, taking my elbow. "Let's get you out of the cold and something hot to drink."

I don't argue and follow behind as the man leads me into my own house.

Only . . . it's not.

I gaze about the foyer, and I don't recognize it. There are black-and-white photographs framed over the fireplace, the furniture is old-fashioned, yet new, and the woman walking in our direction in the dress and apron is someone I've never met in my life, even though she seems vaguely familiar.

"Dale, what in the world?" she exclaims, and she grabs me gently, patting my cheeks with her hands. "Can you hear me, dear?" she asks, her nose in my face.

"Yes," I tell her. "I'm fine. Just cold."

"Well, I imagine you are," she tells me. "Marina!" she calls over her shoulder, before turning back to me. "You look almost my daughter's age and size. We can borrow some of her dry clothing while we heat you up."

Marina?

As in . . .

My grandmother appears behind the woman, only it can't be my grandmother because this girl is around my age, and . . . she looks like every picture I've ever seen of Gran from when she was young.

Maybe I do have frostbite. *Of the brain.*

"Hello," Gran says to me with her young mouth and twenty-two-year-old skin. "Are you okay? Where in the world did you come from?"

She rushes to her mother's side. My *great-grandmother*? The woman in the photo over the mantel. The serious photo.

"I'm Marina," young Gran tells me, as she pulls off my coat. She eyes it oddly, shaking it. "What's your name?"

"Piper," I tell them, and I feel a bit faint.

"What are you doing up here?" she asks. "Who are you with?"

Both women and the group of men wait for my answer, and with the facts being what they are, rather unbelievable, I choose not to share them.

In short, I lie. There's no other way.

"I don't know," I tell them. Lying about it isn't too hard, because I'm absolutely confused. Did I hit my head? *Am* I confused? Am I dreaming? "I can't remember."

Their heads all snap back in unison, their eyes wide.

"You mentioned a man," Dale reminds me. "Someone named Dan. Do you remember him?"

"I thought I did," I tell them. "When I first opened my eyes, I remembered him. But now everything feels cloudy." I have to lie because the truth no longer makes sense. What seems to be happening can't possibly be real, yet when I pinch my hand to make sure, I feel the pain. I stare around in confusion, and a group of equally confused faces stare back.

"I think she might need a doctor," Dale says. "We should send word into town."

"It's getting dark now," the woman says. My great-grandmother. With that in mind, I know her name is Sophie. "We'll have to check tomorrow."

"I'm fine," I announce. "Maybe I'm just dreaming. Am I?"

"I'll go in the morning," Dale says, turning toward the kitchen. I know, because this is my house. But not my house. And Dale is *Eberdale*. A family name. He's my great-grandfather.

"I think you should lie down," Sophie tells me, and I've never heard a better idea. She and Gran escort me upstairs. As we turn the corner, I wonder which room they'll put me in. They walk right past my actual bedroom and choose the one next to it. A much smaller room than mine.

But they don't know I know that.

I sit on the bed, and Sophie bends to unlace my boots. "These are intricate," she says, as she both unties and un-Velcros them. She eyes the Velcro with interest, as though she's never seen it before.

I automatically reach for my phone, so I can google when Velcro was invented.

But my phone isn't in my pocket. Just my grandfather's compass.

"What year is this?" I ask politely as Marina, my grand-mother, lifts my legs onto the bed.

She and Sophie stare at me in concern.

"Nineteen forty-four," Marina says slowly.

"So World War II is still going on," I say as I settle into the pillows. This room has rose wallpaper now, and I'm not a fan. Oh, and *I'm in 1944.* My head spins a bit, just like my compass had spun earlier.

"Yes, the war is still going," Sophie says. "We don't know when it will end."

I do.

May 8, 1945.

But obviously I don't announce that.

That would ruin the dream. And this must be a dream. This can't actually be happening.

"I have a very vivid imagination, and I miss my grand-mother very much," I murmur. *Yes, that's what this is.*

"Pardon?" Sophie asks.

I swallow. "I said, I think I'll surely feel better if I rest for a while."

"You're probably right," Sophie agrees. She pulls a blanket over me. "You rest, and I'll check in on you later."

"Thank you so much," I tell her. She smiles.

"It's my pleasure. I don't get female guests here, so it'll be nice to chat. When you're feeling better, of course."

She and Marina slip out, and I lie completely still.

Maybe I'm having a very lucid dream, and I'm actually still in the snowbank. Maybe I'm dead. *Is this heaven?* I pull out the compass and look at it. The hands are frozen now, broken. No matter which way I aim it, they stay the same. I lay it on the nightstand and stand up.

I feel like I'm in an episode of *Supernatural* or *The Twilight Zone* as I creep to the door and open it just a crack, peering out.

They're gone now.

I tiptoe quietly down the hall, trying to get my bearings.

I look into my actual bedroom, and now it's someone else's. A man's.

I examine the walls and am startled to find the magnolia wallpaper that I'd helped strip from the walls when I was a kid. Only, it's not faded now.

There are knickknacks and photographs that I don't recognize.

I creep back down the hall and linger near the railing overlooking the great room below. Voices drift up.

"Can't imagine what an unchaperoned girl is doing up here," a man says.

"She thinks she lives here," Dale says. "She knows the name of the lodge."

"She's probably from town," Sophie says.

"But how did she get up here? She should know never to hike during this time of year," Marina says.

"Well, it don't rightly matter," another man says. "She's here now. As soon as possible, we need to send word down to the town doc and let them know that we've got a girl here, in case anyone is missing her."

"What if we can't?" Marina asks. "It's supposed to get bad today. You know as well as I do that any day now, it'll be too snowy to get to town until the big thaw."

"Don't borrow trouble," Sophie answers. "If it's clear enough in the morning, we'll send someone to town. Albert, could you go?"

"Of course," a man answers.

Someone claps her hands, then Marina speaks. "I can't believe it. Finally! Another girl!"

I can hear them walking, so I bound back down to the bedroom they'd left me in. I quietly slip back into bed.

I stare at the rose-patterned wall as I try to wrap my head around this.

"Mama, that elk stew smells delicious," Marina says from downstairs.

"It always goes over well with the boarders," Sophie answers. I sniff the air, and sure enough, something does smell amazing. My stomach growls in reaction. I haven't eaten since Ellen's sausage this morning.

Ellen.

Home.

My belly clenches. What must they be thinking? Dan, Ellen, Shelly. Do they think I'm dead?

"I can make the cornbread, if you want," Marina tells Sophie. Their voices get farther away. It feels like my hold on reality fades with them. I know that whatever this is shouldn't be happening, yet here I am, in my house but not my house.

I'm going to have to roll with whatever punches come my way.

I'm also going to have to lie my pants off. Which is unfortunate, since I'm really horrible at it. Gran always knew when I was lying, but she'd never say what my tell was.

When Marina comes to get me for dinner an hour or so later, she brings with her a clean dress.

It's definitely vintage, robin's-egg blue, with buttons. The slim-silhouette A-line skirt would fall at my knees.

"I brought you something dry," she tells me. "It's freshly laundered. And it's time to eat. Are you hungry?"

"I'm starving," I tell her honestly.

She beams. "Then you've come to the right place. My mother always makes too much food, even with rationing."

Rationing?

"I can't wait," I tell her. I wait for her to leave so I can get dressed, but she doesn't. She pulls my elbow, helping me to stand. Then she helps peel off my clothes.

"These are interesting," she tells me, eyeing my snow pants. "Where did you get them?"

"Amazon," I answer without thinking. She looks at me.

"Where?"

"Um, a store where I'm from. Idaho."

Lord, I hope they don't ask many questions. I know nothing about Idaho.

"You live in Idaho? What are you doing here, then?" Marina asks, folding the turtleneck that I'd just handed her. "Is your husband away in the war?"

"I'm, uh, not married yet," I tell her. "I don't think. I'm not wearing a ring."

"Me either," she says, as if she's confiding in me. "I've got a good-looking fiancé, though. I'm just hoping he comes back."

He will.

"He will," I assure her.

She helps me shimmy into the dress, and it fits me fine, although it's a little snug in the chest.

"You're curvier than me," Marina, my gran, says, eyeing my chest enviously. "I've got little goose eggs myself."

My cheeks flush because this is my gran talking.

"I didn't mean to embarrass you," she says. "Being closed off up here, I sometimes forget my manners."

"It's okay," I assure her.

"My mother said you can stay as long as you need to," Marina tells me, linking her elbow with mine as we walk down the stairs. "It might be impossible for us to get to town right now. We'll have to see. If it is, you'll stay here until we can."

"This is very kind of you all," I tell her.

She nods. "We just hope you get your memory back, so we know how to contact your folks."

"Me too," I tell her. "It's the strangest thing."

"It must be awful," she decides. "Not knowing where your people are or even who *you* are."

"It's a very odd feeling," I tell her honestly, as I look around the dining room. A record player plays Bing Crosby's "White Christmas." I'd forgotten how a record even sounds . . . crackling and distant.

"We hope you're hungry," Sophie says, as she walks to each man seated at the table and serves him cornbread.

"I am," I assure her. "Starving, actually."

The men go around the table and introduce themselves to me as I sit. There's Edward, William, Albert, Frank, Charlie, and Joseph. As I glance at them, I realize they all have something in common. They're either older or injured.

William, Albert, and Frank are older . . . in their forties. Joseph and Edward each have a physical issue. Joseph has missing fingers, and Edward has a disfigured ear.

Edward catches me staring.

"My brother shoved me into the campfire when I was seven," he says cheerfully, taking a big bite of stew.

"I'm so sorry," I tell him. He shrugs.

"I'm used to it now. You just gotta talk into my good ear. I can't hear a lick out of this one."

I nod.

"You can call me Joe," Joseph tells me, and he's got the brightest, most sparkling blue eyes.

"And you can call me Piper." I return the favor. Everyone stares at me now, since I have an odd name. So now I'm the odd girl they found in the snow with no memory and a weird name. Perfect.

Have Piper aircrafts even been invented yet? Feeling fairly confident that they were built in the twenties, I speak up.

"My dad was a pilot," I tell them, leaving out the part where I was conceived in a Piper. "So I was named after an airplane."

"Ohhh, that's charming," Sophie says with a smile. "I love interesting stories. Do you remember your father's name?"

I shake my head. "No. I remember him, but I can't see his face clearly or remember his name. It's the strangest thing."

"You must've hit your head, girlie," Edward says. "You'd better rest up."

"Thank you so much for your hospitality," I tell them all. "I don't know what's happening, but I'm so grateful you found me."

"Don't you fret," Sophie says, patting my shoulder. "Edward's right. You must've hit your head. You'll remember soon enough. This happened with ol' Tom Ford, do you guys remember?" She glances around the table, where everyone is nodding. She looks at me.

"He had an accident at the mill, fell into the metalworks. He didn't die, but he hit his head mighty hard and couldn't remember a thing for close to six months."

"But it all came back to him?" I ask quietly.

She nods. "Oh, yes. He was lying in bed one night, doing absolutely nothing of note, and all of it came rushing back. It darned near gave him a heart attack, he said. But he remembered, and so will you. And when you do, we're here to help."

She takes her seat, and I pick up my spoon to take a bite, but everyone holds hands. Marina holds hers out to me, and I pause.

She lifts an eyebrow and nudges my hand.

Ohhh. I wrap my fingers around hers, and with Edward's on my other side, as Dale says a prayer.

He thanks God for my arrival, for my safety, and for the hands who prepared the meal.

When he says "*Amen,*" everyone repeats it and digs in to their food.

After a minute, Sophie exclaims, "Oh, dear. I forgot the peaches. They're from a batch I canned this past summer, and they're delicious. I thought having a special guest for dinner is the perfect occasion to serve them."

She stands up and, immediately, every man at the table stands.

I pause, staring at them.

This is what having manners looks like.

They don't sit until she returns and takes her seat.

Everyone acts as though the simple canned peaches are made of gold, and each person carefully spoons out a couple of slices onto their plates, saving them for dessert.

Not only is this a different time, but honestly, it feels like an entirely different world. The entire ambience feels different. More serene, cozier, yet more formal. There are no cell phones beeping or vibrating. There's no TV in the background.

Marina laughs at Albert—and *her face*! I've missed it so much. It's unlined now, and her eyes sparkle with life. This is Gran as I never knew her, but she is most certainly my gran.

Bing sings, the fireplace crackles, and I take another bite of the savory, homemade stew.

Everyone at the table chats and laughs, and as we eat together, I come to the conclusion that whatever is happening . . . is going to be interesting. Or educational. Or terrifying.

Or all of the above.

CHAPTER FOUR

After dinner, the men slip away, leaving Gran, Sophie, and me to clear away the dishes and clean the large kitchen. Soon, as I'm scrubbing a pot in the battered farm sink, I smell smoke from a pipe.

They're smoking indoors.

Because this is 1944.

The smell permeates the room quickly, and before I can mask my reaction, Gran catches sight of my face.

"Men are smelly creatures, aren't they?" she asks, as she swings around to put the glass milk pitcher into the fridge. The fridge is a relic, of course, but also rather new. It's mind-bending. I'm using antiques . . . when they weren't antiques.

"Nothing smells better than a freshly bathed man, though," Sophie speaks up, and Gran . . . *Marina* . . . rolls her eyes.

"Daddy smells like campfires," she tells her mother. Sophie nods, a loving expression in her eyes.

"He does. Except for when he's freshly bathed."

She towels off the last pot, and I pull the drain from the sink.

"Let's put the strainer in there," Sophie says quickly, settling the screen into the drain. "These old pipes get clogged easily."

Because there's no garbage disposal, I realize.

"I'm sorry," I tell her. "I wasn't thinking."

"How could you know this old house is antiquated?" Marina asks me. "It should be a museum, not a home."

"Marina!" Sophie chides. "This is our home. It was your father's home, and his father built it with his bare hands. It will be in our family for generations to come and will outlast us all. At least, that's the plan."

"As I said," Marina grins, "it's old and should be a museum."

"But you love this house," I protest, and then realize I shouldn't know that. "I mean, anyone would," I backpedal.

"Oh, she's too young to understand what tradition and family mean," Sophie interjects, and Marina rolls her eyes behind her mother's back. "She just wants to live in the lower forty-eight, where there are more exciting things to do."

"I think any girl my age would," Marina replies, defending herself. "Aren't I right, Piper?"

Both women look at me expectantly, and I'm a deer in the headlights.

"Um," I stammer, and Sophie laughs.

"It's fine," she assures me. "Both places have merit."

I visibly relax, and she laughs again.

"We give Marina too much leeway," she tells me. "But she means well. She's a good girl."

"Usually," Marina amends.

Now it's Sophie rolling her eyes.

"Don't give Piper the wrong idea," she tells her daughter.

"You're a good girl and you know it. You've just got a bit of a spunky mouth."

"Strong women run in our family," Marina tells me. "So I learned from the best."

I can't help but wonder if it's true. *Does it run in our family? Did Gran think I'm strong?*

I realize that I'm already referring to the gran I knew as *Gran*, and *Marina* when I'm thinking about the young girl in front of me.

Separating them in my mind might be the key to not losing it.

See? I tell myself. *You're strong. You're adapting. You've got this.*

"Oh, you." Sophie sighs, shooing at her daughter with her hands. "Go on, get. Take your smart mouth and go make sure the men have towels. It's bath night."

"Bath night?" I ask before I can stop myself.

Sophie nods. "We need to conserve electricity right now, so Friday night is bath night."

"For all of us," Marina adds. "I'm sorry. It's awful. Sponge baths every other day."

"Marina, land sakes. We're blessed to have very little impact from this war," Sophie rebukes her. "If we can only buy a little sugar or can only bathe once a week, it's nothing compared to the sacrifices our boys are making over there."

"I know, Mama." Marina sighs.

"So I don't want to hear you complain about this again."

"Yes, Mama," Marina agrees with another sigh.

"It won't be for much longer anyway," I speak up, and immediately feel like clapping my hand over my mouth. "It will surely be over soon," I add.

"I don't know," Sophie answers. "We keep hoping, and it just never happens."

"Nothing can last forever," I say brightly.

"It's almost like you haven't experienced an Alaskan winter," Marina says, with a wink. "Because I assure you, it lasts forever."

"What did I just tell you?" Sophie says sharply. "Stop complaining, missy."

"Sorry, Mama."

Marina is contrite now, and she turns to me. "Want to help me pass out towels?"

"Marina, don't enlist our guest to—"

"It's okay," I interrupt. "I'd love to. Truly."

Sophie nods with an approving smile, and I hurry to keep up with Marina as she practically darts from the room. I turn down the hall to the laundry room, but Marina continues on, so I turn around and join her.

She leads me downstairs, which at this moment in time isn't finished yet. Gone are the wooden beams and brick walls of the wine cellar. It's now a very, very rustic laundry area, with concrete walls and just a couple of single lightbulbs hanging from overhead. An old washing machine sits in the corner, and makeshift clotheslines are stretched from one side of the room to the other.

This is the laundry room now.

She grabs dry towels off the lines and tosses them to me to fold. Soon enough, we each have an armful, and we head back up the wooden stairs.

The men are all extremely happy to get their towels, and I feel a little like Santa Claus as I hand them out.

Bing Crosby is singing on the record player again, its crackling sound adding a festive flair to the evening.

"We get the record player tonight too," Marina tells me, her eyes sparkling. I'm seeing now that Friday nights are an event here. "So hurry and take a bath, and we can dance!"

Her enthusiasm is contagious, and I rush to the bathroom, eager to see what 1944 deems as entertainment.

I'm derailed for a minute as I realize that there's no shower. Only a claw-foot bathtub.

How am I supposed to wash my hair like that?

As if on cue, Marina taps on the door, then thrusts a bottle of shampoo at me.

"Here, you can borrow my shampoo. Just don't use too much; I don't get another card for more for a couple of months."

Rationing. I forgot.

"Thank you," I tell her sincerely. "I'll just use a dab."

She grins. "Just leave it in there. I'll bathe next. Remember— just two inches!"

"Two inches?"

"Of water, goob!"

"Two inches of water?" I repeat dumbly.

"Boy, you really did hit your head, didntcha? You can only use two inches of water," she says slowly. "Because of the fuel rations. We have to limit how much fuel we use. So we can't use a lot of hot water. It takes too much fuel."

She's speaking to me like I'm a child, and I appreciate it.

"Okay. Two inches. Got it!" I promise.

She's not convinced.

"So get wet, turn the water off, lather up, then turn the water back on and rinse."

"I will."

I close the door and do my best. Craning my neck to get my head submerged under the water spout proves to be a feat, but I somehow manage.

When I open my eyes, Marina is sitting on the toilet lid.

I screech, fighting the urge to grab my towel and cover up.

She giggles. "You forgot to bring your clean dress. And here, let's wear stockings tonight. You can borrow a pair of mine. I'll draw on yours, and you can do mine."

I have no idea what she means, but I know I'll find out soon enough.

"Okay," I agree, and my teeth are chattering now. "I'll be out in a minute."

She slips out, and I dry off. I pull the stockings on, then button my dress.

I open the door, and she's standing outside with her towel.

"Just give me a minute, and we can pin our hair," she says, and she closes the door behind her.

Only six minutes later, she appears in my bedroom doorway with hairpins and a felt-tip pen in hand.

"Turn around, I'll do you first," she instructs. I turn, and she drops down to her hands and knees and draws a careful line up the back of each of my legs.

It's a strange fashion trend, I decide, as I return the favor. But then again, people in the nineties tight-rolled their jeans. So trends don't always make sense.

"Here," she says, and she thrusts bobby pins into my hand.

She stands in front of the mirror and pins curls around her face. She catches me watching.

"Don't tell me you've forgotten how?" She lifts an eyebrow. "Oh, boy. Come here. I'll do it."

She's got me pinned in two minutes.

"The fireplace will have them dry quicker than you can shake a crow at."

"O . . . kay," I say.

"Your hair is so shiny," she says admiringly. "What do you use? Egg yolk and mayo?"

I wrinkle my nose. "No. Olaplex."

"Ola-what?" Marina asks, as she messes with her own pins, making sure they aren't stabbing her in the scalp.

Ola—hasn't been invented yet.

"You know, I can't remember the name of it," I lie, thinking longingly of my luxury shampoos and blow dryers lined up in my bathroom at home. In my home *time.* Lord, this is getting mind-bending.

"Well, if you think of it, let me know," she says absently. "Rations have to lift at some point, right?"

I nod. "Soon," I tell her. "Surely."

I examine myself in the mirror, and Marina bends over to pinch my cheeks.

"For color," she says, then does her own. "Come on, girlie. Let's get downstairs. Oh, wait! We forgot the most important part!"

She proudly pulls out a small tube of lipstick from her pocket.

"Montezuma Red!" she declares, leaning over to apply it in the mirror. I search my memory and recall vaguely that women in this war era wore this shade to thumb their noses at Hitler, since he was known to hate red lipstick.

"How did you get your hands on this?" I ask her. "With supply so low?"

"I saved my rations and had to order it in. It took months, but it was worth it."

She holds it out to me when she's finished, and I apply it, careful not to waste any of the precious commodity. As I examine the finished product, with my hair pinned and my vintage dress, I look like I've stepped off a wartime poster. It's a strange feeling. Rather than reading about the war era in a history book, I'm living it. *Right now.*

The fire is roaring as we descend the staircase, and Sophie and Edward are cutting out gingerbread man chains from parcel paper. Sophie looks up with a smile, her tired eyes sparkling.

"Marina, come hang these over the mantel. And why are you downstairs with your hair pinned up?"

"So that it can dry by the fire, Mama." Sophie nods, accepting that.

"Well, take them out and get presentable the moment it's dry."

"Yes, Mama."

It occurs to me that in the forties, they have different sets of manners. In the twenty-first century, I wouldn't have thought too much of being "unpresentable." But here, it's an issue.

Interesting. I wonder how much more I have to learn.

The air is festive tonight, excited, and I have to admit, it's contagious. Marina and I hang the paper garland over the fireplace mantel, and Sophie lights candles and stirs spiced apple cider. When she turns away to do something else, my great-grandfather Dale dumps a bit of something from a flask into the steaming cider pot.

He catches me watching, winks, and holds a finger to his lips.

I nod with a grin and motion that my lips are sealed. The scent of the cider changes to something slightly alcoholic as it wafts through the room, but no one seems to notice.

"Can you save a dance for me?" Edward asks with a shy smile. He aims his good ear at me so he can hear my reply.

"Of course," I tell him. He beams. As he walks away, his fingers flutter to cover his scarred ear, a subconscious thing that I've noticed him doing.

"You just made his entire life," Marina tells me as she slides in next to my hip. "He's so shy, I'm surprised he had the gumption to ask!"

"He's sweet," I answer. She nods in agreement.

"It's too bad about his bum ear," she replies.

"Why? He can't help it."

"I know. But he couldn't go off with the rest of the boys to Europe, and so now he feels like he let everyone down." Marina's mouth purses. "You know how boys can be."

"Surely he's relieved that he didn't have to go," I reply.

Marina looks at me like I've grown a second head. "He's not yellow," she says incredulously. "He just has a bum ear."

It takes me a minute to realize she thought I'd called Edward a coward.

"Of course!" I agree quickly. "I'm sure he wanted to go support his friends."

"And the country." She nods firmly. "We might be Alaskans, but we bleed red, white, and blue too."

"Alaska isn't a foreign country." I chuckle. She glances at me sharply.

"I know. But tell that to half of America, who worry about how close we are to Russia."

That hadn't occurred to me. But yes, in the forties, that was probably a concern.

"You definitely bleed red, white, and blue," I assure her.

Pacified, she pulls me to the side of the room, where she takes my pins out and arranges my hair. When I look in the mirror, a 1940s pinup girl stares back.

"Holy crow," I murmur.

Marina smiles widely. "Don't you love Friday nights?"

She links arms with me as we turn to rejoin the room. Charlie, Frank, and Albert are sitting at the dining room table enjoying hot cider, while William, Edward, and Joe shuffle a deck of cards and prepare to play a game.

Dale and Sophie emerge from the kitchen with nuts and popcorn, and Sophie tucks in a stray hair. Her cheeks are flushed, and Dale slaps her lightly on the butt when he thinks no one is watching. Sophie quickly looks around to make sure no one saw, and I look away.

The record changes to a big band tune, and amid the saxophone notes and the chatter, no one but me notices a loud knock on the door.

I cross the room and pull it open. The wind swirls in powdery snow and frigid air.

There, in the middle of the snowy swirl, stands a tall form with broad shoulders, slim hips, and bright green eyes.

A smile forms on masculine lips, lips perched above a cleft chin. Dark hair curls beneath the edge of a stocking cap.

"Excuse me, miss. I've been letting a room down the mountain at Essie Klein's house, but she's taken sick, and I'm hoping that you have a room to spare."

His voice is so husky it's practically indecent.

"Lane Patrick Hughes, is that you?" Sophie calls above the din. Someone turns off the record player as Sophie joins me at the door. "Boy, get in here or you'll catch your death," she chides him as she pulls him inside. Dale slides past to grab an army duffel bag from outside the door.

"Of course we've got rooms," he booms. "And for you, after what you did over at Kasserine Pass and then coming to help out around the barn here sometimes . . . there won't be a charge, and I don't want to hear another word about it."

Lane opens his mouth, then closes it.

"Thank you, Dale."

Dale carries the duffel bag past us and toward the stairs. "I'm going to put him in Marina's room," he calls over his shoulder. "Marina, you can sleep with Piper."

"Is Essie all right?" Sophie asks Lane, her eyebrows knit in concern. He nods.

"It seems she will be. She had a bout of pneumonia and needs to rest now without worrying about taking care of me. Mr. Klein helps as much as he can, but he's not feeling much better than she is. I figure I'll go down and make sure their fire doesn't go out, and maybe take them a bowl of soup or something every day, if I can buy one off of you, ma'am."

She waves her hands at him. "Lane, you haven't changed a bit. Your mama would be so proud if she could see you now, may God rest her soul."

"Your pap too," Marina says as she joins us. "They sure loved you, Lane."

"I only wish they could've known I was going to come back safe and sound before they died," Lane says, a bit softer now. "My mother worried so much."

"She had faith in you, though," Sophie tells him. "It never crossed her mind that you wouldn't come back to her . . . because you promised you would. She told me, 'Sophie, that boy always keeps his promises. I raised him right.'" Sophie smiles gently at him. "And she was right. You do."

Lane closes his eyes for a brief moment, and in that moment, his face looks so travel-worn and weary. Then he opens them, and the melancholy moment has passed. "Thank you, Sophie."

"Now, let's get these cold things off of you, and you get your behind over there to that fire and get warmed up." She starts pulling off his coat, and he winces in pain.

"Oh, dear," Sophie gasps, yanking her hands away. "I'm sorry."

"It's okay," he assures her. "It's just slow healing. The bullet broke a small piece of my shoulder bone off. It's lodged in there good and tight, and sometimes, when I move just right, it gives me trouble. But otherwise, I'm right as rain."

"Oh goodness," Sophie says, her hands fluttering like a nervous bird's wings. "Piper, dear, can you take him to the kitchen where it's nice and warm while I hang up his coat to dry?"

I nod and lead the way to the kitchen. Trays of toasted nuts are on the counters, cooling and filling the air with a nutty, rich scent. "It's warmest over here," I tell him, guiding him to the front of the oven.

He eyes me curiously as he joins me. "Did Mrs. McC call you Piper?" he asks, his eyes twinkling.

"Yes." I nod. "I know. It's strange."

"Not strange," he says slowly. "Unusual. And interesting. Which I get a feeling suits you just fine."

His tone of voice and handsome face make my cheeks flush. And suddenly, in this warm small space, in the proximity of this handsome man with sparkling eyes who is, by all appearances, some sort of war hero who recently lost his parents, my ovaries decide to betray me, and they flutter wildly to get my attention.

The problem is, when they do, it's like sensory overload, and the room spins, my cheeks get hot, and the last things I remember are Lane's green eyes gleaming with concern and his strong arms darting out immediately to catch me before I fall to the ground.

CHAPTER FIVE

I've never passed out before, but when I come to on the settee in front of the fire, with everyone gathered around me in concern, I realize I should do it more often because it certainly makes a statement.

"Oh my gosh," Marina says when my eyes open. "You scared us! Did you drink too much of the cider?"

"I hadn't had any yet," I tell her. "I don't know what happened."

The room spins for a second, and I squeeze my eyes closed.

"Maybe you stood up too fast," Sophie decides, and I don't have the heart to tell her I hadn't been sitting down.

"I'm sure that's it," I assure her, opening my eyes and trying to focus. "I'm truly fine. Please, don't let me interrupt this evening. Everyone is having so much fun."

"You ninny," Marina says. "Of course we're worried about you. You have amnesia already. We don't want anything else to happen to you."

"You have amnesia?" Lane, who I hadn't noticed was next to my ear, asks.

"She knows her name," Marina tells him. "That she's from Idaho. A couple vague things. Nothing more."

"How did you get here?" he asks, interested now.

"She doesn't know," Marina says patiently. "I just told you. Honestly, Lane. You'd think you were the one who'd gotten thumped on the head, not Piper."

"Marina," Sophie says warningly, nudging her daughter.

"It's okay, Mrs. McC," Lane answers. "Marina has always treated me like the brother she doesn't have."

"That's no excuse," Sophie murmurs, but her tone is less severe.

"He used to tie my braids together in school," Marina explains to me, rolling her eyes.

"Don't forget the crickets I put in your boots," he adds helpfully.

"That too," Marina says drolly. "You knew I was scared of crickets."

"I was just trying to help you conquer your fear." He shrugs, but his grin is anything but angelic.

I can't help but smile as I sit up, and the room wobbles a bit. Could this be a by-product of time travel? I mean, I did somehow pass through almost eighty years. That's bound to take a physical toll on a body.

I rub at my temple, and the fuzzy feeling clears.

"I'm fine," I announce again, standing up. "I'm sorry to alarm everyone."

"You can't get out of a dance with me so easily," Edward declares, as Lane supports my elbow. I'm thankful that he absorbs my weight as I stand. He does it quietly, without a show, and for that, I'm thankful.

"Of course not," I agree with Edward, still leaning ever so slightly on Lane. "I'll be ready to two-step in no time at all."

"I don't know what a two-step is, but we're gonna fox-trot till the sun comes up!" he answers happily. Sophie lifts an eyebrow.

"I mean, until a respectable hour," Edward corrects himself. I smile.

"I look forward to it."

"Let's get you some cider," Lane suggests, his voice low near my ear.

"It's spiked," I tell him.

"Let's get you some water and *me* some cider," he amends. I smile again.

"Deal."

He guides me to a wing-back chair by the fire, the very one that I'd passed out in the night before the Norton party left for their expedition. It's practically new now and just as uncomfortable as ever.

"You stay put," he instructs. "I'll be right back." A dimple appears on his left cheek, a surprise glimpse of joy on a face that has seen so much battle. As he walks away, I know I need to learn more about this man. He's like no one I've ever met before. He's responsible, gallant, kind, gentlemanly, yet I can tell he's got a wicked sense of humor that he hides in order to be respectful.

"The Greatest Generation," I mutter, repeating something

my gran had said a hundred times before, as I start to see what she meant.

"What?" Marina says as she plops on the arm of the chair.

"Nothing. I just feel silly. Everyone is going to think I'm some weakling."

"No one is a weakling in Alaska," she answers firmly. "If you're here, then you're worthy."

"That's true," I agree.

"Lane's taken a shine to you. He never likes anyone."

"That can't be true," I answer, as I watch him fill up a cup with cider and then disappear into the kitchen, presumably to get a glass of plain water for me.

"It's very true." She nods. "I've known him a long time. He's never had a special girl. He never wanted one."

"I wonder why?" I ask, trying to seem casually interested.

But Marina stares at me knowingly.

"He told me once that he wants what he wants. That he's willing to wait for the perfect thing. Here in Alaska, we don't always get the choices everyone else gets in the lower forty-eight, whether it's a car, or a coat, or a person. But he said he's willing to wait."

"How long ago was that?" I ask.

She shrugs her slender shoulders. "I dunno. High school."

"The war might've changed that," I suggest. She appears doubtful.

"I think it actually just strengthened his resolve."

"There's nothing wrong with that," I declare. She agrees.

"No. Not if there's something *worth waiting for.*" She winks and stands up, swaying a bit to the sound of the big band song coming from the crackling record player. "Don't forget to dance with Edward, if you feel up to it. He's really looking forward to it, and he's sweet."

She wanders off, and I notice that one of the lines I drew up the back of her stocking is a bit crooked by the knee. I hope she doesn't notice.

I'm watching the paper gingerbread man garland flutter in front of the fireplace when Lane returns with a glass of icy water.

"Drink up," he instructs me. "You might be dehydrated. I saw it all the time out in the field."

The *battlefield*, I realize. I obediently take a drink.

"Being dehydrated can cause all kinds of issues," he tells me. "I saw soldiers pass clean out just like you did. Especially if they were standing at attention for too long with locked knees."

"Did it ever happen to you?"

He shakes his head. "Nah. I drink too much." He lifts his cup and takes a long draw of the spiked cider as if to prove it. But then he laughs. "I don't want you to get the wrong impression. I haven't had a drop of liquor since I came back."

"When did you get back?" I ask, sipping my water again. It tastes clear and pure, without any kind of filtration.

His eyes cloud over for a scant moment. "Four months ago."

"Oh, boy. And your shoulder still gives you so much trouble? You should go see a specialist."

"They aren't exactly a dime a dozen up here," he points out.

He's got a point. Nineteen forty-four Alaska is even more remote and rugged than twenty-first-century Alaska.

"Does it scare you that you've lost your memory?" he asks, changing the subject.

It's a blunt question and one that no one else has asked. I try to imagine what it would be like if I had truly lost my memory. Of course it would be frightening, so I tell him so.

"Yes."

"It would come in handy to lose memories . . . if we could pick and choose," he says in a low voice, and that cloud hovers over his face again, making me scared to think of the things he'd like to forget.

"Do you have any brothers or sisters?" I ask. He shakes his head.

"No. I'm an only child. My ma had a hard time getting pregnant with me. They considered me their miracle."

"Same," I tell him. "So we've got that in common."

"My folks are gone now."

"Also same," I tell him. He eyes snap up and meet mine.

"You remember that?"

"It just now came to me. I remember abstract concepts. Like, I get the feeling that I'm all alone."

"I am too," he says softly, and his hand reaches to squeeze mine for a brief and respectable moment. Then he puts his back in his pocket.

"But that's okay," he adds. "It just means that we can write history however we want it to be. No expectations, no excuses, and no one telling us what to do with our lives."

"That's true," I agree. "But with so many options, and no one giving input, it seems like too big a decision to make."

"Nah," he argues. "It just means that we have to clear our heads and listen. We'll figure out what we want."

"You sound pretty sure of yourself."

"I am," he agrees. "A person has got to be, don't you think?"

It's a sexy trait, I decide. He's self-assured but not cocky. He's . . . capable. Talking to him, I have no doubt that he'll do whatever he sets out to do, and more than likely, he'll do it with his own two hands. It's admirable and a very different attitude from that of men from my own generation.

It's refreshing.

Sometimes progress isn't all it's cracked up to be, I decide, as I think of men with manicured hands and briefcases. Not that there's anything wrong with that either. Lane is just different.

Men here are different. They don't keep their faces buried in their phones, because they don't have phones. They actually engage in conversation, and they appear to have stringent manners. It's so odd.

"You're not on a different planet," I mutter to myself. Lane, who had been staring out the window at the swirling snow, pivots toward me.

"Pardon?"

"You must be happy to be home," I say instead of repeating myself.

"Yes and no," he answers. "Yes, I am. But no, I'm not. I hate leaving my buddies there without me."

"You can't help what happened," I tell him. "They know that, I'm sure."

"I tried to get them to let me heal up and then send me back," he says, a slight wooden tone to his voice. "But no dice. I'm damaged goods now."

"You are not. But the good side to that coin is now you're home."

"Yes and no. My home is gone, burned to the ground. My parents died in the fire. My buddies are all still out there, fighting the good fight. I should be there with them."

"But instead, you're sitting here with me, safe and sound. I get it. You feel guilty."

He shrugs. "I guess I do. I have friends who didn't make it. They'll never get to go home, where they have families waiting for them. Yet here I am . . . home with no home to return to. It's practically a waste."

"You have survivor's guilt," I tell him.

"That's not a real thing," he says uncertainly.

"It is. But that's neither here nor there. You survived for a reason. You'll figure out what it is."

"I'm glad you have faith in me," he says, smiling now, his dimple reappearing. I fight the urge to put my finger in it.

I stand up and sway once again.

"Goodness. I still don't know what's wrong with me," I tell him. "It's so strange."

"It's probably me," Lane says seriously. "Ladies swoon in my presence all of the time. I overwhelm them, I guess. It's a gift and a curse."

I laugh at his good-natured audacity. "I bet it is. You'd have had a girl in every port, if you weren't so worried about them hurting themselves by fainting in your mere presence. You're quite a gentleman, if you think about it."

"I was a soldier, not a sailor," he tells me. "So I didn't have ports. But even if I were a sailor, I wouldn't do that. I'm a one-woman man."

He says that so firmly, so . . . honorably, that I swear my ovaries twitch again.

"They don't make them like you anymore," I tell him.

He shakes his head and rolls his eyes. "You really do have a head injury."

"Hughes," Dale calls from the table. "I need ya over here, son." The men around the table hold their cards as they wait, and Lane turns to me.

"It's a pleasure to meet you," he says, his warm eyes meeting mine.

"I'll be seeing you again," I remind him. "Since you're living here now."

His cheeks oh-so-briefly flush. "Very true."

He lifts his fingers in an old-fashioned tipping-the-hat gesture and then joins the men.

When I move to Marina in front of the fire, she's twirling her hair, her eyes sparkling.

"Do not let Mama see you glowing like that after you talk with Lane, or she'll make him sleep in the barn," she warns, only half joking, I'm sure.

She glances up. "There's Edward. While you're dancing with him, I'm gonna see if I can bum a smoke off Frankie. If I can, I'll meet you outside."

Before I can retort, Edward fills my frame of vision, a blush dusting his pale cheeks.

"You free for that dance?" he asks nervously. I smile to set him at ease.

"For you, always," I tell him. He holds his arm out, I take it, and he leads me four steps to the makeshift dance floor. Dale, after abandoning his card game, is spinning Sophie wildly, far out of time with the music, and judging from her grin, she's loving every minute of it.

Edward carefully puts his hand at my waist and looks into my eyes.

"Is this fine?" he asks, unsure.

I nod. "It's perfect."

We sail in a small circle, with Edward relaxing just a bit after a minute or two.

"You're not half bad," he says, and I choose to interpret that as a compliment.

"You too," I agree.

He beams, and the song comes to an end. We walk to the side, and he eyes the half-empty bowl of cider.

"Would you like a refreshment?" he says formally.

I shake my head. "No, thank you. You go ahead."

He makes his way over, light on his feet and humming.

"You made his entire life," Sophie tells me, as she pats her hair back into place after the vigorous dancing. "You're a very sweet girl."

"He's nice," I tell her. She nods.

"Most people here are."

Marina has returned and grabs me now, whirling me around

the room, the music spinning around us and through us, and I never in a hundred years would've thought that such a simple evening could be so much fun.

Outdoors, the snow falls and the wind howls, but here inside, we are cozy, and warm, and festive. Everyone is flushed and laughing, and I understand why Friday nights are everyone's favorite. They are an *event*.

Later, when Marina and I lie in my bed, she giggles.

"Your face when you came to, and Lane was right here! It was priceless!"

"You've got an evil streak," I tell her, but I'm not at all surprised. Gran always did have a sharpened side. It's nice to see that it was innate rather than developed over time.

"I do," she agrees cheerfully, as we huddle for warmth. The hot water bottles that Sophie placed at the end of our bed, tucked into the covers, warms my toes.

"I'll be honest with you," she says. "I've never seen him look at anyone the way he looked at you tonight. Don't hurt him, Piper, or I'll have to kill you."

She's only half kidding, and I know it.

"I'll do my best."

"I'm serious," she says. "He's a good guy. He doesn't deserve heartbreak."

And I'm not from this time.

Surely, I'll be able to go home, and then I'd leave him here.

"I hear you," I answer. "I don't intend on breaking his heart. You're giving me far too much credit. My womanly wiles haven't been developed yet."

"I think they're just fine," she says with a wink. "Lane is special, though, Pippie."

That name sends a jolt through me. It's something that my gran had called me since I was little. My head yanks up and I stare at her. Does she remember?

Her expression is blank and startled as she looks back at me. No, she does not.

I relax.

"What in the world is wrong with you?" she asks, reaching over to cover my shoulder with the blanket. "I'm just saying, go easy on my friend. He's grieving his parents. He's all alone. Essie told my mother last month that he's got shell shock. He has nightmares."

Shell shock.

PTSD.

"That poor man," I murmur, thinking of his mischievous, kind eyes and the way he'd quietly supported me when I'd stood up.

"He'd never want you feeling sorry for him," she says firmly. "And don't you dare tell him I said anything. I don't know the specifics anyway. I doubt anyone does."

She snuggles in and goes to sleep, and I watch the snow drift against the windowpanes for hours, thinking of my situation. With the snow piling up as quickly as it is, I doubt they'll be able to get to town to ask about me, because they don't have snowmobiles, which is good.

It buys me some time.

But then what?

At some point, the snow will melt, and everyone in town

will say they have no idea who I am or how I got here. What will I do then?

Will I ever be able to get home?

Is it possible?

I didn't choose to come here, it just somehow happened.

How, then, can I get home?

It seems like, since I'm not supposed to be here, and it defies the natural order of things, I surely can't stay here forever.

But then again, maybe I happened upon a strange wormhole in time or something, and tumbled into it, and unless I find it again, I'll be stuck here.

It hadn't occurred to me until this moment . . . *I might never get home.*

This isn't a dream.

I find myself wishing I'd watched more sci-fi movies so that I'd know more about this subject.

I'm in a situation that shouldn't be scientifically possible, and there are no guidebooks or instruction manuals to help me figure it out. I don't have Google. I don't have a phone.

I can't simply say, *Siri, how do I get home?*

I'm stranded in 1944.

There's a beautiful, haunted man down the hall from me, and if I fall for him and then somehow *am* able to go home, I could break his heart, and that would be the singularly most vicious thing I've ever done.

I'm not a cruel person.

Even still, when I finally fall asleep, I'm thinking about the strong, steady feel of his hand on my back as he'd guided me across the room.

CHAPTER SIX

When I wake, it's still dark, and Marina isn't in bed with me. Her side of the bed is stone cold, an indication that she's been up for quite a long time. I bolt out of bed and get dressed, immediately guilty.

They're housing me; the least I can do is make sure I help around the house.

I patter down the stairs and rush toward the kitchen, where clattering sounds indicate breakfast is being made.

The hushed voices, though, stop me in my tracks.

They're talking about me.

"Jed Atkins and his boys went out yesterday and searched. There is no one else out there," Dale says, almost ruefully. "Whoever was with her, if anyone was, is gone."

"She didn't just wind up here alone," Sophie answers. "A young girl like that didn't just show up in Alaska, Dale."

"I know." He sighs. "And I know what it means. She was with someone, and that someone is . . . gone."

As in, *dead.*

I swallow hard. Surely Dan isn't dead. I'd assumed that

I was the only one to travel here. It hadn't occurred to me that the process might have brought him here, too, might've killed him.

"Come spring, when the snow melts, whoever she was with will be found."

"It'll kill her," Marina says, clearly troubled. "We've got to do something, Pop."

"You know there's nothing we can do," Sophie interjects. "The snow last night has made it impossible."

"They shouldn't have been out in the elements. Everyone knows that."

"I just can't rightly figure out what they were doing," Dale muses.

"It'll all come out in the wash," Sophie decides.

"You know, eavesdropping is considered rude by some," a low voice says near my ear. I whirl to find Lane.

His hair is combed, his shirt is tucked, his eyes are devilish.

"I—I . . ." I have no excuse. I stare at the floor, my cheeks on fire.

"I don't blame you," he says quietly. "You must feel so lost."

"I *am* lost," I answer.

It's not a lie. I'm lost in *time*.

"Not true. You've been found, by some of the kindest folks in Alaska. You lucked out there."

I nod. "I agree."

He holds out his arm. "Let's get some food in your belly. Everything will feel better after that. Sophie makes the world's best biscuits and gravy."

True to my suspicions, it tastes just like what my gran

would eventually come to make. I shovel it in my mouth with abandon, and only notice a few minutes later that everyone is staring at me.

I pause, swallow hard, and reach for coffee.

"I'm sorry," I say, patting my mouth primly with a napkin. "It's just so good, Sophie. It tastes like what my gran used to make."

Marina's head snaps up. "You remember?"

I shrug. "I remember that. I don't see her face, and I don't see her name, but I see the food she used to make." I feel horrible lying, particularly when I see the sympathy on everyone's faces.

I swallow hard again.

"It's a good sign," Dale decides, sipping his strong coffee. "I have no doubt that everything will eventually come back to you."

"And until it does, you're safe and sound here," Sophie reminds me, depositing two more biscuits onto my plate.

Lane watches in admiration as I load them up with gravy. "I haven't seen anyone eat like that since back in the mess hall," he announces.

Marina scowls at him and swats his shoulder. "Don't make her feel bad," she tells him. "She needs some meat on her bones, anyway."

"I'm not making her feel bad," he answers. "It's a compliment!" He turns to me. "Right?"

I don't see how.

"If you say so," I agree amenably. He smiles over his cup, his eyes crinkled at the corners.

"You want to burn off those biscuits?" he asks.

I'm cautious.

"How?"

"I'm going to take care of the herd while I'm here. You can help."

"Lane Hughes, she is not going to traipse out and about in the cold to help you feed reindeer." Sophie clucks. She continues on about how I'm recovering from an injury, et cetera, et cetera, but my mouth has dropped open.

"Reindeer?"

Lane nods in satisfaction. "Reindeer."

"Yes," I say immediately. "I'd love to see them."

"Oh, girlie, you don't know what you're asking." Sophie sighs. "Dale started a herd a few years back, and they're huge. Their water troughs need the ice broken, they need hay, the barn needs to be mucked out, and it's frigid outside, as you well know."

"Let her see them, Soph," Dale interjects. "They might do her good." He turns to me. "They're the gentlest creatures you've ever laid eyes upon," he tells me.

"But why do you have them?" I ask.

He stares at me. "I like them." He shrugs. "They're indigenous to Alaska, you know."

I do know. In the wild, they're caribou. They're only "reindeer" when they're tame. I'd seen that wild doe just before I came here.

I also know that our family has never, ever had things, pets, or products that don't somehow make money for the business.

"Don't they eat a lot?" I ask curiously. I mean . . . *rations*.

Sophie *hmmph*s now and I can see it's a sore subject.

"They're mostly free-range in the summer," Dale says. "And in the winter, they eat lichen under the snow. It's why their hooves are so sharp, so they can paw away the snow. I'm thinking that someday, after the war, we can have a reindeer petting zoo. Children will love it."

My immediate question is . . . are there enough children in this area to warrant having a petting zoo? But I don't ask, because Sophie is already disapproving, and Dale obviously loves the reindeer.

"Land sakes, Dale," Sophie mutters. "Your head is always in the clouds."

"Let's go," Lane suggests.

Gladly. I hate awkwardness of any kind, but particularly when a married couple disagrees on something and I have to witness it. It makes me feel like I'm watching something I shouldn't be.

"Go with them," Sophie tells Marina, who groans. Her mother shoots her a sharp look, though, so Marina stands.

I scramble up, put my dishes next to the sink, and rush out to bundle up.

Marina is already in the foyer, pulling on an overcoat, her father's from the looks of it. She grumbles and shoves a canvas overcoat at me.

"Where's mine?" I ask, confused.

"Yours must've been very old. I hung it up to dry, and when I went to check on it, it had literally fallen apart."

My North Face parka that was only a few months old? That literally makes no sense. But I don't argue. Instead, I pull the canvas coat on. It draws less attention to me anyway, when I look like they do.

"This is the last thing I wanted to do this morning," Marina says, stuffing her arm into the armhole. "Playing chaperone for the two of you. Why can't you just play footsie under the table like normal people?"

"No one actually plays footsie," I tell her, skirting her implications. "And no one needs to chaperone me."

"Do you have any idea how cold it is out there right now?" she demands, gesturing toward the windows. Through them, I see the floating white snow, the frost on the glass.

"Subzero," I answer cheerfully, pulling on a hat.

"I know I say this often, but you can really, really tell that you hit your head," she advises me. I grin.

"Oh, come on. Let's get some fresh air and stop bellyaching."

I leave her sputtering as I pull open the heavy front doors. The winter air immediately freezes my nose closed.

Marina hooks me from behind with a scarf, tossing it around my neck like it's a lasso and I'm a wayward calf.

"I swear, it's like you *want* to catch your death," she grumbles. I twirl the scarf around my neck and mouth a few times, and the two of us crunch across the snow to the barn behind the lodge.

She slides open the heavy door, and we step inside.

The sweet smell of hay rushes over me, and I spin around, taking in the rustic surroundings. The barn is thick, old wood. It's dim in here and apparently kept as warm as possible for the animals.

Toward the back of the barn, I can see furry bodies moving in an indoor corral.

I peer closer and the forms of giant reindeer appear.

I'm like a bee to honey as I head for them.

Marina trails much more slowly, and I am in heaven as the curious creatures approach without fear and nuzzle me. One, two, three of them sniff at me, nudging my hand and my pockets.

"Watch out for that one!" Marina calls, gesturing to the reindeer on my left. He eyes me and promptly nibbles a bit too hard for comfort on my hand. "He bites," she finishes limply, too late.

"Thanks," I tell her wryly, rubbing my arm.

"Roger is a good boy," she croons, rubbing his face. "He just gets a little . . . pushy when he's hungry."

She pulls out a carrot and sticks it unceremoniously into his mouth.

"You've got three reindeer," I say in wonderment.

"No," she answers. "We've got ten. The others must be out back. We leave the back door open during the day. Daddy must've opened it before breakfast."

"Ten reindeer," I repeat dumbly.

She wrinkles her forehead. "Well, ten and a half. If you count Nugget."

"Nugget?"

It's at this very moment that a small flash of grayish brown comes flying in from the back gate and careens toward us.

A baby reindeer skids to a stop in front of us.

"Is that a baby . . ."

"Nugget," Marina confirms. "This is our baby reindeer, Nugget."

I squeal in absolute delight and drop to my knees, smothering the adorable animal with kisses on his sweet, fuzzy nose. His eyes are coal black, like a teddy bear's, and he might be the cutest thing I've ever seen.

When I voice that to Marina, she laughs. "Don't be deceived," she warns. "He's also the orneriest. Seriously, guard your pockets—he's a world-class pickpocket."

He looks at me with the cutest expression, and I notice as he backs up that his leg is crooked.

"Oh, no," I say, bending to examine it. "What happened?"

"He was born that way," Marina answers. "It doesn't seem to cause him any pain."

"Poor little guy."

"Again, don't be deceived," she says. "He's got a great life. Every doe in the herd takes care of him."

"They all look like does," I mention, scanning the herd that has accumulated in the corral. "None of them have horns."

"Antlers," Marina corrects. "And reindeer are interesting. They *all* grow antlers, males and females alike. They lose them once a year or so, like these all have. And then they grow back later in the year."

"I didn't know that."

"They're pretty interesting," Marina says, rubbing the neck of one. "And these are very tame. When they're wild, they're called caribou."

"I *did* know that," I concur.

"I see you've met the household menace," Lane interjects,

approaching from the front of the barn. He carries two buckets of steaming water.

"How do you know? You just got here last night," I point out.

He laughs. "I didn't arrive from China," he answers. "I've been staying at the Kleins' . . . just down the mountain. I come up here to help out from time to time. I can personally tell you, this little guy is a scamp."

"I think you've been maligned," I tell Nugget. His ear twitches, and it's almost like he's agreeing. Lane and Marina laugh.

"Yep, he's got you wrapped around his hoof already," Lane observes. He nudges past us and into the corral, where he sets the buckets down next to the frozen water troughs. He grabs a pickax and rams it into the ice, over and over, before he then pours the hot water on top. The reindeer gather around curiously, sniffing at the steam, and then lap at the water.

"They're simply magical." I sigh happily.

Marina doesn't seem annoyed anymore as she smiles. "I'm glad you like them. They're a heck of a lot of work."

"Your mom doesn't seem to like them much," I point out. She sighs.

"My father . . . he gets big ideas that don't always pan out," she offers simply. "My mom has to be the down-to-earth one."

"He's a dreamer," I answer. "There's nothing wrong with that."

"Tell that to the sixty cases of snake oil in our basement that he bought before the war. He thought it would make us rich to resell it. Or the plan he had of building custom furniture."

"He makes incredible pieces," I say defensively, thinking of the heavy armoire in my bedroom back home.

"How could you possibly know that?" Marina demands. "Although you're right. He does. But then the war happened, and . . ."

"And nothing has been the same," I finish for her.

She nods.

"Well, all I'm saying is the world needs visionaries, so it's a good trait to have."

"Don't let Mama hear you talking like that," Marina warns. "Or you'll get on her bad side."

"Do you remember when he wanted to sell wolf pelts to the lower forty-eight?" Lane asks Marina.

"You can't hunt an endangered species," I say with a chuckle.

"Endangered?" Marina lifts an eyebrow. "You get some crazy ideas, girlie."

Being an endangered species probably isn't even a thing in 1944.

Sheepishly, I shrug. "They just seem too beautiful to kill."

"They are beautiful," Lane agrees. "They also are predators that kill our farm animals."

"That's the cycle of life." I shrug again. "I don't mean to be flippant, but they've gotta eat too."

"Would you say that if one ate Nugget?" Marina asks, her eyes narrowed. "It's not actually so cut-and-dried."

"Nothing ever is," I agree.

"Anywho," Lane drawls. "Who is mucking stalls?"

Marina and I both point to the other.

Lane laughs.

"I'll do it. Who can get a few flakes of hay down from the loft?"

"I can," I answer.

"And since you already broke the ice in the troughs, I'll just be over here supervising," Marina attempts.

Lane rolls his eyes. "Nice try. You can gather eggs since we're out here already."

"Oh, boy-o." She sighs. "You're worse than Mama."

As I climb up the wooden ladder to the hayloft, I gaze down at Marina . . . my gran. She's so different now. So girlish, so immature. She wasn't born perfect after all.

Currently, she's kicking at the ground while she pretends to gather eggs, while Lane mucks the stalls seemingly without even breaking a sweat.

I'm covered in itchy hay by the time I return to them with a few two-inch-thick flakes.

"Toss 'em in!" Lane calls. "They'll love you forever."

I hurl them over the gate, and the herd converges to munch.

"I'm not exactly on their mind right now," I say wryly, watching the melee unfold. Lane laughs, and behind us, Marina crows in disgust as she steps in reindeer scat.

"Lane, you missed a spot," she grumbles, holding up her foot.

He tosses her a shovel, which she easily catches in her gloved hand.

"That's not what I had in mind," she says ruefully. He grins again.

"I'm sure it wasn't," he agrees cheerfully. The sleeve of his coat has slid up, and a jagged scar shows on his wrist. It's angry and red, recently formed.

"What did you do in the war?" I ask, making conversation.

Marina shoots me a glance, warning me. *Be quiet.*

My head yanks back.

I hadn't meant any harm, but Lane's face is closed off now.

"Just an ordinary GI, ma'am," he says. The forced cheerfulness in his tone is apparent.

I've messed up again. People didn't talk about this stuff in the forties. Talking about feelings and intimate details just wasn't done.

Dang it.

"Well, I'm not sure if I told you last night, but thank you for your service," I tell him, trying to backpedal. "We appreciate you."

He smiles gently now. "You're welcome. I wish I could've done more. I'm gonna go check the cistern."

He heads out of the barn, with a steady swagger and broad shoulders.

Marina turns to me.

"What in the world . . ." She sighs. "Piper, I swear. Were you born yesterday? Don't make him sad. He's suffered enough already."

"I didn't mean to," I tell her. "I swear."

"I know. Your social graces are just lacking from your injury," she says, but I can tell she's doubting it at this point. She's generally just wondering if I were born in a barn.

"What is a cistern?" I ask curiously. I've heard the word before but never bothered to find out what it is.

She stares at me with an expression that I'm rapidly memorizing because I'm seeing it so often.

"It's where the rainwater is collected off the roof," she explains. "It falls onto the roof, then collected in a pipe that runs into a storage tank."

"And then what? You water the animals with it?"

"We drink it, goof." She shoves my shoulder playfully.

"How do you filter it?"

"Why would we need to?" she answers my question with a question. "It's clean rainwater. Lane is just checking to make sure the pipe hasn't busted from freezing. We probably won't need the cistern water—it's a backup source."

"Oh."

There's literally no way I'm going to keep from getting caught. They're going to realize that I know absolutely nothing about life in the forties, and I don't have Google to help a girl out right now.

The best way forward is to just try to keep my mouth shut, I decide. The less I say, the less I can mess up.

"Let's gather the eggs while we're out here," Marina says. She picks up an empty bushel basket and we head to the back corner of the barn, where a chicken coop stands. "Hello, girls," she greets the clucking birds.

They eye us suspiciously as we invade their musty, warm space.

"This thing is insulated really well," I say in admiration.

Marina glances up from sticking her hand under a hen. "When my dad builds something, he does it right. He built the dining room table and the wing-back chairs in front of the fireplace. They'll probably last a million years, sadly. They're the most uncomfortable chairs I've ever sat on."

I don't disagree. And it makes sense now why Gran insisted we keep them.

"They're beautiful, though," I answer.

She hands me a large speckled egg.

"Pop likes beautiful things. These reindeer . . . do you know why they're here?"

I shake my head.

"Because they're so tame and friendly, he thinks they'll be good for the men. For Edward, and William and Frankie. For Lane. For Albie. For everyone. He asks them to chip in and 'help take care of the reindeer,' but actually, he wants the reindeer to soothe their souls."

"Therapy animals," I murmur. She raises an eyebrow, and I shake my head. "Your dad has a soft heart."

"Don't say that," she snaps, and already, I've said the wrong thing. "He does not. He just cares about people. He's every bit as tough as anyone else. You're staying here under his invitation. You shouldn't bite the hand that feeds you, girlie."

She stomps out in a huff and I chase after her.

"Marina, I didn't mean that in a bad way," I insist. "I was paying him a compliment. Too many men, in my opinion, don't allow themselves to be kind. They're too focused on being manly all of the time. Your dad is manly *and* he's kind. I admire that."

She narrows her eyes but pauses and lets me continue.

I try to think of how to explain toxic masculinity without actually explaining it. It's a theory that hasn't been thought of yet.

"He's a good man," I say instead, limply. "I'm grateful for him and for your entire family."

She relaxes now. "I'm sorry. I didn't mean to snap at you. It's just a sore subject with me. I don't like it when anyone says anything about my pop."

"No, of course not. But who in the world would say *anything* derogatory about your dad?"

"Alaska is a hard place," she finally answers. "People don't always realize that you don't need to be a hard person to live here."

So, gossip and perception mattered in the forties too. Some things never change.

"Your dad is special," I say. "In a very good way. You're lucky to have him."

Her face softens, and she smiles. "I think so too."

"The cistern is fine," Lane says, stepping forward in a swirl of snow. "It's coming down again." He looks at us. "What did I miss?"

"Not a thing," Marina assures him.

"Good. Your dad wants to cut down a tree for Christmas and needs you girls to pick it out. He's waiting on the porch."

Marina exchanges a glance with me. It roughly translates into *See? My dad is amazing.*

I smile back at her in confirmation, because he truly is.

CHAPTER SEVEN

Your mama wants a nice tree for the men," Dale tells Marina as we tramp through the snow, examining pine trees within walking distance of the lodge. "It's good for their morale."

"Daddy, Mama hates the pine needles on the floor," Marina says. "You're the one who likes it."

He smiles, his mouth and eyes the only thing not covered by his scarf and stocking cap. But his eyes twinkle warmly, regardless of the chill in the air.

He doesn't confirm or deny. He simply says, "Don't let your mama fool you. She likes it too."

"No doubt," Marina agrees. She points into the distance. "There. Look at that one."

"Yessiree," Dale agrees, gazing at it. "Looks to be about nine feet tall, full bottomed, perfectly formed. Nicely done, young lady."

He marches ahead to examine it more closely and waves when he determines that it is the one. He spreads a canvas tarp on top of the snow next to the tree.

Marina and I join him as he drops to the ground on his back and hacks away at the trunk with a handsaw.

It takes him less time than I would've thought, and soon, the tree topples onto the canvas.

"Good job, Daddy," Marina tells him.

"Hold that end, honey," he instructs her, gesturing toward the corner of the tarp. He threads a rope through a large grommet and then tosses the rope to Marina for her to do the same.

Before I know it, we're pulling the tree on its makeshift sled back toward the lodge.

"Do you remember anything about Christmas in your home?" Dale asks as we tug. "Do you decorate a tree?"

I think of the giant tree, similar to this one, that we've always put in the great room, how we always decorated it together until my parents died, and then my gran and I carried on the tradition alone, and how I'd forgotten to put the traditional heirloom strings of bells on it.

"No," I reply. "I can't remember."

"Don't fret about it none, you hear?" he says. "It'll all come back."

I nod. "I know. It has to."

We tug the tree up the front steps, and the door opens. Sophie waits, pointing to a spot near the fireplace.

"Over there," she directs. "If you must drag an entire tree into my living room."

She clucks and Marina rolls her eyes.

"Notice how she's already popped corn to string for it," Marina whispers in my ear. I giggle and eye Albert, who is standing in the doorway to the kitchen with a giant bowl of popcorn in his hands.

Sophie looks at me. "What are you girls getting on about?"

"Nothing, Mama," Marina says innocently. "Piper's just excited. She doesn't remember Christmas at her home."

"You poor thing." Sophie clucks again. "Don't you worry. We'll give you a beautiful Christmas. It might not be the same as before the war, but don't you fret. It'll still be nice. I'm going to have you girls string the popcorn for the tree."

Marina winks at me, and I force myself not to laugh.

Dale isn't the only softie in the house.

Albert carries the bowl to the dining room table, where string, scissors, and large needles are already laid out.

Sophie turns to Marina. "Be a dear and run downstairs to fetch the ornaments."

Marina trots off, and Sophie turns to me.

"If you don't mind, you can get started with Albert. Be sure to keep an eye on him—make sure he doesn't eat all of the popcorn."

I grin. "I love popcorn."

"Oh, boy. This Christmas tree is doomed."

She waggles her finger toward us before she heads down the hall.

Albert is chewing when I reach the table.

"Sophie will kill us if we eat the popcorn," I tell him as I steal one morsel.

He shakes his head. "Her bark is worse than her bite."

He hands me a threaded needle. "Ladies first."

I thread piece after piece while Albert works on another.

His hands are big and calloused, and he doesn't wear a ring. He's friendly but formal.

"What do you do for a living, Albert?" I ask politely. He's

clearly better at sewing than I am. His fingers are deft and precise.

"I'm a logger. Same as Willie and Frank. They stay up here in the winter to work. After the spring breakup, they'll head back to Anchorage to be with their wives."

"Oh my word. They don't see their wives all winter?"

"Why, no," he answers. "They can't get down the mountain in weather like this, miss. Their wives keep their houses going until the men get home."

"Why don't they just get jobs in the city?"

Albert glances at me. "Logging is what we know, miss."

Hoping he doesn't think I've insulted him, I smile. "Don't call me miss, please. I'm just Piper."

"Well, just Piper, what's your favorite Christmas carol?"

"'Rudolph, the Red-Nosed Reindeer,'" I tell him.

He shakes his head. "I don't know that one."

"Oh, come on." I nudge him, and then sing a few bars. He still shakes his head, and I realize that maybe it hasn't been written yet.

"How about 'The Little Drummer Boy'?" he asks.

I start singing, and he joins in.

We sing as we thread, and it seems as normal as can be.

"My wife used to love that one," he tells me when we're finished. "It was her favorite."

Used to. Was.

Those are past-tense words. I swallow hard.

"Do you want to sing it again?" I offer gently. He nods.

I start singing, and he joins in, his face soft, his eyes glassy.

Even when we're finished, he continues humming.

"I'm sorry for your loss," I tell him without meeting his gaze.

His jaw clenches ever so slightly. "Thank you. It's been over a year now, but some days, it feels like yesterday. Like maybe even if I think hard enough, I can open our front door and walk in, and she'll still be there."

The other men have wives to go back to, and he doesn't.

I'm not equipped to deal with this.

Or am I?

It's not the same, but my parents did die in a plane crash on this snowy mountainside. I know a little something about grief.

I can't share with him that I understand the overwhelming emotion, the way time drags and flies at the same time, and how there's a lump in your throat that you can't swallow for months and months afterward. I can't share any of that, because I'm not supposed to remember the details.

"I can't imagine how you feel," I say softly. "But that seems pretty normal."

"There is no normal now," he says astutely, knotting his row and clipping the thread. "There's only *different*."

I think back to how this lodge felt different after my parents died. It was the same building, but when it was only Gran and me here, the dynamic changed. It was different, even though it was the same.

"It'll get easier," I tell him gently. "I'm sure."

He nods but doesn't say a word. How can he? He can't see it yet. He can only see the present, and the present is painful. I make up my mind to pay him a bit of special attention if I can, to help his holiday feel less lonely.

After we've threaded all of the corn, draped it around the tree, and I'm walking away down the hall, I can still hear Albert humming "The Little Drummer Boy," over and over.

"Lord," I say as I close the bedroom door behind me, and Marina looks at me from the bed, where she sits surrounded by papers. "Albert's story is sad."

She nods. "By all accounts, his wife was a lovely person."

Her hand flits from paper to paper, as if she can't decide which to land on.

"What's all that?" I ask, stepping over to her.

"Letters from my man," she says cheekily, giving me a wink. "He's in France."

My granddad Ollie.

I smile. "Tell me about him."

I perch on the edge of the bed.

"Oh, boy. I could talk about him all night. You know, I'll just read you one."

She lifts a letter, the paper visibly dirty. She reads his words lovingly, each one forming a love song of their own.

"'To my favorite girl,

"Lord, I miss your pretty face. Nobody here keeps me in line quite the same as you do. Baby, I know it's hard that you won't get letters this winter, but don't worry. By the spring thaw, I'll surely be there to deliver them in person. And I'm better than an ol' letter, right?'"

Marina pauses. "He's a bit confident," she tells me. "But he wears it well."

I smile.

"'Danny Boy and Short Stuff . . . you asked me about them

in your last letter. Short Stuff is really tall, and Danny Boy is Danny. Anyway, both of their girls sent Dear John letters. Can you believe that? We're over here trying to do something good, and those dames stomped on their hearts. Short Stuff handled it better than Danny Boy. He was a wreck, and darn near got us killed awhile back from not paying attention. Anyway. Months ago, we each got an anchor tattoo on our forearms. Now, before you get angry, my love, we decided that the anchors stood for our girls—and how you're with us through thick and thin, reminding us of what we have waitin' at home.'"

She pauses again and looks at me almost wearily. "What could I say to that? Because of course Mama isn't going to like that when she sees it, but he's still the boy I'm going to marry. So she'll have to get over it, and his reason is so *sweet.*"

She looks back down at the letter, and continues.

"'So you can see how they're extra upset now because tattoos are permanent and their girls weren't. I told them: They didn't have to stand for those girls in particular. They could stand for their future wives. That seemed to help.

"'Since this is the last letter till spring, I'll leave you with this. Nothing will happen to me, my girl. Don't worry your pretty head for even one minute, because before you know it, I'll be there with you. France is beautiful here in the countryside, but it doesn't hold a candle to you. I can't wait to see you soon, and I can't wait for you to be my wife. That compass you gave me for luck is holding up just fine, and someday soon, it'll lead me back home to you. Don't you doubt it.

"'All my love, your American Hero.'"

She smiles with watery eyes. "He wears it well," she reminds me of his confidence. "The compass was my dad's. He got it in the First World War."

The compass had been Dale's? That's something I didn't know, or at least didn't remember. I wish that I had paid more attention to Gran's stories when I was growing up. To be honest, at the time, they had seemed so hard to relate to. I hadn't been there and I didn't always know who she was talking about. So it was difficult to get into her stories.

When she'd left me the letter with the compass that is currently in my pocket, and yet apparently also somehow in France, I wish she'd told me the story again. But all I had was her promise that it would always help guide me home.

I reach into my pocket, my fingers touching the cold brass.

I hadn't known it was a family heirloom. I guess I'd thought she'd gotten it from a guest. It hadn't occurred to me to be curious.

I also hadn't known that Dale had fought in World War I. Now it makes sense, how he wants to care for men who don't have anyone else.

"Well, your young man will forever be known to me as A.H.," I tell her. "American Hero."

She giggles. "Never let him hear you say that. His head will get too big for his neck to carry."

We laugh and she refolds the letters, placing them back into their envelopes. I look at the battered envelopes with bright postage, all sent from different places, all slightly dirty or torn.

"I can't wait to hear his stories about all of these places," Marina says, stacking them into a neat pile and tying them tightly with twine. "And what all he has seen."

"He might not want to talk about it," I say. "But I think we should encourage them to. They don't have to suffer in silence."

She looks confused, and I remember that men used to be expected to suck it up and not talk about their experiences like this, which might be perceived as weakness.

"Yeah," she agrees, without understanding what I'm saying, and I let it drop. I don't know a lot about the space-time continuum and whatnot, but from every movie I've ever watched, you should never tamper with time. I should try not to change anything.

But Lord. The realization slowly dawns on me that I could literally change the course of history, maybe. I could leave a note that JFK shouldn't take that ride in the motorcade, or someone should check on Marilyn Monroe the night she dies, or . . .

I forcibly stop those thoughts. Because . . . I could also leave a note telling my parents not to take that flight that day.

Then my parents wouldn't have died, and Gran wouldn't have carried the guilt of telling them it was safe to fly. It hadn't been her fault—the weather had been safe. She'd had no way of knowing that the deicers on the plane would fail.

But no one could ever convince her of that . . . that it hadn't somehow been her fault.

She carried that guilt until she died.

What could happen if I just made that one tiny change? In the big picture, it surely can't affect the world if two people just . . . don't die. Two people.

It's a thought I can't stop going over again and again throughout the evening.

I could write a letter explaining everything, and then leave it somewhere that someone will find it in the future.

Obviously, I can't say anything else in the letter about JFK or Marilyn, because those changes would affect millions in one way or another and that was surely interfering too much with the fabric of time. That would surely bear too many consequences. But this? Two people? One married couple in Alaska? That wouldn't affect anyone but me and Gran.

To distract myself from the thoughts at dinner, I pass the butter beans and turn to Dale.

"Marina told me the story of your compass today," I tell him. "It's so sweet that you let her send it to her fiancé."

Sophie clucks. "Let? We didn't know. If he doesn't come back, that piece of history dies with him, Marina."

"That's the whole point, Mama," Marina assures her. "He'll move heaven and earth to get that compass back to me. That's why I sent it."

She's pleased with herself for her strategy. And while I do have the benefit of knowing that it all turns out well because my granddad didn't die in the war, I do have to admit her plan is clever, and I tell her so.

"Don't encourage her," Sophie chides me.

"She gets her cleverness from her father," Dale interjects with a wink.

"Are you saying I'm not clever? I thought you were smarter than that!" Sophie chucks her half-eaten dinner roll at him, which he catches neatly and tears off a big bite.

"Of course not. My wife is the most beautiful, intelligent woman in the world."

Marina blinks. "Ew."

Sophie blushes and laughs.

The men chat back and forth, and it's halfway through dinner when I catch Lane staring at me.

His gaze is so direct, so honest, so forthright that it causes a physical reaction in me. I almost have trouble breathing as I think about how everything about me is a lie to him.

Everything but my name.

The energy in the air whenever the two of us are near is palpable. It's like nothing I've ever experienced in my "real" life. It must be the chemistry that romance books always reference. It's a live wire of electric current that connects us whenever our eyes meet.

As they do right now.

The edge of his lip tilts up.

I don't look away.

Marina clears her throat lightly, noticing.

I blush and turn to start a conversation with Edward, only to realize that I'm not on the side with his good ear.

I'm batting a thousand tonight.

Shoulders slumped, I chew a bite of beans and stare straight ahead, trying not to look in Lane's direction.

It proves impossible, and I reluctantly look at him.

He's waiting with a self-assured stare and a grin to match.

As I swallow, the cad has the nerve to wink at me.

Marina kicks me under the table, and I yank my attention over to her, as she pointedly chats about the Christmas tree and how we'll need to hang the ornaments after dinner.

After we clear the dishes and dry the pans, she turns to me.

"Were you dizzy in there?" she asks. "You can't flirt with Lane Hughes like that out in the open! Mama will make him sleep in the basement."

"Oh. Great. Did anyone else see? But I mean, you noticed it, too, right?"

"That he was staring at you like you were something to eat? Yes, I noticed."

I feel my shoulders relax.

Lord. I do want his attention.

I mean, to be honest, the odds of me somehow getting back to my own time are slim. Probably nonexistent since I don't know how I got here in the first place. It's not like I can just retrace my steps.

So, if I examine it through that lens, then engaging in a romance with Lane Hughes wouldn't be cruel of me after all.

I find myself disappointed when he excuses himself right after dinner and I don't see him the rest of the night.

That is, until he wakes the entire lodge by screaming in the middle of the night.

CHAPTER EIGHT

Marina and I leap out of bed to find Sophie and Dale already rushing into Lane's room. They close the door, but before they do, I catch a glimpse of Lane, wild-eyed and crouched in the middle of the bed. His eyes are vacant, like he's not even there.

He screams a few more times, in abject horror, his voice thick and guttural, before I hear Sophie's soft voice and then Dale's.

They manage to quiet him, and those of us congregated in the hall try not to look at each other or acknowledge that we're witnessing such a private moment. Lane wouldn't want witnesses to this.

"Well, good night again, everyone," I tell the boys. They nod, clearly agreeing with my unspoken assessment, as they all head back to their rooms. There's nothing to see here. We have a silent agreement not to acknowledge it.

"Poor Lane," Marina breathes as we climb back into bed. Our hot water bottles for our feet are still warm. "Did you see the look on his face? It was like he'd seen a ghost."

"It *was*," I agree. "Ghosts of his own."

"Poor Lane," she says again. "Tomorrow, we must promise to pretend not to know about this at all."

"Of course," I say quickly. "I'd never want to make him feel bad."

"He would too," she tells me. "To have everyone see him in that state . . . he'd just die. Maybe he won't remember a bit of it."

"We can hope," I tell her. We snuggle together for warmth, and I don't know what time it is when I finally drift back off to sleep.

At breakfast, I can't tell if Lane remembers or not. He doesn't show it one way or another, but he *is* uncharacteristically quiet.

When Marina, Sophie, and I are washing the breakfast dishes, I see him through the window over the sink slip away to the barn. I wipe out the cast-iron skillet without using water, as Sophie had shown me, and place it back on the stove.

"I think I'll go gather eggs," I say to no one in particular. Marina eyes me knowingly. Sophie smiles.

"That's so kind of you, dear. Thank you."

I bundle up, and at first when I enter the barn, I don't see him.

It's not until after I've collected the eggs and my eyes have adjusted to the dim light that I see his silhouette high above me, sitting in the loft.

"Hey, I'm out here collecting eggs," I call out. "Do you see any up there?"

He's quiet for a minute before he calls back, "You do realize that chickens don't fly, right? I mean, not very high."

"So that's a no?"

I think he chuckles, but I can't be sure.

Without waiting for permission, I climb the ladder to join him.

"I'd forgotten that . . . about the chickens," I tell him.

He glances at me from where his legs dangle over the edge of the loft, his arm slung along a wooden beam.

"Yeah. They don't fly. Not very high. They run real quick, though. My friends and I used to play a game in the summer. Did you know if you hold a chicken's head under its wing, it'll fall asleep in a few seconds?"

I shake my head.

"So, we'd see who could start with one chicken and then finish the whole flock before the first one woke up," he says with an embarrassed grin.

"Farm life was wild and crazy," I tease. He smiles good-naturedly.

"You don't remember if you grew up in the city or on a farm?"

I shake my head. "No. Nothing." I tap my temple. "It's empty up here."

He laughs. "It's not empty. It might not hold memories right now, but you're not empty-headed."

"A compliment! Thank you!"

"I dole them out when they're deserved," he says, unchagrined.

His thumb taps the side of his leg, the only indication that he's anxious. What has him on edge? His nightmares from last night? Being here in close quarters with me?

"I remember them," he tells me quietly, ending my curiosity. "The dreams. I saw your face last night. I didn't mean to scare you."

"You didn't," I assure him. "I was just worried about you. I wasn't scared. Do you want to talk about it?"

He lifts an eyebrow. "About the nightmares I get almost every night? No thanks."

"It's normal, you know," I tell him. "After something traumatic . . . to be tormented by it. I can't imagine what you saw, and I'm sorry you had to see it."

"I'm fine," he says stiffly. "But thank you."

"You're not fine," I answer. "Not yet. But you will be. Time heals, I promise."

"How can you possibly know that?" he asks me, and given that I supposedly have no memory, it's a valid question.

I shrug. "I just do."

"Well, then, I'll choose to believe you," he decides.

"I'm a trustworthy sort," I tell him.

"But wouldn't everyone say that?" he wonders. "It's not like you'd announce to me that you were otherwise."

"You do have a good point," I agree.

"My mom used to tell me that I'm a pill," he says. "So it's okay if you agree with that."

I grin. "Your mother was correct."

"She'd say, 'Lane Patrick Hughes, you're a pill, but you will at least *act* like a gentleman.'"

"You do," I assure him. "So she'd be proud about that."

"A compliment!" he exclaims, mimicking me from earlier. "Thank you!"

"I dole them out when they're warranted," I banter back. He grins.

"You're witty," he tells me. "I like that."

"My gran used to say my tongue is too sharp. But truth is, I got it from her!"

He lifts an eyebrow. "Another memory?"

"A vague one. They trickle in randomly, without details or context."

"Hang in there, kid," he says. "They'll all come in soon."

"They're not teeth," I remind him.

"No, you've got a full set of those already."

"I do," I agree.

He glances at my hands, which I'd stupidly forgotten to put gloves on. He pulls off his own and hands them to me.

"No, I couldn't." I try to push them back, but he refuses.

"Just put them on, Ace."

"Ace?"

"Your dad was a pilot, you're named after a plane, you've got a crack sense of humor. It seems to fit."

He doesn't know that it fits even more than he knows . . . because I'm a pilot myself.

I pull the gloves on, which are already warm from the heat of his hands. "In that case, thank you."

"I think I'm going to hike down to Mrs. Klein's and take her some breakfast. Would you like an outing?"

"Yes," I answer immediately. He smiles in satisfaction.

"Let's go, then, kid." He stands up, then grabs a wooden-seated rope swing that had been secured to the beam. "You first."

I stare at him.

"What do you mean?"

"This is the quickest way down. Unless you're scared."

The swing is hooked to a wooden beam in the loft's ceiling, and I'd have to trust that rickety old rope not to break as I leaped out from a perfectly good loft *and* trust the swing to support my weight.

"We used to play with this when we were kids."

"You and Marina?"

"Yes. Along with a few others."

"Do you know if it's been used since then?"

"Not a clue," he says honestly.

"Then I'll take the ladder," I tell him.

He clucks at me like a chicken, but I ignore him, focusing on descending the rungs of the ladder without breaking my neck.

When I reach the ground, he stands high above me, poised to leap onto the swing.

"I'm not sure you should do—"

He leaps, his tail end landing on the wooden disc seat and his arms curling around the rope.

He swings in a wide arc, back and forth many times, before the swing finally comes to a stop and he steps off it.

"Very dramatic," I commend him.

He bows.

A small bleat echoes through the barn, and Nugget careens around the corner.

"Does he ever walk?" I ask, laughing as he bumps my pocket lightly, hoping for a treat. "It's almost like someone has conditioned him into thinking there are treats in pockets," I observe.

Lane grins. "Don't look at me," he declares.

Nugget headbutts his pocket, like he's done it a hundred times before.

"Traitor," Lane mutters to him.

I laugh, and honestly, there's nothing cuter than a handsome man and a baby reindeer.

"I'll bring you treats tonight," Lane tells him quietly.

"I heard that," I call over my shoulder as I head for the door. "I'm gonna go change my socks for our hike."

Sophie doesn't make a fuss at all about us hiking out in the elements, once she hears that we want to take a care package to Mrs. Klein. She takes the eggs from me and starts to boil a couple. When they're done, she packs a knapsack with food, includes the hard-boiled eggs, and hands it to Lane when he comes in.

"If she and Fred need to come stay here, you bring them back," she tells him. "We can help."

"They're too stubborn," Lane tells her. "But thank you."

"You're a good boy, Lane Hughes." She pats his back before turning to me. "Piper, did you put on several pairs of socks?"

"Yes, ma'am. I can barely wiggle my toes at this point."

"Good. You don't need frostbite."

No, I do not.

"I put a couple issues of *Good Housekeeping* in the bag," Sophie tells us. "They're from last year, but they'll still give her something to read."

She pats me on the shoulder. "Don't let Lane go too fast. Remind him that your legs aren't so long. And get back before dark. Once the sun goes down, it's far too cold for you to be out."

I nod. "Will do, Sophie."

"Marina is getting a sniffle, or I'd send her with you."

I glance at Marina, who is cozied up in front of the fireplace. She winks at me over the rim of her mug.

"Feel better soon, Marina," I say wryly. She smiles at me from behind her mother's back.

"Don't worry about her," Sophie tells me. "I'm baking bread today, and she's going to help."

"I am?" Marina asks. "I might sneeze everywhere, Mama."

"The heat in the kitchen will do your sinuses good," Sophie tells her daughter, and Marina's face is priceless.

This is 1944. Did she really think her mother was going to let her lounge in front of the fireplace all day when there's bread to be baked?

Marina sticks her tongue out at me, and drawing a parallel between this ornery girl and my gran becomes currently impossible. She waggles her fingers behind her ears for good measure, and I grin at her angelically.

This must be what having a sister feels like.

If I change my parents' fate, could I end up with a sibling? Maybe even a sister?

It's an intriguing thought.

"You ready, Ace?" Lane asks. I nod, and he opens the door.

The swirling snow greets us as the sunlight filters down through the powder in the air.

Lane sets out at a brisk pace, but it's clear that he's slowing himself for me. I step it up, determined to not slow him down.

Yes, his legs are longer.

But little do they know, I'm a twenty-first-century independent woman. No man needs to slow down on my account.

I'm half dead by the time we see the chimney from Essie Klein's cabin poking through the trees, wisps of smoke curling into the clouds.

"Almost there," Lane calls back to me.

I nod, because I'm too out of breath to speak, because I've been hiking nonstop in three feet of snow for two hours.

But by God, I've kept up.

I haven't had to rest, and I declare that a win.

As we wait for Mrs. Klein to answer the door, Lane gazes at me.

"You're impressive," he decides. I nod, trying my very best to hide how heavily I'm breathing.

"I am," I agree.

"Are you getting ready to pass out?" he asks, his eyes twinkling. "You seem a bit winded."

"Not at all," I manage to say calmly, while my lungs internally combust. "I'm just eager to meet the famous Mrs. Klein."

The door is opened a scant moment later by an elderly man in overalls with faded blue eyes.

"You two better git in here," he tells us, ushering us in. "There's a storm coming."

"What?" I turn around and eye the clear sky. "It seems fine."

He rubs at his elbow. "I can feel it, missy. Mark my words. Now, come on in here."

The fire is low but still burning, and before Lane takes his coat off, he heads back outside to haul in more wood.

Mr. Klein introduces himself and sits me down in front of the fire with a cup of hot tea.

"I don't want to hear no arguments," he tells me sternly. "Your lips are blue. I already heated up the water for my missus, so you timed this just right."

"How is Mrs. Klein?" I ask, glancing around. She hasn't made an appearance yet.

"She was just laying down a spell, but I'll go get her now. She'd want to see Lane. She's taken that boy under her wing, and she's the biggest mother hen you've ever seen in your life."

"Are you talking about me, dear?" a slightly frail voice asks.

A stocky older woman with steel-gray curls steps up to the fire and sits across from me.

"I'm Essie Klein, dear," she tells me. "I'm going to assume Lane brought you here, although why he'd drag you through the elements for this is beyond me."

Her voice is stern, but her soft eyes betray her fondness for him. They also show a marked curiosity about *me*.

As Lane carries another load of wood in to stack near the fireplace, he calls to her.

"Mrs. Klein, meet Piper. She's a guest at Great Expectations, and she wanted to accompany me today to check on you."

"Young man, why in the world would you think that I'd want you out in the elements to check on me?" she asks him sharply. "Fred and I have survived here for decades. I don't need you risking your life to *check on me*."

Lane doesn't even pause. He stacks the wood, then turns to her, grabbing her in a big bear hug, lifting her off her feet.

She squawks a bit, then pats at her hair when he finally sets her down.

"It's good to see you, Essie," he says with a grin. "I've missed you."

She flushes a bit. "You should be at the lodge," she chastises him. "Sophie needs help with her workload, I'm sure."

"She's fine without us," I assure her. "She and Marina are baking bread today."

"Oh, I bet Marina's fit to be tied, then. She's a good-hearted thing but a bit lazy."

Lazy? My gran? It's such a funny notion that I almost laugh.

"How are you feeling, ma'am?" I ask her, and she scowls at me.

"Don't call me ma'am, young lady. And I'm fit as a fiddle."

However, as she utters the last word, it catches in her throat and she coughs.

"I see that," Lane says. "Come sit down, Mrs. K."

"I'm going to get you some hot tea with a splash of whiskey to warm you up," she argues, but Mr. Klein is already carrying a cup into the room.

"I've already got it, Ess. Sit yourself down."

She doesn't argue with her husband, and half sits, half melts back into her chair.

I can't help but notice that her face is pale, paler than I assume it should be.

"Sophie sent you some elk stew, boiled eggs, and thick sandwiches," I tell them both, opening the knapsack. "I just need to heat the stew. Could you point me to your kitchen?"

"You don't have to do that—" Mrs. Klein begins, but her husband cuts her off.

"It's just through there." He gestures to a door. "Let me show you."

He leads me into a compact kitchen space, which, though small, has a charming table with a red-checkered tablecloth and a cast-iron stove.

I pour the soup into a pot, and Mr. Klein lights the stove.

While I unwrap the sandwiches from their wax paper and lay them onto plates, Mr. Klein slices the eggs, then stirs the soup until it's ready to dish into bowls. He inhales deeply.

"Lord, that Sophie is a good cook," he says, and I notice his hands are bent and calloused from what I imagine are years of hard work.

I nod in agreement. "She makes the best biscuits and gravy I've ever had."

"Truer words have never been spoken," he agrees.

"I heard that," Mrs. Klein calls.

Her husband smiles impishly.

"Oops."

Lane joins us just in time to carry the two hot bowls of soup to the table. As Essie approaches, she glances toward the window.

"You're not going anywhere tonight," she tells us. "Piper, you can sleep in Lane's room, and he can make up the sofa. You can't hike back up the mountain until the snow breaks."

"If this don't just beat all," Fred says, staring outside. "It came outta nowhere."

"Sophie will be worried," I point out. But Lane shakes his head.

"She'll know that I wouldn't trek you up the mountain in this." The responsible, gentlemanly, and perhaps even slightly protective tone in his voice sends a thrill through my belly. Because yes, I'm a strong, independent woman, but dang. Sometimes, for just a minute, it's nice to be taken care of.

I meet his gaze, and my chin comes up a bit.

He notices, and the corner of his mouth twitches.

"But you can take care of yourself, can't you?" he asks, his voice low. I stare him straight in the eye.

"Of course."

"Of course."

"Well, I'm glad that's settled," Essie says from the table, sipping soup as she watches our exchange.

"What did we settle?" Fred asks, turning away from the window.

"I'm not exactly sure, dear. But I believe we just decided that Piper can take care of herself."

"In this weather?" Fred snorts. "Not likely. A gnat has more meat on its bones than you."

"Speaking of, we'll need to feed you," Essie says, thinking. "What do I have that's enough for a growing man?"

"I'm not growing," Lane tells her. "And you do not need to feed us. We ate a huge breakfast. We won't have you going to any trouble. We can wait till morning."

"Pish. It won't be a trouble. I have some nice two-day-old bread, and we still have sweet cream butter. You can have butter sandwiches. I have some bread-and-butter pickles down in the larder too."

"We'll be fine, Mrs. Klein," I tell her. "Truly."

"As long as I have your word that when you get hungry, you'll make a sandwich."

She's relentless, so I'm quick to agree.

"I absolutely will," I promise, and she is satisfied with that.

It's when Fred and Lane are out milking cows and I'm clearing Essie's dishes that I notice her chest rattle when she coughs. She tries to cover it up, but too late.

"Mrs. Klein, how are you feeling, truly?" I ask her.

"Nothing that some rest won't cure," she tells me stoutly.

"It's okay to need time to rest," I reply. Her lined face indicates that she's never known a day without hard work in it. "I'd love it if you'd allow me to take care of the house tonight while you take the night off."

She starts to argue, but I hold up my hand. "I insist. You take a seat over by the fire, and I'll clean up these dishes, and Lane can tell me anything else that needs done."

She's tucked cozily into her seat when the men return, and I'm wiping off the table.

Fred seems astounded. "Ess let you in her kitchen to clean it?"

"I guess it's my natural charm," I say with a grin.

"She's persistent," Essie says without opening her eyes.

"I am," I agree. Fred grins too.

"Well, I'll be. Essie met her match."

I swat at him, and Lane laughs.

"We brought you two buckets of milk," he says to Mrs. Klein, then turns to me. "What do you want us to do with it?"

I stare at him blankly.

Do with it?

"The cheesecloth to strain it is in the drawer by the icebox," Essie says, again without opening her eyes.

It takes me 2.7 seconds to realize what is expected of me.

I scan my memory, trying to think of any possible time—in a history book or at a heritage fair—where I'd learned what to do with raw, fresh milk.

"I'll show you," Lane offers, eyeing my expression. "You don't remember, do you?" he asks softly, as we hunt for the cheesecloth.

I shake my head.

The sympathy in his eyes causes me immense guilt, guilt that I try to brush away. It's not like I chose this. I would never choose to lie to anyone like this. But if I told them the truth, they'd think I was insane.

"Here we go," Lane murmurs, pulling a ream of the woven cloth from the kitchen drawer. He unfolds a square, cuts it, then digs in the cabinets for two pitchers.

"Here's what you do," he says. "You cover the top of the pitcher with the cheesecloth, and leave just a little bit of give so the milk won't run off the sides. Then, you just pour the milk through the cloth."

He demonstrates, and soon, the milk has been strained, and the fat has been scraped into a bowl to save for butter making.

"You make your own butter?"

"Essie and Fred do, because they've got cows and fresh milk. Sophie and Dale trade fresh meat for butter, because Dale and the men hunt."

"That's nice. So everyone gets what they need."

He nods. "That's the idea. Out here, we have to depend on each other. The war won't last forever, but even afterward, life here in Alaska isn't the same as it is elsewhere."

"No, it's not."

"We take care of each other."

"I respect that," I answer. And I do. I wish it were still like that in the present day. The world evolved, but some of the evolutions weren't for the best. For instance, in the present day, my family owns this entire mountain. Whatever became of everyone else who lived on it? To Fred and Essie? To the other neighbors I've heard mentioned every now and then?

They have their own sparse community here, something this mountain lacks in the future, and I can't help but wonder when and why that happened. Gran would never have bought them out without their say-so.

As Essie exhales in her sleep, her breath catches, and she coughs. I catch Lane's eye.

"Could you show me to your room?" I ask. "I'd like to lie down for just a bit."

"Of course."

He guides me to the plain, neat room, and I turn to him once we're inside.

"Lane, can you hear her breathing? I don't think we should leave her here. She needs medicine."

"She sounds better now than she did," he says, his dark eyebrows knit together. "I think she's on the mend, honestly. Something about being here, Ace, is that when we get sick in the winter, we have to make the best with what we've got. We can't just run to town to get what we need."

I hadn't thought of that. They can't just run down to a corner Walgreens.

"Do you include medications in your supplies when you stock up for winter?" I ask him.

He nods. "When we can. Extra medication is scarce right now because of the war. Along with everything else, right?" He grins ruefully. "They had some antibiotics, but they took them all when Essie first took ill. Since she already had that round of medication, I truly think she's on the mend."

"That's what she wants you to think," I tell him bluntly. "She's stubborn."

He studies me.

"You've got her number already, don't you?"

"She's not hard to figure out."

"But *you* are," he says.

"Not really," I answer. "I'm just a girl who doesn't remember who she is or where she came from or where she's going."

Because sadly, that last part is the truest thing of all.

I have no idea what is going to become of me, now that I'm stuck in 1944 without a way back home. There, I might not have known what I wanted to do, but I had options. I knew I could sell Great Expectations and live from the profits, or I could hire a business manager to run it and go off and do my own thing.

But here . . . Great Expectations isn't mine.

I no longer have options or prospects.

I'm just a girl living at the mercy of a good-natured family who doesn't know they're my family.

How will I support myself if I can't get back home?

"What a mess." I sigh.

"She'll be fine," Lane tells me, not knowing that I'm no longer thinking about Essie.

"That may be true, but I do think we need to come check on her more often."

"It's a deal. But for now, I can't be in here any longer, Ace. It looks bad."

We're alone and unchaperoned again.

I sigh once more.

While 1944 manners and decorum are refreshing, it can still feel a tad confining, always having to worry about reputation and appropriate behavior.

I shove at his arm. "Well, go on, then, before I can no longer control myself in your presence."

Lane's head snaps up, his eyes wide. When he realizes I'm joking, his eyes narrow.

"You're far too gullible," I tell him, laughing. "Has anyone ever told you that?"

"No," he confirms, his eyes narrowing even further.

"Oh, good! Then I'm your first."

I flounce past him, hoping for a theatrical exit, but I trip on his boot and go flying. Luckily, Lane has reflexes like a ninja, and his hand shoots out lightning fast to grab my arm, preventing me from sprawling onto the floor.

As I decide how to regain my dignity, he asks, "Has anyone ever told you you're really clumsy?"

I shake my head, already seeing where this is headed.

"Good. Then I'm your first."

He smirks and walks out, claiming my dramatic exit as his own.

CHAPTER NINE

The cast-iron stove puffs away as we eat dinner, creating necessary warmth in the cabin. The atmosphere here is quieter and calmer than it is at the hectic lodge. Outside, the wind howls, but in here, we're cozy and warm.

"You must call me Essie," Mrs. Klein insists as I offer her another piece of toast and a pickle. She takes the pickle, then smiles at her husband.

"Do you remember when we canned these last summer?" she asks. "You said we were doing too many, that we'd never eat them all."

"Yes, dear." Fred sighs. "You were right, of course."

She smiles sweetly. "I was."

"But in my defense, I didn't know we'd have young Lane Hughes letting out our room," Fred adds.

"That is true," his wife concedes. "But still. A wife always knows."

No one argues, and she's satisfied as she finishes her dinner.

"Lane, would you be a dear and read to us?" Essie asks. "I do love a deep reading voice, don't you, Fred?"

Fred doesn't seem to care one way or the other, but Lane obediently takes the book that Essie holds out. I smile when I see the cover.

The Little Prince by Antoine de Saint-Exupéry.

"Oh my gosh, I loved that book when I was little," I gush. "My gran used to read it to me."

Lane looks surprised, then pleased that I had a memory, but Essie stares at me.

"It was only published last year," she tells me. "My niece left it when they were visiting with their little ones last summer."

"Oh. I must be thinking of something else," I stammer. Lane takes pity on me.

"She has a head injury," he offers. Fred is instantly intrigued and sits down next to me.

"Do you remember anything at all?" he asks.

"Just bits and pieces, here and there. Nothing of any importance."

"Well, don't that just beat all," he says to Essie. She nods.

I get self-conscious and grab dinner dishes to carry to the sink. Lane follows, close on my heels, two plates in his hands.

"Are you okay?" The look on his face is truly concerned. "It must get tiring answering questions."

"It does," I admit, picking up a dishcloth. "It's just so frustrating that I can't remember. My memory has holes, and there's nothing I can do about it."

"Time heals everything," he assures me, picking up a dish towel, something I feel certain isn't a manly thing to do in 1944. I wash a plate, rinse it, and hand it to him. He dries it and puts it away. "At least, that's what people tell me, including someone in this very room."

Me. Drat.

"Well, let me know how that works out for you."

He glances at me, and I cringe. "I'm sorry. I didn't mean that as harsh as it sounded."

"I know," he says easily.

"You dry a mean dish," I tell him, changing the subject as I hand him another plate.

"Trained by the United States government," he says, thumping his chest. "Us GI boys are self-sufficient, ma'am," he drawls.

"The ladies will like that," I tell him. He wipes at the plate, his biceps tightening as he does. His high-waisted slacks are held up by suspenders, and his hair has a dip in the front, before it ends in a curl. Even though the style here is different than I'm used to, he sure wears it well.

"I know you've bumped your head, so you might not realize this," he says, "but this is Alaska. There aren't many 'ladies.'"

"There's Marina," I point out.

"Yes, there's Marina," he concedes. "There's also ol' Mrs. Hensen in town. She's probably a hundred and four nowadays."

"There's more women than that," I say with a laugh. "There's Sophie."

"Sophie's married." He shrugs. "I was only talking about single and available."

"There really aren't any other women?"

"Not single ones. Not many."

"So I'm a hot commodity," I realize. His lip twitches.

"Well, I don't know if I'd put it *that* way, but yes. Eligible women are in short supply here."

The knowledge that, if I were stuck here and had to stay, I could have my pick of men is an intriguing thought that I can't ignore.

But then again, as Marina told me herself . . . who knows which men will come back? Men my age are in short supply here too.

Except for the very handsome man in front of me.

The one whose voice makes my knees quiver just a bit.

"Are you going to read when we're done?" I ask him.

He shrugs. "It makes her happy. So yes."

"You're a good man, Lane Hughes."

"So they say." He sighs, as we head back into the living room.

Essie and Fred are settled in chairs near the fire, and Lane picks up the book, sitting on the stone fireplace surround. He begins to read, and my eyes flutter closed as I curl up on the sofa and listen.

The crackles from the fireplace and the rhythmic low cadence of Lane's voice, combined with the cozy warmth, is too much for my brain to ward off, and before I know it, it's dark and Lane is quietly waking me up.

Essie and Fred are gone, and the room is awash in moonlight.

"I told Essie I'd make sure you got to bed," he tells me. He's bent over me, and the moonlight makes his skin almost glow.

"You can just take the bed," I tell him. "I'm fine out here."

"She'd string me up in the morning," he argues. "Come on, Ace. The room is yours."

With a sigh, I stand up and follow him down the hall.

He walks me to the door, and I pause there. He's so close, he smells so good, and his eyes shine in a particular way that I can't put my finger on.

"Good night," he says softly, and, like a complete gentleman, turns and leaves me alone.

I feel disgruntled, and it isn't until I'm crawling into the cold sheets, my skin puckered from the chill, that I realize why.

I'd wanted him to kiss me.

I'd wanted him to kiss me.

The thought hits me hard in the chest, almost taking my air.

I haven't been interested in someone in . . . so long. And now, now I find someone? *Now* I'm focused on someone?

I should be focused on getting home, which would mean leaving him behind.

I curl on my side and stare out the window at the starry night, recalling the way Lane's voice had sounded while he was reading.

You, you alone, will have stars that can laugh, he'd read.

If stars can laugh, they're certainly laughing at me right now, and the predicament I'm in.

I flip over onto my other side, staring at the door.

Wouldn't it be amazing if he'd just step back in? If he'd sit on the edge of the bed and read me to sleep?

I sigh at the thought.

Then I somehow drift into sleep, very aware that the handsome man consuming my thoughts is right down the hall.

I don't know what time it is when I wake up or even what woke me.

I'm still for a moment, my eyes open wide as they try to adjust to the dark.

And then I hear it again.

A whimper.

A low, anguished whimper.

I'm out of bed before I can think twice, padding down the hall in my bare feet.

It's Lane, whimpering in his sleep.

He's thrashed around enough that he's half on the sofa, half on the floor, and his shirt has somehow come unbuttoned. He yanks it away from his neck in his sleep, as though it is suffocating him.

"Lane," I murmur, shaking his arm gently. "You're dreaming. You're okay."

He doesn't answer; instead, he turns over, yanking at the blanket.

I don't expect it when he shouts, "No!" and lunges from the sofa, spinning in midair and landing in a crouch in front of me.

His eyes have a wild gleam, and I know that Lane isn't staring at me right now.

He's staring at his personal demon.

"Lane, wake up," I tell him. "Wake up."

"Why are you here?" he hisses. "You're dead."

"Lane, wake up," I plead, as his eyes narrow.

"You're dead," he says simply. He grasps my wrist tightly, too tightly, and I beg him to let go. But his grip is a vise, and he seems to have no intention of loosening it.

"You died," he says again. "Stop haunting me."

His words are blurry and thick, those of a person in the grip of sleep.

"I'm not dead," I tell him. "My name is Piper, and I'm not dead. Wake up, Lane."

"You left me, like everyone else. Cecile," he says now, his voice cracking.

His face is so anguished, so haunted, that tears well in my eyes.

Who is Cecile?

"I'm not Cecile," I tell him. "I'm alive."

"Come here, then," he murmurs. "If you're alive."

He pulls me down onto the sofa with him, where I rest against his hard chest. He seems to relax when I'm in his arms, and his fingers absently stroke my hair.

"You're safe," he tells me, his lips in my hair. "I'll keep you safe now."

I try to get up, because this isn't a situation we should be in. Not here.

But he won't let go. He's caught in the dream of holding his Cecile, and he half sings, half hums a French song.

A French song, and a girl named Cecile.

I'd bet anything that he was in France and his girl was French.

The thought of someone else being his girl causes my belly to tighten, even though I have no claim on him and don't have the right to be territorial.

But still.

I'm here now, and his arms are around me.

His face relaxes, although his grip doesn't. It's like he's afraid to let go, afraid I won't come back. Because I'm guessing that Cecile didn't.

Something happened to her.

Everything about this man makes my heart hurt. He's lost his parents, gone to fight in a war that tortures him while he sleeps, and he's apparently lost a woman, as well.

I let him hold me for a while longer. I'll just let him fall into a sound sleep, and then I'll slip back down to my room.

The trouble is, I don't wake up until the room is flooded in sunlight, and Fred is standing over us.

"Oh, girl." He sighs. "Now look what you've gone and done. Be gone with ya—get back down to the bedroom before Ess sees ya."

I leap to my feet, as Lane sits up, rubbing his eyes in confusion.

"What in the world . . ." he's saying as I flee the scene.

I close the bedroom door behind me and lean against it.

What will this do to me here?

Will Essie tell everyone? Will my reputation be ruined? How does this sort of thing work in 1944?

I make the bed, taking my time. I can't bring myself to face anyone out there, most particularly Lane, not when I think of the look on his face as he'd realized the situation.

He was appalled that he'd been sleeping on the sofa with me.

That stings.

I mean, I'm not a 1940s pinup girl, but I'm not minced meat either.

It's twenty minutes before I shore up my resolve and open the bedroom door.

Lane stands there.

"Piper," he says, uncertain. "Can I . . . Can we . . . talk?"

"Out here in the hall," I tell him. "I wouldn't want anyone to get the wrong idea."

He flinches.

"I don't know what happened," he tells me. "How . . . when . . ."

"I woke up in the night," I tell him. "You were . . . distressed. I went out to check on you. You grabbed me and didn't want to let me go."

"Oh, no. I didn't mean to," he gasps. "I would never . . ."

"I know," I tell him quickly. "You were dreaming, Lane. You weren't awake."

His head drops, his chin on his chest. Red stains his cheeks, and he won't meet my gaze.

"Lane, if you ever want to talk, I'm here," I tell him softly. "You can talk about anything, and I won't judge you."

"You're very kind," he says, still not meeting my gaze.

"I mean every word. Sometimes, it helps to talk to someone who isn't involved in the situation."

"I'm sorry I laid a hand on you," he says, his voice gruff, and he still doesn't look at me. "That's not me, I swear it."

"I know that," I tell him. "And you didn't *lay a hand* on me. You didn't hurt me."

Not *really*.

"Lane," I begin hesitantly. "Who is Cecile?"

Lane freezes. "Why do you ask that?"

"You thought I was her. In your sleep. You didn't want to let her go."

"I can't talk about that," he finally answers stiffly. "I'm apparently not fit for human interaction now," he adds, and he spins and stalks down the hall.

When I join Essie and Fred in the kitchen a few minutes later, I'm still a bit shaken, and Lane is outside doing chores.

"What's got into him?" Essie mutters. "He barely said a word."

"It's hard to say," Fred answers, giving me a look. He doesn't want me to upset his wife.

Message received.

"The snow stopped," Essie tells me. "You can hike back to the lodge today, if you want."

"We'd better," I tell her, trying to focus on the elderly lady in front of me instead of the smoldering and tortured man who is currently outdoors working his angst off. "We'll bring more food next week."

"We thank you kindly," Fred says.

Essie seems pale and tired, and I make her a cup of rich coffee, taking care not to spill any of the precious grounds. Her coffee supplies are running low.

"How do you feel today?" I ask her.

"Fit as a fiddle," she answers, which is a total lie, and I know it.

"You know, we could stay awhile and help," I offer.

She's already shaking her head, a proud mountain woman if there ever was one.

"I'm fine," she says firmly. "It's not much more than a cold. It'll linger, and then someday, it'll pass."

"Well, if you need us, you just ring."

"Our shortwave is busted, but don't you worry about us. Lane will come to look in on us."

I don't feel comfortable about leaving, but they're insistent. When Lane comes in from outdoors, they tell him the same thing, and nothing we can say sways them.

"I can stay here with you," Lane offers. "I don't want to be a burden on you, Essie, and I wouldn't be. I can take care of *you*. You don't need to take care of *me*."

"Oh, pish, Lane," she dismisses him. "We don't need taken care of. Be gone with both of you. We'll be fine here."

Lane loads them up on wood, then we set out back up the mountain.

"Why won't they just let us help them?" I ask Lane as cold bites at my face.

"You'll find that people around here are very self-sufficient, to a fault. She's not up to having a boarder, but she's too proud to let me help. I have to respect that, or it would be insulting to her. But trust me, I'll be checking on them."

"But it's more trouble for you to hike down here every week than it would be if you just stayed at their house," I point out. He nods.

"I know. But it's not my logic we have to defer to here. Essie's got a gruff exterior and she's proud, but she's a very kind woman."

"I can tell," I agree. "And Fred is the same. He didn't have to stay quiet about me waking up with you on the sofa . . ."

Even from behind his cap, I can see Lane's face explode into flame.

"They're good people," he says, and then he stomps ahead to forge the way, and also to get away from my prying eyes.

He makes a point of staying at least ten paces ahead of me the entire hike. He makes sure to check on me from time to time, glancing back to make sure I'm okay, but he doesn't invite any further conversation.

I have to respect that.

When we reach the lodge, Marina catapults out of the door, down the front path, and into my arms.

"God, you were gone forever," she exclaims. "Come inside. Mama's using some sugar rations for Christmas cookies."

She links arms with me and half drags me into the house. Lane quietly takes his boots off by the door and makes his escape to his room. Marina glances at him.

"What's with him?"

"I don't know. He's just in a quiet mood, I guess."

She's not convinced, but she doesn't press. It seems unlike her, but I don't question my good fortune. Instead, I follow the smells of baking to the kitchen, where Sophie is rolling out sugar cookies.

"Piper!" she exclaims. "How are Essie and Fred?"

"They greatly appreciated the food," I tell her. "I think Lane should've stayed to help out, but they wouldn't hear of it."

"Pride comes before a fall," she says, shaking her head. "But we're all a little proud up here, aren't we, Marina?"

Marina, who is currently trying to nonchalantly steal cookie dough, nods.

Sophie slaps at her hand. "Nope. You can have two cookies tonight, when they're done."

Marina's shoulders slump. I find it ironic, since Gran used to shoo me out of the kitchen when I was little and she'd bake cookies, for the very same reason: I tried to eat the dough.

"Lane seems down in the mouth," Marina announces.

"I don't think he is," I argue. "He just feels bad about the Kleins. They won't let him help."

"Is that all?" she asks. "He can take another trip next week. We'll pack them up more food."

"They've got livestock to take care of, and . . ." My voice trails off, but Sophie interjects.

"We all do here, darling. It's fine. We'll help out as much as we can. We look out for each other here."

And they really do. It's uplifting and lovely.

I tell her so.

She shrugs off the praise.

"It's nothing that anyone else wouldn't do," she says.

That's not true in the twenty-first century.

But since I'm not currently *in* the twenty-first century, I follow Marina upstairs, where she wants to try something new with my hair.

We sit on the bed and chat until it's time to help Sophie start dinner.

CHAPTER TEN

It's not until Sophie calls for us that Marina turns to me, a strange expression on her face.

"What happened with you and Lane?" she asks, as she stands up. "I haven't seen him like that in . . . *ever.*"

"Nothing happened. At all!" I assure her. "He's carrying some baggage from the war. That's all. I didn't do anything."

"I wasn't saying you *did* something, dummy," she says impatiently. "I'm just saying that I know something happened, and because I'm nosy, I'd like to know what it is."

I sigh. She's as determined now in her younger age as she was in her older years.

"He had a nightmare," I tell her quietly. "A bad one. I got up to make sure he was okay, and he thought I was someone else."

This has her attention.

"Who?"

"A woman named Cecile."

Marina's brows furrow. "I don't know anyone named Cecile."

"No, you wouldn't. I think . . . I think he met her overseas. I'm not sure, but he was humming a French song."

"In his sleep?"

I nod. "Yeah. He wouldn't wake up."

"Hmm. Maybe he met a girl over there. Maybe he's going to bring her here after the war," she suggests. She catches sight of my face. "I'm sorry, Piper."

"No . . . it's . . . she's dead."

Marina's eyes widen.

"What?"

"Yeah. I don't know how, and I don't know who exactly she is, but he certainly cares about her. He thought I was her. He grabbed me, held me close, and we slept like that on the sofa."

Marina's eyes are practically bugging out of her head now.

"What?"

"I know. He wouldn't let go—in his sleep—and I acciden-tally fell asleep, too, and then Fred found us in the morning."

"Oh my gosh," she breathes. "Fred found you? Not Essie?"

"Not Essie," I confirm.

"Well, you lucked out," she decides. "Fred probably won't say anything."

"The whole way back here, Lane wouldn't talk about it. He's humiliated and upset, and I hate it."

My shoulders slump, and Marina rubs the one closest to her.

"It'll be okay," she says. "We'll find out what this is about. It makes sense, though. I know he was in France. He was in the Battle of Belgium."

I scan my memory for historical facts. The Battle of Bel-gium . . . If I remember correctly from school, a lot of people died, and it ended with the German occupation of Belgium.

"When was that?" I ask.

"It was when he was injured," she says. "This past fall. September."

"I bet she died in that battle," I say out loud. "So, he lost his parents and then Cecile."

Marina sucks in a breath. "Oh, Lane."

I nod. "It's bad, Marina. He's not okay."

"None of them are," she says quietly. "Not a one. My fiancé tries to hide it, but he talks about it in his letters. He's seen things. They all have."

Sophie yells for us again, impatient this time.

We rush to the kitchen, where she's stirring a large pot of soup and slicing homemade bread.

She stares at Marina sternly. "Go ahead and set the table, miss," she says. She turns to me.

"Piper, dear, could you get out the butter and then put two sugar cookies on saucers for each place setting?"

"Of course," I tell her quickly.

I'm carrying the saucers out to the table when Lane appears. His hair is damp, so he must have run it under water.

"Well, hello," he says to me, completely normally. "I see you're the bearer of joy tonight." He gestures toward the cookies. "The men will love you forever."

"Well, I aim to please."

I set the saucers down and head back to get more. He follows.

"I'll help."

I glance at him. He's making reparations for something he couldn't help.

"Lane, it's fine. I've got it. I don't think Sophie wants any men in her kitchen." I laugh, but I'm not sure that I'm wrong.

"One thing about Sophie," he tells me as we turn the corner into the kitchen. "Guests get away with murder."

Unfortunately for him, Sophie is turned in his direction, and her eyes narrow.

"Lane Patrick Hughes, get out of this kitchen before you mess up my organization."

I giggle.

"I can see that," I tell him. Sophie looks at me sharply.

"What's so funny, you two?"

"Nothing at all," Lane assures her before I can rat him out. "I'm just excited for the sugar, so I was going to help Piper carry the cookies to the table."

"Piper can do it," Sophie tells him. "I don't trust you not to sample the wares, Lane."

She's talking about the cookies, but the incident on the sofa is fresh in both Lane's and my minds, and so he flushes again.

It's amazing to me that such a confident, manly man is reduced to blushing simply because of me.

Back home, Shelly would take one look at him and breathe, *Now*, that's *a man*.

And he is.

She wouldn't be wrong.

"I'll just go join the others, then," he says now, with a slight bow toward Sophie.

"Thanks, Lane," I call after him.

Sophie eyes me.

"Be careful, Piper," she says. "You don't even remember who

you are. It would be a shame if you have a husband somewhere, and you got Lane's hopes up."

"I don't have a husband somewhere," I assure her.

"How can you know that?"

"Well, I'm not wearing a ring," I tell her. "And I just think . . . I'd *know*."

She appears unconvinced.

"Just use caution," she says simply. "I don't want anyone under my roof hurt. In any way."

Her message is loud and clear, and I nod.

When she disappears into the root cellar, Marina, who's returned from setting the table, looks at me.

"Now you've done it," she says. "Her eye will be on you both now. She never misses a thing, trust me."

"I'm not doing anything wrong," I say firmly. "Neither is Lane."

"Not *now*," she says simply.

"Not ever," I tell her, although saying that aloud hurts my heart more than I could've imagined. "He's in love with a dead girl."

Sophie reemerges with a jar of canned carrots, and our conversation stops. If Sophie notices, she doesn't say anything, thankfully.

We assemble around the dining room table, where Dale says grace before everyone digs in with gusto.

The stew is rabbit, and while I never would've tried it back home, it's delicious here. The broth is simple and savory, the flavors are vivid and unencumbered by preservatives. The bread is the same way. Thick and hearty, without the added sugars that bread companies use back home.

William asks about Essie, so Lane gives him an update, and William offers to take turns hiking down to help. Then Albert says that he'll pitch in, and before we know it, each man, including Dale, has agreed to help.

"What shall we do tonight?" Sophie asks as everyone finishes up. "We could play rummy."

"I'm going to puff on a pipe for a while, dear," Dale answers. The other men mumble their agreement with that.

"I think I'll go check on Nugget," I tell everyone. "I haven't seen him since I left."

"You haven't eaten your cookies," Sophie points out.

"I'm saving them for later," I tell her, taking a small nibble. "They're so delicious, Soph."

She beams.

The men eye my cookies, and I hold up a hand. "Don't you even think about it. I'll have to hide them so you can't find them."

"Now you see why I eat everything right away." Marina laughs. "They're scavengers. And watch William. He's got a hopeless sweet tooth."

William laughs good-naturedly and doesn't deny it.

"I'll go out with you," Joe tells me. "I'll break the ice on their water troughs tonight."

"I just did that this morning," Dale tells him.

"It's okay. I don't mind doing it again," Joe answers. Marina kicks me under the table and shoots me a glance.

Joe wants to spend time with me.

Dang it. The last thing I'd ever want to do is hurt that gentle soul.

"I'd love the company," I tell him.

Marina kicks me again.

"Ow," I mutter. *What is she expecting me to do? Crush his feelings right here in front of everyone?*

"I don't have all of my fingers," he tells me. "But the ones I do have are at your service."

He grins and I wince, trying not to glance at his poor right hand. It's missing three fingers, with only his index finger and thumb remaining.

I carry my dishes to the kitchen, where Marina is hot on my heels.

"You can't lead him on," she tells me firmly.

"I'm not," I hiss. "I don't know what you want me to do here. Embarrass him in front of everyone?"

She recoils, as if I'd struck her. I sigh.

"I'm sorry," I tell her. "I didn't mean to sound so harsh. I'm exhausted. I obviously don't want to hurt that sweet man. What do you suggest I do?"

"Viable women here are rare," she tells me. "You have to be prepared for them to swarm you, and be very clear when you're not interested."

"Okay," I answer. "I will be. But in private. Not in front of the whole table."

"You're such a sweet girl," she tells me, patting my hand. "You'll get the hang of it."

Ohhhh. She's trying to help me because she thinks I don't remember how to rebuff a man's advances.

Gah. I keep forgetting that I'm supposed to have forgotten literally everything.

"Thank you for looking out for me," I tell her. "I'll be okay, though. I think that kind of thing is instinct. Like muscle memory."

She looks satisfied, even though she's probably not sure what muscle memory is. I keep finding myself using phrases and words that haven't been coined yet in the forties. It's frustrating.

"I'll help Mama with the dishes," Marina tells me. "You go ahead. Let him down easy. But also clearly."

"I will," I promise.

I bundle up and toddle out to the barn, my arms so bundled that I'm like the Michelin Man. The door is open, which means Joe is already here.

I catch sight of him at the back of the barn, surrounded by the curious reindeer. Nugget, of course, is front and center, nuzzling his pockets for a treat.

"Don't tell anyone," he tells the tiny deer, digging out a mushy carrot from his stew. Nugget sniffs at it, looks at it curiously, tilting his head one way then the other, and decides to eat it.

"You're a softie," I tell him, as I approach. "Don't worry. I won't tell Sophie."

"How can you resist this face?" he asks me, gesturing at Nugget's teddy-bear eyes.

I shake my head. "Well, I certainly can't."

I pull out a piece of cookie and offer it.

Nugget eats it in one gulp and hunts for more.

"No more, little one," I tell him. "I'm sure sugar cookies aren't good for reindeer. People either, but that doesn't stop us. We're gluttons."

"Oh, a little treat here and there doesn't hurt anyone," Joe says.
"True."

I try not to, but I glance at his hand, wondering once again how it happened. He catches me, and I flinch.

He smiles. "It's okay. It's kind of hard not to wonder. It was a grenade."

I freeze. "A grenade?"

"An Mk 2, to be exact. I was in a foxhole, and it got tossed in. I caught it and attempted to throw it back, but it detonated as I threw it."

"Oh my gosh. You're lucky it didn't take your whole arm," I tell him. "Or worse."

"I know," he agrees. "That's what the doc that patched me up kept saying. That I'm lucky. It's a miracle. It doesn't really feel like a miracle, but I guess things could always be worse."

"So you were over there," I say slowly.

He nods.

"Thank you for your service," I tell him.

He nods. "You're welcome."

He's uncomfortable with the gratitude, something I always notice about military men (and women) when you thank them. It's like they never know quite what to say, even back home.

"You were very brave," I continue. "The world needs more men like you."

He's surprised by that. "The world is literally full of men exactly like me," he says. "Only most of them have all of their fingers."

He chuckles, but I know it's a sore spot. How could it not be?

"Are you right-handed?" I ask.

"I was." He nods. "I'm learning to be a southpaw now."

"Oh! I can help with that," I tell him. "We can practice lettering, if you want. I can draw up some makeshift primers, and we can practice writing with your left hand."

"You'd do that?" He glances at me.

"Of course! It's the least I can do to thank you."

"Well, thank you," he tells me.

I realize suddenly that I'm not doing a good job of sending a clear message. My heartstrings have been pulled by this noble, gentle man.

"I'd do it for anyone," I tell him. "You are all heroes."

There. That should help.

We play with Nugget for a bit longer, laughing as he loses his balance and almost careens into the barn wall.

"Joe," I say softly. "I need to be open about something. I can't get involved with anyone right now since I can't remember who I even am."

He blushes, and I feel awful. But I know it's the right thing to do. I don't want to hurt anyone. I wish my heart would pay attention to that and stop being so interested in Lane, but one thing at a time.

"You're a wonderful man. And some woman will be lucky to have you."

Joe nods. "Thank you." His cheeks are still cherry red, and he pointedly stares at Nugget.

"Did you know that he'll play fetch?" Joe asks.

"Like a dog?"

"Exactly like a dog." He nods. "Watch."

He wanders to the tool bench in the front of the barn and comes back with a small rubber ball.

He throws it, and Nugget takes off running.

A minute later, he trots back with it in his mouth.

"The tricky part is getting him to drop it," Joe says, trying to entice the reindeer into doing just that. Thankfully, Nugget's antics take the awkwardness from the moment, and now we can laugh as the baby reindeer runs around in a circle, flaunting the ball in his mouth, clearly making this a game.

"I've never seen a wild animal with so much personality," I say.

"He's not really a wild animal, though," Joe points out. "He was born here, in this very barn. He's never known the wilderness."

"Oh, well, that makes more sense, doesn't it?" I croon to the baby. He rubs my elbow with his head but runs when I try to get the ball. "You're a scamp!" I call after him.

He looks back at me as though he's laughing.

"Marina has tamed him," Joe tells me. "He's a pet now."

I nod. "I can see that."

But my gran tamed him? She's always been adamant that if something isn't helpful on the property, we don't need it.

"Oh, boy," Joe exclaims, looking past me through the window. "You can see the northern lights!"

We hurry to the door and step outside, and sure enough, the sky is awash in a rippling, shimmering, green glow.

"I missed this when I was overseas," Joe says, staring up in wonder. "It never gets old, does it?"

"No, it doesn't," I agree.

The sky glimmers and gleams, like green silk unfurling across the night. Stars twinkle throughout, and like always, I'm in awe of nature as I stand and behold it.

"I missed it too," Lane says from behind us.

We turn in surprise.

"There was this one night, I was standing watch, and the only thing that kept me sane was looking up at the stars and imagining *this*."

I swallow hard, a lump quickly forming in my throat as I think of him, so far from home, and how scared he must've been.

He holds out a single sugar cube on his palm, changing the subject.

"Sophie sent this for you to give to Nugget," he tells me. "You should feel flattered. She would never usually give up sugar like this."

He drops the sugar into my hand, and Nugget comes flying.

"He's got a built-in radar," Joe says, chuckling.

He licks my palm, nibbling the sugar. He laps at my fingers, hoping for more.

"That's it, buddy," I tell him, stroking his soft nose. He nibbles lightly at my fingertips. "I love him so much," I tell the two men. "He's so so adorable."

"He seems a bit partial to you too," Joe points out.

"He's not fooling me—he just wants more sugar."

Nugget blinks innocently, and we all laugh.

"Dale is going to read the Christmas story when you guys come in," Lane says, and if I didn't know better, I'd think it was a hint.

"The Christmas story?" In my head, I'm thinking of the movie with the kid and the BB gun and the tacky lamp made to look like a woman's leg in fishnets.

"From the Bible?" Lane answers, his eyebrow lifted.

"Ohhhh. Of course."

The Bible. Duh, Piper.

The values here are so refreshing.

We head back toward the house, pausing to wait for Joe as he slides the barn door closed and fastens it with the chain.

We've reached the lodge when we hear the unearthly, guttural growl.

I'd know it anywhere, having grown up in Alaska.

It's the very distinct sound of an annoyed grizzly bear.

CHAPTER ELEVEN

We all freeze, watching the huge shadow lurking in the perimeter of trees.

"You're supposed to be hibernating," I tell it softly.

One giant paw steps into the moonlight, followed by another.

"Damn it," I mutter.

"Get behind me," Lane says, stepping in front.

"Back up," I say quietly. "Slowly."

We start edging backward, toward the barn, the three of us moving in tandem.

The massive bear is out in full sight now, standing completely still, his black eyes glittering as he watches us. He must weigh over a thousand pounds. Goose bumps lift the hair on my neck.

"Something must've disturbed him and he came out," Joe says. The bear's ear twitches.

He huffs again, warning us.

But lucky for us, he hasn't charged yet.

I reach behind me, feeling for the barn. When the wood

bumps my hand, I grasp for the door, trying to slide it as quietly as I can.

The bear doesn't miss a thing. His eyes glitter, and he huffs again warningly.

"I don't think he means any harm," Lane says. "Open the door."

"It won't open," I answer. "I can't get the chain off."

Lane reaches over, slowly, and drops his large hand on top of mine. I pull out of his way, but not before a jolt of electricity shoots up my arm from the touch of his skin.

Focus, Piper. Your life is in peril.

I hear the chain drop, hitting the barn wall as it does, a sign that Lane was successful. Unfortunately, the bear hears it as well, and rears up on his back legs, bellowing in our direction.

Lane shoves the door open and we all three tumble inside, our legs tangled, as the bear lunges toward us. Joe jumps up and pulls the door closed, just as the bear slams into it.

Lane springs to his feet, helping Joe hold the door closed.

The bear paws at the wood, already understanding that he needs to slide it open to get to us.

"Smart devil," Joe says. I lend them my weight and strength as the bear, much larger than us, tries to break the door free.

"Damn it," Lane says as the bear hurls his weight into us. He huffs on the other side of the door, furious with us for daring to be in his path. Lane cringes from pain, because his wounded shoulder is taking the brunt of the bear's force.

"If he breaks through . . ." My voice trails off, because we're all quite aware of what that would mean.

The bear slams into the door once more, and this time, it sounds like the wood cracks.

"Oh, no," I gasp.

And then there's a gunshot.

And then silence.

The bear stops huffing, stops clawing.

We barely even breathe as we listen.

"Go on, get out of here," Marina shouts. "Go!"

It sounds like the bear is lumbering away.

"You guys can come out now," she calls.

Lane opens the door, and we find Marina standing with a shotgun in her arms.

"You just saved our lives," I tell her, before I rush to give her a hug.

"You're lucky. I'd stuck some milk in the snow to chill it. If I hadn't come outside to get it, I wouldn't have known. Right place, right time, I guess."

"Thanks, Rina," Lane tells her. "I owe you one."

"Thanks for holding the door, guys," I tell the men. "If I'd been alone, I'd be a goner. I'm not strong enough to hold him off like you did."

It's a stark reminder that this world is vastly different from my own, a place with every modern convenience. This is truly a wilderness.

Marina ushers us into the house, where she leaves the shotgun by the back door.

Inside, gathered around the dining room table, the rest of the group laugh and chat over gin rummy. They hadn't heard the gunshot.

Dale's face is priceless as we explain.

"You're telling me . . . my girl is a hero," he announces.

"We'll make that barn a tribute to your bravery, Rina. May that door be preserved forever!"

"Oh, yes, dear," Sophie says, patting his arm. "Maybe we should give tours!"

She's kidding, but she's obviously proud.

"You always hope you're doing a good job raising your child," she says. "But when you hear something like this, where your daughter risks her own life to save someone else's, you know that you're doing something right."

Marina blushes. If Sophie is anything like Marina turned out to be, she doesn't often dole out praise. It was earned, not overly given.

Dale rubs his chin thoughtfully. "I'll make a table out of that door," he decides. "We'll tell this story forever."

Marina blushes even more, and we gather in the living room.

The fire crackles while Dale begins to read.

His voice is sure and warm as he reads the story of Christmas from the Bible.

I scan each face in the circle. Edward's eyes are closed, Albert's hands are clasped, Marina smiles slightly, Sophie rests a hand on Marina's arm. Joe watches me, then looks away when I catch him. Frank, William, and Charlie listen attentively.

It's Lane who holds my attention.

He's staring out the window, seemingly listening to Dale, but his mind isn't truly here. That's apparent in his absent gaze. In his mind's eye, he's somewhere else. He stares at the night sky, perhaps reliving what had just happened, but maybe he's in France again with Cecile. It's impossible to tell from his expression.

I'm turning my attention away when he shifts his head and meets my gaze.

Unlike Joe, he doesn't look away.

His green eyes are stormy, a sea of unrest.

I don't look away either.

We stare into each other's eyes for long minutes, until Dale is finished reading.

There's something powerful about staring into someone's eyes for so long, like we somehow just breached a level of intimacy reserved for lovers.

For instance, I know now that Lane has a ring of darker green on the outer rim of his iris. I know that there are tiny flecks of blue making his eyes almost seem turquoise in the firelight.

I wonder what he saw in mine?

We just faced down a bear together. Between that and staring into each other's eyes . . . we're on a new plane tonight.

I can tell he feels it too.

Unfortunately, Marina noticed as well, and brings it up when we climb into bed with our hot water bottles.

"What's happening, Pippie?" she asks.

I shrug. "I don't know. I wish I did."

"Do you feel something for him?"

"I just met him." I laugh. She's the one shrugging now.

"Sometimes, that's all it takes. My father knew when he set sight on my mother."

"At first glance?"

She nods. "You can ask him to tell the story. He loves retelling it."

"Did you feel that way about your fiancé?"

She laughs. "Not really. We grew up together; he pulled my pigtails when we were kids."

I hadn't known that she'd grown up with Gramps. Goodness, I wish I'd paid more attention when she was alive. Although . . . I have her now.

"What's he like?" I ask. "Boyfriend?"

"Boyfriend?" Marina laughs. "He has a name."

Yes, but he's my grandfather, so I don't necessarily want to think about that as she's telling me about their relationship.

"*Boyfriend* has a nice cheeky ring to it, though, doesn't it?" I wink at her.

She has no way of knowing that I totally stole that from *One Tree Hill*. Thank you, Brooke Davis!

She laughs. "Well, *Boyfriend* is pretty amazing. I just can't wait till the spring breakup so I can get to the post office and check for new letters. I miss hearing from him. I miss hearing his voice too."

I think of Lane's voice and the husky rasp it gets when he's tired. My belly twinges.

"I like him," I blurt out. "Lane, I mean."

Marina stares, then blinks.

"But I don't even know who I am. Maybe I won't be able to stay here—and I'd end up leaving him, just like Cecile did. I could never do that to him."

Marina's face falls.

"We don't know for sure that Cecile was his girl," Marina reminds me. "It's possible she wasn't."

I consider that for a second.

If that was true, then I wouldn't be quite as selfish if I allowed myself to get close to him. While there's always the chance that I'll get to go back home, it makes it a little less bad if I take that risk knowing that he hadn't previously lost a woman he loved.

"I just wish there were some way to know," I murmur.

"I can look through his stuff," Marina offers. "I'm really good at being quiet. It gets on Mama's nerves. I'm always overhearing stuff I'm not meant to."

"Hmm. I'm listening," I tell her, urging her to continue.

"Well, tomorrow morning, when he goes out to do chores, you go with him to keep him occupied a bit longer. Ask questions about the chores, or whatever, just do something to buy me time. I'll go through his stuff and hunt for letters to her."

"That just seems so invasive." I sigh. It's the 1944 version of going through someone's text messages.

"I mean, it totally is. But do you want to pass up an opportunity that could put your worries to rest?"

"Okay," I relent. "But only look until you find confirmation that she's his girlfriend. *Was* his girlfriend. Don't read really personal stuff, Marina."

She nods. "I won't. Probably. Unless it seems *really* good."

"No," I answer. "You can't."

"Okay, fine." She pouts. "No need to rag on me. I get it."

She eyes me, waiting to see if I'll relent.

"Some rules are meant to be broken," she announces, when I don't. This version of my gran is baffling. I had thought Gran was born with a rule book in her pocket.

But not *this* Gran.

"Not this rule," I answer. "I mean it."

"Fine," she says, and I'm pretty sure she means it this time. "Just keep him occupied in the morning."

"Will do."

"Now, going back to rules," Marina says, as she reaches under the bed. "I snuck this from Lane's room—*my* room—earlier today, which is why I know for a fact I can sneak in and out of there without anyone knowing. Under no circumstances are you to tell my mother about this, okay?"

I nod. "Of course."

She sets a hot plate up on the bed.

I stare at it, not connecting the dots with why this hot plate breaks any rules.

"We can't use extra electricity," Marina reminds me, reading my mind. "And, I don't want to seem selfish, but I have a stash of snacks that I collected before the winter freeze."

I wait now, amused.

She pulls up a can of beans next, followed by a can opener.

"A can of pork and beans?" I ask, my eyebrow lifted.

"Don't knock it until you try it," she warns. "After a long day of work, nothing tastes better than this, Pip. Besides, I saved several lives today from a fifteen-hundred-pound bear. I think I've earned this."

She plugs in the hot plate and opens the beans, setting the can straight on the warmer.

"The bear was closer to a thousand pounds," I correct her. "Twelve hundred, tops."

"Don't diminish my heroism," she chides me. "That bear was enormous and you know it."

"I know it!" I agree. "I was just saying it didn't weigh fifteen hundred."

"Details," she mutters, stirring the beans with a contraband spoon. She blows on the bite, chews it, then smiles in bliss before she offers me the next bite. She cups one hand beneath the spoon to catch any drips, just as older Gran had done when she fed me as a child.

I swallow.

"Won't your mother see the empty can in the trash?" I ask, after we've eaten most of the beans.

Marina glances at me. "Not when I hide it under other trash, goof."

"You're sneaky," I point out to younger Gran. She rolls her eyes.

"Not sneaky," she corrects. "I prefer *crafty*."

I don't point out that it's virtually the same thing.

"Well, you were right. Nothing tastes better than that after a long day," I tell her. She grins.

"Told you so."

She carefully hides the evidence, and snuggles back into bed with me.

As we huddle together for warmth, she pipes up. "I do really think it at least weighed sixteen hundred, though, Pip."

I smile and close my eyes.

CHAPTER TWELVE

"So, fellas," I say over breakfast, as I let a bite of scrambled eggs cool before I eat it. "How much do you think that bear weighed?"

Marina stomps on my foot as she rolls her eyes.

"Hmm," Joe speculates. "I think it looked near a thousand pounds. What do you think, Lane?"

Lane thinks on it. "I think nearer twelve hundred."

"That's *exactly* what I thought too," I tell him proudly. "Marina thought it weighed two thousand."

She rolls her eyes again, and Sophie interjects, "Don't do that, dear. Your eyes will get stuck like that."

Which is literally something Gran used to say to me as a child.

"Regardless, I still think saving three lives is a bit impressive," she says innocently as she takes a bite.

The men chuckle and Sophie rolls her own eyes.

I think it might be this moment when I fall in love with Gran's motley family, my own ancestors, and the boarders, who are such an integral part of my family's story.

Seeing them like this now . . . they're real in a way that simple stories of them could never be. They're far from the black-and-white, two-dimensional photographs that hang in the great room back home.

They're real, and they're honestly just like me. They laugh, they cry, they band together like a tribe.

Finally, Lane pushes away from the table. "I'll go get the livestock fed," he says. "Ace, I think you should help. I know it was scary yesterday, but you should get back on the horse, so to speak."

He thinks I'm too afraid to go back to the barn.

"That's an excellent idea," I tell him, to his surprise. "I think you're right. I'll get right back on that horse."

He seems proud of himself, and I feel a twinge of guilt.

I'll be helping him while Marina rifles through his letters.

I jump up and rush to get bundled up, before I change my mind.

In the light of day, the barn door damage is impressive. The bear's claws gashed into the wood at least a quarter of an inch.

I run my fingers over the jagged grooves.

"Careful, you'll get a splinter," Lane says from behind me. "You should've worn gloves." He shoves the door open, presumably so I don't have to even touch it.

We've barely stepped inside when Nugget starts bleating excitedly.

"He thinks you brought a treat," Lane tells me.

"And he's right," I answer, digging for the crust of toast I'd brought. He nibbles it. "You're a carb man," I tell him. "Same."

"You're no *man*," Lane says, and I think it's a compliment. So I smile.

Nugget's ball is lying near the gate, so while Lane breaks the ice, I toss the ball for the baby reindeer.

"I've never in my life seen such a thing," I say in wonderment as Nugget retrieves it again and again.

"Me either," Lane calls back. "He's cute as the dickens."

While Nugget tosses the ball into the air and watches it fall back down, I turn to Lane.

"What's your favorite part of being back in Alaska?" I ask. His parents are gone, but there's got to be something good about being home.

"The air here," he says immediately. "It smells like Alaska. Clean and wild."

I have to agree. I'd said the same thing many times, and Shelly always thought I was nuts.

"It's more than just mountain air," I agree with him. "It's something very specific to Alaska. It feels like . . . home."

He nods. "Exactly."

Swinging the ax with his uninjured shoulder, he breaks through the top of the second trough, then uses the ax head to crush the ice into slush.

"I'll get the hay," I tell him before I head up to the loft. Nugget follows me with his eyes, waiting for his alfalfa treat.

There's not an open bale, so I call down to Lane.

"Do you have a pocketknife?"

"Yup!"

I head back down the ladder to retrieve it. When I turn around, I find Lane taking off his parka to dig in his pocket for the knife. He drapes the coat over the gate when he's finished.

He holds the knife out to me. "Don't run with that," he teases, his eyes sparkling.

"I'll try not to."

It's harder to climb the ladder the second time.

"I've gotta get into better shape," I mutter. I glance over my shoulder at Lane, who is now mucking the stalls.

"You know, you probably should go easy since you tweaked your shoulder yesterday," I suggest.

"I'm okay," he calls.

"That's what Essie says too," I answer.

He grins.

"Are you comparing me to a one-hundred-and-nine-year-old woman?"

"She's not one hundred and nine, and yes."

He throws back his head and laughs, and honestly, it's a joy to behold. Sometimes he's so serious, so tortured, that it makes me feel like I somehow help him when I make him laugh.

I vow to myself to do it more often.

I'm trying to come up with another joke when I look back down at him, and I see a large bloodstain spreading on his shoulder.

"Oh my gosh, Lane!" I exclaim, rushing back down the ladder, forgetting the hay. "You're bleeding."

I make a beeline for him, and without thinking, I reach for the buttons on his shirt, trying to see the damage.

His fingers take over for mine, and once again, electricity jolts through me like lightning when our fingers touch. He unbuttons his shirt, pulls it down, and I see a scrape on his shoulder.

"It's just from yesterday," he tells me. "It's not my war wound, if that's what you were thinking. That was stitched up."

I can clearly see the scar in question. It's healing rather nicely from what I can tell.

The angry scrape next to the scar is the culprit now.

"You were bracing all of your weight on your wound." I sigh. "Lane, are you okay? Does it hurt?"

"It's fine," he tells me, and his voice is suddenly gentle. His eyes are soft for a scant moment. "I'll live."

"I was afraid your war wound had broken open. I'm glad to see that's not the case. We do need to wash this scrape, though. Did you wash it yesterday? I can see traces of wood in it, Lane."

"I didn't scrub it, no," he admits.

"It could get infected," I answer. "We've got to clean it. I'll grab the hay for the deer, then we're going straight to the house to take care of this."

I scale the ladder, no longer caring about the burn in my thighs.

I fly back down the rungs and toss the hay to the reindeer, before sternly waiting for Lane to pull his coat on and join me.

I close the barn door behind us this time, although Lane mutters disapprovingly.

"Hush," I tell him. "Enough with the toxic masculinity."

He stares at me drolly. "That sure is a fancy way of saying something."

And it's not a phrase that's been coined yet. I sigh. It's harder to not give myself away than one might think.

I know that we haven't been gone anywhere close to long enough for Marina to hunt through his things, but that's no longer important. What's important now is patching up this selfless man.

When we come through the back door, Sophie greets us.

"I saw you coming," she says. "What happened?"

"Don't worry," Lane tells her. "I just scraped my shoulder yesterday during the bear incident. It's fine."

"There's bits of wood in it," I tell her over my shoulder as I pull Lane toward the kitchen. "It needs to be washed out or it could get infected."

Sophie doesn't ask how I know about the wood pieces.

I realize that once again, I've broken protocol. I sincerely doubt I should've been in an empty barn with a man whose shirt was off. And in fact, I had unbuttoned half of those buttons.

I blush.

Sophie notices but doesn't say anything.

Instead, she maneuvers Lane into a chair and unbuttons his shirt herself, then examines the wound.

"Piper, can you run upstairs and ask Marina for a pair of tweezers?"

"On it!" I call, racing out.

Marina is emerging from Lane's room as I round the corner upstairs. She looks up, startled, then is relieved to find that it's only me.

"We need tweezers," I tell her, pulling her toward our room.

I fill her in as she sifts through the contents of the top dresser drawer.

"Oh, Lane." She sighs. "He's such a ninny sometimes." She glances up at me. "And, in case you were wondering, there's no evidence of a girl in Lane's room. No letters, no photos."

"None at all?"

She shakes her head. "Not a one."

I exhale, and my shoulders relax.

"Not a one?" I repeat.

"Not a one," she says again, with finality.

"If I told you how relieved I am, it would be embarrassing," I tell her. She grins.

"I got that feeling."

She hands me the tweezers.

"Go get 'em, Ace."

Lane's name for me.

"You really do hear everything, don't you?" I ask her.

She grins sweetly. "I've got ears like a bat and feet as light as . . ." She pauses, thinking. "Feet as light as a snowshoe rabbit."

"That's light," I tell her.

"Indeed."

When I reenter the kitchen, Lane is leaning over the giant farm sink and gritting his teeth as Sophie washes his scrape, which is actually more of a deep gouge.

"Ow." I flinch. "That's gotta burn."

"It does," Lane agrees, his pleasant tone in direct contrast with his scowl.

"This just goes to show, don't tangle with bears, Lane Hughes," Sophie says.

"I'll try to avoid it in the future," he tells her.

I try to hand her the tweezers, but she shakes her head. "You've probably got a steadier hand," she tells me.

I bend over his shoulder and examine it, instantly finding the largest piece of splinter.

I gently prod at it, trying to nudge it into an upright position that would make it easier to grab.

"Is now a good time to tell you that I've never done this before?" I ask.

"Not really," he answers.

"Too late."

Water droplets run down his tight bicep, curving over the bulge of muscle. He's muscular in a slender way rather than an overly bulky, bodybuilder way. I like it.

I quickly grasp the wood and nip it, lifting it away.

I exhale.

I did it.

Sophie holds out a towel, and I wipe the splinter onto it, then rinse the tweezers in hot water before I go in again.

I repeat the process five times, removing five different fuzzy splinters.

After I've finished, Sophie washes the wound one more time.

Marina has joined us with a square green tin.

"I brought some Bag Balm," she tells us, setting the tin next to us.

I open the lid and the familiar smell wafts out. I breathe it in.

"My grandmother used to use this on me," I tell them.

"You just remembered that?" Marina asks.

I nod. "Smells jar memories."

"That's a fact," Sophie says, as I smear some of the sticky ointment onto my fingers, then slide it gently over Lane's scrape. "I can't smell banana bread without thinking of my own grandmother and her kitchen."

"Did she give you her recipe?" I ask, trying not to notice the rigid muscle beneath my fingers or the way Lane is so, so close. "My gran used to make delicious banana bread too."

"Yes, she did. I try to keep my mother alive through her recipes," Sophie says. "To her, food was love. She loved cooking for her family. So every time I make one of her recipes, I think of it as though it's still her, loving me."

"I love that," I tell her, thinking of how her mother's love had been passed to her, then through her to Gran, who passed it to me. "A mother's love can go a long, long way."

"Yes, it can," she agrees.

"You're all done," I tell Lane, lifting my fingers. He opens his eyes and looks me in the eye.

"Thanks, Ace," he says. "It barely hurt a bit."

"Is that why your forehead is sweaty?" Marina asks with a chuckle.

He scowls good-naturedly. "You don't have to notice every little thing, Rina."

"I can't help it," she announces. "I'm basically super-human."

"Then you won't mind making the corn chowder tonight," Sophie points out. "There are jars of canned corn in the cellar. The milk is in the icebox."

"I was hoping for meat tonight," Marina tells her mother.

Sophie winces. "I'm sorry. Our meat rations have dwindled, I'm afraid, due to feeding more people than I'd planned on."

"Oh, no, because of me?" I ask, mortified. *If they're running out of meat because of me . . .*

"No, not you, dear," Sophie answers. "I wasn't planning on a full house of boarders this winter. Albert and Joe were surprise additions."

"And now Lane and me," I say.

"You don't eat more than a mouse would," Lane says. "I, on the other hand . . . Why didn't you say something, Sophie?"

"I will never turn someone away from Great Expectations Lodge," she says firmly, lifting her chin. "We never will, will we, Marina?"

"Of course not, Mama," Marina answers. She's already walking toward the root cellar door.

"We have plenty of other things to eat," Sophie says. "I don't want anyone to give this another thought. One way or another, we always make it through."

She turns to Lane. "Lane, I'm going to bandage this, then you go upstairs and put on a clean shirt."

"Yes, ma'am," he agrees.

"Piper, in that drawer over there, there's clean flour sacks. Cut them into long strips, would you?"

Flour sacks?

"Of course," I tell her. I open the drawer and find a stack of laundered cloth sacks, stamped with Gold Medal Flour's label. I had no idea flour used to come in cotton sacks.

I obediently cut one into strips and hand them to Sophie.

She applies them to the salve-covered scrape.

"There you go," she says, after she's arranged them to her satisfaction. "All fixed up. We'll re-dress this tomorrow."

Sophie insists that Lane join Dale in the chairs by the fire, and after a quiet afternoon, I help Marina fix the corn chowder. None of the men complain about soup for dinner, and in fact, they thank Sophie for the meal, just like always.

While we're cleaning up, Sophie turns to me.

"Thank you for your help with Lane. Have you ever thought about being a nurse? Maybe you *are* a nurse?"

"I don't think that suits my temperament," I tell her honestly. "I'm kind of a *walk it off* girl. That doesn't work too well for nurses, I'm sure."

Sophie laughs. "Probably not. It just seems like so many girls your age are doing their nurse's training so they can help the cause."

All of a sudden, I feel self-conscious. I have a very good reason for not doing something for the war effort: I'm not from this century. But obviously, I can't say that, so instead I'm stuck feeling guilty.

"Don't feel bad," Marina tells me. "I didn't want to be a nurse either. I hate the sight of blood." She shivers now at the thought.

Marina washes the dishes and hands them to me to dry.

I dry them and hand them to Sophie, who puts them away.

We might not have a dishwasher here, but chatting while doing these chores makes the time pass quickly.

When we return to the living room, Dale is asleep by the fire, snoring.

Sophie clucks. "Every single night, he falls asleep in that

chair. Then I have to rouse him to come to bed, and it's a whole ordeal."

"He also snores quite loudly," Marina chips in.

"I heard that," Dale says without opening his eyes. "I'm checking my eyelids for holes."

"Me too," Lane says from the other chair, also keeping his closed.

"Men." Marina sighs loudly.

"You don't know the half of it, girl," her mother says wryly. "Dale, do you want to wake up to read for a bit?"

"I will if you want me to," he answers, his eyes still closed.

"If I didn't, I wouldn't have asked you," Sophie says cheekily.

"She has a point," Lane says.

With a sigh, Dale sits up and holds his hand out for a book. Marina passes one to him, and we all settle in to listen.

Dale's gruff voice covers us all with its calm notes, and the fire feels so cozy and warm.

The wood planks in the walls smell like cedar, and the tree smells like pine. With the popcorn strings and colorful ornaments hanging around us, it almost feels like we're in a Hallmark movie.

No wonder Gran had always loved Christmas.

The wind howls outside, but in here, we're snug as can be, and happy and warm.

Nineteen forty-four isn't so bad, I decide.

When Dale is finished reading, I go around with Sophie to turn off lights and blow out candles. I make sure the doors are locked, although it's from habit. There's no one out on the mountain in this weather who could possibly break in.

It's a safe feeling.

Knowing that we're isolated because of the extreme weather probably should make me uneasy, but it does the opposite.

I know we're safe here, and we're surrounded by good people.

Nineteen forty-four isn't bad at all.

Marina and I head upstairs, where she rolls my hair into curlers for tomorrow.

She turns around, and I return the favor, although my hairdressing skills aren't nearly as adept as hers. She's kind enough not to point that out.

"Boyfriend is fine," I tell her firmly as we roll down the covers and situate our hot water bottles in the bottom of the bed. "I feel it."

"I hope you're right," she answers. "Every day, I hope you're right."

"I'm seldom wrong, honestly," I say with a giggle.

She nudges my shoulder, and I can almost hear her rolling her eyes.

"Be careful, or your eyes will get stuck like that."

"You can't see my eyes," Marina said. "You have no idea if I—"

"Did you roll your eyes?" I ask patiently.

"Yes."

We both giggle.

"What's it like in Lane's room?" I ask her curiously, pulling the covers up over her cold shoulder.

"It's very neat in there," she says. "It's empty. He doesn't have much with him."

We cuddle together for warmth.

"You should definitely shave your legs this Friday," Marina advises me, her calf brushing mine.

"You're not exactly a baby's bum yourself."

She giggles and doesn't deny it.

We fall into silence and my thoughts drift to Lane and the ever-so-slight day-old scruff he had on his jawline today.

"There wasn't one single trace of Cecile?" I ask Marina.

"Not one trace."

I smile and drift right to sleep.

CHAPTER THIRTEEN

The next morning, there's evidence of bear tracks around the house.

When I come downstairs, the men are examining them outdoors.

"He's taken a liking to us," Dale tells Marina and me when we step out on the porch to watch.

"Well, I don't like *him* much," Marina answers.

"He's just trying to survive," I remind them. "Same as any of us."

"You are a tenderheart," Marina announces. "It's kill or be killed here, Pip."

"I know," I say. "It's just . . . he didn't ask to be here either."

I think of the Norton party back home and how happy they'd have been to encounter a grizzly to take home as a trophy. It tightens my stomach. While this bear is dangerous, he's still not a sport. He's a living creature, the same as any of us.

"That's neither here nor there," Dale declares. "He'd kill the reindeer if we allowed it. You wouldn't want that."

"Of course not," I agree quickly.

"Well, once a bear has come out of hibernation and lingers like this, it only means one thing," Albert says, coming to the porch. "He's hungry, and he likes something here."

"Not for long," William says from behind us. "Soph's digging a bear trap out from the barn."

"Oh my gosh, no," I gasp. "Those are barbaric."

They all look at me as I mentally picture the bear with his leg trapped in the steel jaws. I shudder.

"We can handle it some other way," I suggest. "Steel traps are cruel."

"It won't be humane if he kills one of *us*," Lane says slowly, eyeing me.

"I know, but it's in his nature. He doesn't know better. We do."

"I could use the meat," Sophie says as she joins us. "We're out."

I can't argue with that. I like meat as much as the next person, when it's meant to be eaten. Just not for sport. That's over the line.

"If you cook it right, it tastes like pork," Dale tells the men.

"My ma used to make it," Albert says. "It was gamey but good."

"I can cook the game out," Sophie tells him. "But I couldn't find the trap."

"So, first we have to get the bear," Lane points out. "And Piper here doesn't want to use a trap."

"There are more humane ways," I insist again.

They stare at me, waiting.

"Well, we can just wait him out. He's clearly hanging

around. We'll just hunt him the old-fashioned way." I shrug my shoulders. "It's not rocket science. We'll put out bait and wait."

"But we won't put the bait in a trap?" William asks, confused.

"No," I tell him impatiently.

"What kind of bait?" Lane asks curiously. "We're out of meat. Bears eat meat."

"Well, I don't know. But we'll figure something out. Maybe *you* can sleep out here and be the bait."

"No, thank you," Lane answers wryly.

"We can try it your way," Dale says. "And Lane isn't sleeping outdoors. But we do need meat, Piper. So if this doesn't work . . ."

He trails off, and we all know what that means.

The inhumane steel trap.

"But we'll try," Sophie assures me quickly.

"Thank you," I tell them. "Truly."

Dale nods, and I think he's hoping we can get the bear as humanely as possible too. He's got a soft heart in there, something that's uncharacteristic for this time and place.

"Thank you," I say again, directing it to Dale. He nods again.

"You're welcome. It won't hurt us to wait a couple of days."

From the barn, I hear Nugget bleating.

"He hears us," Sophie says with a grin. "You boys have spoiled him."

As I listen to the baby reindeer, agitated that he can't get to us, an idea forms.

"We'll use the noise of the reindeer to bait him," I announce.

"Nugget is getting more spoiled by the day and cries when he hears us and can't get to us. Let's bring him into the house a couple of times a day to play, then when we take him back to the barn, he'll be agitated and will bleat like he is right now. One of you can be waiting outside to get the bear in your sights."

"You want to bring a reindeer into the house?" Sophie lifts an eyebrow.

"We can make a makeshift diaper for him," I tell her. "With old material or something."

Sophie doesn't look convinced, but she doesn't say no.

"I'll think about it," she says.

Nugget is in the house by midafternoon, a flour-sack diaper fashioned around his rump.

"He's such a pill," Marina complains after he steals a half-empty bag of cornmeal from the kitchen counter and runs off with it in his teeth.

"True," Sophie agrees as we chase after him, indulging him in his game. "But he's cute as the dickens."

Nugget skids around a corner and collides with William, who plucks the bag out of Nugget's indignant teeth and hands it to me.

"You might not want to let him run in the house," William says, bending down to examine the floor. "His hooves are scratching it."

Sophie sighs and shakes a finger at Nugget. "No more running."

He cocks his head like he's listening, then trots behind us as we make our way back to the kitchen to bake the bread for dinner. As Marina pours the flour onto the counter, Nugget eyes her suspiciously.

"Not all of us can eat grass," she tells him, patting his fuzzy nose. It must tickle him, because he sneezes and flour blows into the air, on the walls, and all over us. It startles him, and he scrambles for the corner counter, knocking off two metal pans, which clatter onto the floor.

"No reindeer in the kitchen!" Sophie decides, when the noise dies down and she wipes flour from her face. "Piper, can you take him elsewhere?"

I pat Nugget's neck, and tug him toward me.

He digs in his heels.

I tug harder.

He sits down.

I put my hands on my hips.

He blinks.

Marina giggles and gets behind the deer, pushing him up.

He stands, begrudgingly, but it takes me luring him with a cracker for him to follow me to the living room.

I sit on the front edge of the stone fireplace and let him nibble at the cracker. I laugh when he licks at my fingers.

"You really *are* spoiled," I tell him.

"He doesn't care," Lane tells me as he steps into the room. "Not one bit."

"You're right," I tell him with a grin.

"He's been in the house for a couple hours. I think we can take him back out now," Lane says. "His mama might be wondering about him."

"She's probably used to his shenanigans."

"That too."

Together we loop a lead rope around his neck and guide him outside. He doesn't love going down the front steps, but after a moment of encouragement, he hops down like he's been doing it all his life.

We lead him out to the barn, and it's funny to watch him skip and hop over the top of the snow. His light weight barely makes him sink into the powdery surface.

It's when we're four steps away from the barn door that Nugget somehow slips the rope and bounds away from us, looking over his shoulder as if to laugh.

"Dang it, Nugget," I mutter, as I slip while trying to catch up to him.

He bounds around the back of the barn and disappears from sight.

I imagine the grizzly lurking somewhere in the trees, and I yell to Nugget.

"We've got to get to him before that bear does," I tell Lane.

"He's tame, but surely he's still got natural instincts," Lane answers.

We jog into the copse of trees, listening for the small crunch of his hooves.

He's nowhere in sight.

"Nugget!" I call.

"You know, your shouting is leading the bear to us," Lane suggests.

He has a point.

"Polar bears are the only bears who hunt humans for sport," I say randomly.

"Grizzlies will hunt for food," he replies.

"And technically, I guess we could be considered food," I point out.

The winter wind stings my cheeks. As I throw my head back, I catch a glimpse of Nugget's tail as he disappears yet again into the trees.

I point, and we sprint after him.

"Snow running should be a thing," I pant. "My quads are *burning.*"

"You're a strange girl, doll," Lane answers, also panting.

I try to catch my breath. "Has anyone told you that women don't necessarily like being called *dolls*?" I ask.

He grabs my elbow as I start to slip.

"No one has ever said that to me," he answers. "What are we supposed to say, then?"

"I have a name," I remind him.

"Where's the fun in that, Pip?" he asks with a wink. Then he focuses on something over my shoulder. "Look."

Nugget has stopped and has his nose to the ground, rooting around.

"Nugget, I swear. You get over here."

He doesn't even look up.

I stomp toward him and realize that he's standing at an unnatural angle. "Nugget?"

His front forelock is caught in ice.

"Oh, dang it. Nugget, just be still."

Lane and I approach, and I pat the baby reindeer to keep him as calm as possible while Lane wiggles his leg, working to free it without cutting the small animal.

When his leg comes free, it brings with it a cloud of steam. "Steam?"

Lane and I look at each other, then examine the hole.

"This must be from the hot spring," Lane says, poking at it.

"Hot spring?" I stare at Lane. "There's not a hot spring in this area."

"How would you know that, Pip?" He raises an eyebrow. "I hadn't thought about it, but it makes sense. There's a hot spring maybe twenty miles south of here. It must originate on this mountain."

"We have a hot spring," I say in wonder, watching the water gently bubbling to the surface.

"It appears we do," Lane answers.

"This changes everything," I exclaim. "Do you know . . . we could have hot baths with more than two inches of water!"

"It's a bit frigid out here to bathe," Lane points out, holding Nugget close to him as he loops the rope back around his neck.

"We could build a little building, like an ice-fishing hut," I suggest. "And we could have *real baths.*"

"So you mentioned," he says, getting to his feet. "If anyone could talk the men into trekking out into the cold to build a bathhouse, it's you."

"I'm not sure if that's a compliment or an insult," I tell him honestly.

He grins. "I haven't decided yet."

"Well, at least you're honest," I mutter. He laughs.

"You could charm the spots off a leopard, Ace," he tells me. "That could be dangerous in the wrong hands, you know."

"With great power comes great responsibility," I tell him blithely.

"Whatever you say, Pip," he answers, turning and striding away. Nugget, the little traitor, trots along with him and never looks back.

We hike back to the barn without a single sign of the bear, and we get Nugget safely secured inside.

True to plan, when we lock the barn door and trek to the house, Nugget bleats indignantly, voicing his displeasure.

"I feel mean for this," I admit, listening to Nugget cry.

"You're a mean little thing," Lane agrees. "This was your idea."

"I know, but that's because it's the most humane thing."

We climb the steps, and I'm startled by Albert, slung in one of the rocking chairs on the porch.

"I'm taking first watch," he says, a twelve-gauge propped on his shoulder.

"I'll take the next one," Lane offers.

"Will's got it," Albert answers.

I leave them chatting about the schedule, while I hunt for Dale. He's beside the fire, in a wing-back chair, his eyes closed.

"I'm not asleep," he says before I say anything.

"I know. You're checking your eyelids for holes," I answer. He smiles.

"There's a hot spring on this mountain," I tell him excitedly. "Lane and I just found it. It's just beneath the surface."

Dale opens his eyes.

"We could build a bathhouse out there," I say. "We could take hot baths, Dale!"

"We could," he agrees. "I wonder what else we could do?"

"You could build a day-spa type of thing," I suggest.

"A what?"

"You could make this a tourist destination," I explain. "You could charge people—someday, when the war is over—to come rejuvenate in the hot mineral water."

"We've already got Baranof Island for that," he scoffs. "I can't see how we'd have enough demand for two. But I'll keep it in mind for the future."

He's humoring me, because he has no idea what a big thing spas will eventually become.

But then . . . as I'm talking with him, something occurs to me.

If I can introduce the idea to him now, and if he acts on it, is it possible that my parents won't die in that plane crash? If they weren't flying guests to the lodge in the ice, it's possible—I mean, theoretically—that they wouldn't be on that plane.

That they wouldn't die.

"It's worth thinking about," I tell him. "When the war is over, people will want ways to relax. This could become a vacation destination for families in the lower forty-eight. They could come see the northern lights. You could offer dogsled rides. Stuff like that. Ohh—people would love to see the reindeer."

"This house isn't a circus, Piper," Sophie says from behind me. She's smiling when I turn to look at her. "But I like your enthusiasm."

"I don't know, Soph," Dale says thoughtfully. "She might be onto something."

"Oh, Dale." She pats his arm. "No one is ever going to want to pay to come here."

She laughs, but I can't help but notice the thoughtful look on Dale's face, and I see it on his face throughout the rest of the evening. He's considering it. That's all I can ask for.

I'd love to be able to tell him that his granddaughter's life is on the line, that she'll die if the path of time isn't changed.

But of course, I can't.

They'd think I'm even nuttier than they likely already do.

Dale eventually falls asleep in the chair by the fire, and as I climb the stairs, hot water bottle in hand for bedtime, I hear Sophie chiding him softly.

"Dale McCauley, I swear. If you're tired, come to bed. Don't sleep out here for everyone to hear you snoring."

I smile gently as I climb the stairs.

Growing up, I didn't have a large family. After my parents died, it was just Gran and me. With some of the staff, like Dan. Shelly came much later, although Ellen was with us from the time I was in elementary school.

It's nice to experience the hustle and bustle of a busy household.

It's nice to see the ribbing and the joking and the comradery.

It's nice to see the somber black-and-white image in the photograph above the mantel brought to life with smiles, and love.

I open the bedroom door, and Marina grumbles at me from the bed.

"You're letting in a draft," she mutters, pulling the covers closer to her chin.

It's nice to see Gran like this.

It's nice to almost have a sister. I used to wonder what it would be like, and now I know.

It's bickering over who gets more space in the bed, who steals the covers, who has to wipe out the cast-iron skillet from breakfast. It's also sharing glances at dinner because of a private joke. Or trying not to laugh when she crosses her eyes behind her mother.

When I get into bed, she yanks the covers over and leaves me with two inches.

I yank them back, and then she rolls into a torpedo, trapping the blankets around her body so I can't steal them.

"You're a pill," she grouses, closing her eyes.

"So are you," I tell her.

But I throw my arm around her shoulders and snuggle in to share the warmth.

We're both out like lights within minutes.

I sleep until the middle of the night. I wake up when I hear the grandfather clock chiming from the living room.

Two A.M.

I'm freezing cold because Marina is still torpedoed in the blankets.

I get up and pad down to the kitchen to heat a bit of milk.

The floor is frigid in the kitchen, and it's when I'm rinsing out my cup at the sink that I see Lane outside in the moonlight.

Sitting on the porch, with the shotgun perched against his shoulder, waiting for the bear.

In the night, I can see glimpses of the soldier he was.

The soldier that he still is . . . the soldier that he hasn't let go of yet.

I see it in the alert way he scans the perimeter, the way his eyes glint in the night, and the way he seems to hear the slightest noise, sitting at attention until he's sure it doesn't bring danger.

He's a man.

A deadly, kind, haunted, handsome man.

I dry my cup, put it in the cupboard, and go back to bed.

CHAPTER FOURTEEN

The next morning, Dale is already out examining the hole Nugget had made with his leg when I arrive in the kitchen to help Sophie bake the biscuits.

By noon, Dale, Albert, and William have built a simple lean-to shed over the hole. They also widened the hole to a size large enough for two people to sit in.

"It's a ten-minute walk, Soph," Dale tells her as he chews his egg sandwich. "The shed isn't insulated, but it blocks the elements. You can take a hot bath, if you'd like."

"And then catch my death of pneumonia when I walk with wet hair back to the house," she answers. "Are you trying to get rid of me?"

He grins. "No, wife. I don't know how to cook. I need you."

She smacks him lightly on the arm, and I laugh.

He's all talk and everyone knows it.

He bundles up and goes back out all afternoon. Marina and I decide to trek out there and see what they've accomplished.

We're astounded; or at least, I am.

It's always taken any boyfriend I've ever dated a while to do a project. They have to look up how to do it on YouTube, then gather the energy and find their tools, then they mess around with it for hours, sometimes stringing it along for days as they take TV breaks.

Not the men here. They mean business.

Marina and I find a fully formed shed with a door on hinges, and inside, they've built a bench for someone to stack towels. The soaking spot is quite large, enough for two people to sit in it at once. The hot water and condensation make the small room feel steamy warm. I find the whole thing surreal.

We have a hot spring on our mountain.

How did I not know about this? How could something so valuable be hidden beneath our noses and we didn't know it?

"I want to try this out today," Marina tells me. "You game?"

"Absolutely. It's only fair, though, that these men get to try it first. They did the work, after all."

"I guess you're right," Marina grumbles.

The men nudge each other, and Dale decides he's going first.

Marina and I take that as our cue to leave. Rapidly.

It's when we're walking back to the house that we find the bear tracks alongside it.

We stop to examine them, noting the way they lead up to the windows. The tracks are bigger than my hands.

"He's watching us," Marina points out.

"He must be very hungry."

"Which makes him dangerous," Marina replies.

I can't argue with her. It does.

"We probably shouldn't walk out to the bath shed without a shotgun," she adds.

I don't argue with that either. I want to be humane, but I don't have a death wish.

When we get back inside, we find Lane coincidentally getting ready to clean his shotgun on the dining room table, the smell of gun oil already permeating the room.

It's a sweet smell that I've always liked, and knowing that we have the protection of several armed men in this house from a hungry bear isn't lost on me.

"Do you know how to do this, Pip?" Lane asks, without looking up. I like the way he calls me Pip, like *Pippie*. It's endearing.

"No, I don't," I admit. "I think I've seen it done. It feels familiar. But I don't like to hunt. I know others do, and I know it's necessary for food, but I just don't like to see it. That's cowardly, isn't it?"

"To not want to see death?" Lane lifts an eyebrow. "Not at all. Pull up a seat, though," he adds, pushing out the chair next to him with his foot. "It's time you learned. Knowing how to operate and clean one of these is essential here in Alaska. You might not want to hunt, but you'll have to protect yourself."

I nod. "Good point." I sit next to him.

"First step, make sure it's unloaded."

He hands it to me. I stare at the gun, then at him. The metal is cold in my hands, and I feel a bit more powerful than I did before.

"Like this." He puts his hands on mine and guides me into sliding back the chamber. His hands are deft, knowledgeable. I find myself wondering how many lives he had to take during the war, and if he remembers each one.

"It's empty," he says, looking into the chamber. "So it's safe."

I feel safer than I have in a long time, sitting so close to him. But I don't say that out loud.

"Now what, boss?"

Next he shows me how to disassemble the barrel, and we lay out the parts carefully in front of us.

"Open that bore cleaner." He gestures to a tin bottle. I do, and hand it to him. He brushes down the barrel and dips a brush in the cleaner.

Then he hands it to me to clean out the barrel.

I do it and hand it back.

"Now, we oil everything so that it doesn't rust," he says.

We dip a rag in the oil, then push it down with the plunger. Then I carefully apply oil to the entire gun.

"Is that enough?" I ask.

He examines every piece.

"Yes, I believe so. Good work. Let's put this thing back together."

Piece by piece, he shows me how until we have a fully operational shotgun again.

"And now you know how to clean a shotgun," he says at the end.

"Thank you," I tell him honestly. "That's a skill that you never know when you might need."

"Well, here in Alaska, you'll need it pretty regularly."

I haven't in my entire life, but to be fair, things are different in the twenty-first century.

"I smell completely and utterly like gun oil," I tell him, sniffing at my arm. "And I don't hate it."

"I've said it before, and I'll say it again, Pip. You're a strange one."

"You know, I'm starting to think that's definitely not a compliment." I laugh, and my hand accidentally brushes his.

He startles and looks into my eyes.

His seem to be bottomless turquoise depths, like the sea.

"It's not *not* a compliment," he says.

"Well, that's glowing praise."

He winks. "Don't fish for compliments, Ace. A girl like you doesn't need to."

A girl like me?

I want to ask, I want to know . . . what he thinks of a girl like me.

But I'm determined not to ask.

I'm as surprised as anyone when the words come out of my mouth.

"What kind of girl am I?" I blink, then maintain his gaze. "I mean, I don't really remember, do I?"

It's probably borderline unethical to use my lie to flirt with this gentle, handsome man, but in this moment, all I want is to hear good things about me roll off his tongue. I don't know why. I just need to hear it.

From *him*.

He's hesitant now, unsure, as though he's afraid this is some kind of trap.

"You're a good girl," he finally says. "Funny, smart, and genuine, Ace. I think you're the whole package."

"The whole package? You didn't mention anything about my looks," I point out.

I'm being shamelessly needy right now, and it's a look that I don't like. But that doesn't stop me from fishing.

"If I were a flyboy, I'd paint you on the side of my plane," he says simply. "Fully clothed, of course," he adds quickly. "Very appropriate."

Which I take to be the utmost in compliments from a World War II solider.

I giggle. "Well, thank goodness for that. I'd hate for my painting to be *in*appropriate." I pause. "Did you ever want to be a pilot?" I ask.

"Nope," he says cheerfully. "I'm afraid of heights."

I stare at him.

"You are not."

"I'm afraid I am. Not being on a ladder or something. Not like that. But of being in an airplane, suspended in the sky. Always have been. Fred Klein was thinking he could show me how to fly his old prop plane in the spring, but I have no desire."

"Why does he want you to learn?" I ask.

"Oh, just so someone else around here knows how, I expect. He's getting older, his eyesight is going bad, and his plane is the best way to get to Anchorage for supplies."

Should I tell him I'm a pilot?

I bite my lip. I could solve that problem for them; I could be someone else who can fly for supplies, but then that creates problems for me. Like, how does a girl know how to fly a plane? And how do I remember how, since I've supposedly lost my memory?

I sigh.

It's something I'll ponder another day.

If I'm here to stay and can't get home, I'll have to broach that topic. But I don't have to today.

"You do smell like gun oil," Lane tells me. "I bet . . . you could take a soak in the newly built bathhouse. I told you that if anyone could manage to talk Dale into it, it's you."

"I honestly can't believe they built it in a day," I tell him.

"It's just a shed," he answers. "It's not Rome."

"Well, that's true. But it's still impressive."

"You're easily pleased, Pip," he remarks as he stands and gathers up his tools.

"That's the first time anyone has ever said that about me," I tell him honestly. He laughs.

"I can accompany you and Marina out to the bathhouse if you'd like to go," he tells me. "I don't feel comfortable with you going alone. Not with the bear out there."

I hesitate.

"I'll stand watch outside," he adds. "It will be completely respectable. I won't sneak a peek or anything."

He seems almost offended.

"I know you wouldn't," I assure him. "But I don't want you standing out in the cold on our account."

"So you want me to sneak a peek?" he asks mischievously. "From inside the shed?"

"No." I chuckle. "Nice try. Maybe you could sit inside the shed, but you can turn the other direction. It's not like we'll be taking all our clothes off."

"Ace, you can't walk back to the house in wet clothes," he points out. "You'll catch pneumonia."

"Maybe Marina has a swimsuit I can borrow."

"She'll need it for herself," he answers patiently.

It's 1944 wartime. Of course they don't have multiple swim-suits. That would be wasteful.

"Well, maybe Sophie, then."

"Maybe Sophie what?" Sophie asks from a rocking chair by the fire. She's working on needlepoint and squints to look into the eye of the needle.

"I was wondering if you have a bathing suit I could borrow?"

She looks up. "I expect I do. It's packed with my summer clothes in the closet, but I can look."

"I thought Marina and I could take a dip in the bathhouse tonight."

Sophie sighs, resting her sewing in her lap.

"I have a feeling all of you will catch your deaths in that thing."

"I promise we won't," I tell her. "We won't get our hair wet, and we'll dry off really well. The heat and steam from the water heat up that little shed pretty nicely."

She sniffs. "I don't want any of you getting sick."

"We won't," I promise.

"If something happens to you, how would I tell your family?" she asks me. "I have to keep you safe until we can return you to them."

I swallow now.

This lying thing . . . it doesn't come naturally to me, and I don't like it. Lying never ends well.

"You're very kind, Sophie. My family, wherever they are, will be grateful, I'm sure."

That's not a lie.

Sophie smiles, and when she does, her face softens, the corners of her eyes crinkling. In this moment, she looks exactly like my mother. The same tilt of the head, the same smile. I never knew that my mom looked like my great-grandmother.

But as Sophie smiles at me, it's almost like my mother is smiling at me, and it pulls at my heart.

There are days, and have been throughout my life, when I just simply miss my mom. There are times when a girl needs her mother, and no one else, not even a grandmother, will do.

Regardless, Gran tried so hard to be everything for me that I needed, and she did such a good job.

I don't think I ever told her how much I appreciated everything she did for me.

She probably never knew.

That pulls on my heart too. I should've told her. I should've been more grateful. Gran didn't have to raise me. But she did. She never even thought twice about it.

Being here now, though, I can see why.

The entire family takes care of each other, including the boarders, and Fred and Essie, and, I suspect, virtually anyone else who needs it. It's in our blood.

Gran saw a need, knew she could fill it, and so she did.

And I know she learned that from the woman I'm talking to.

"You're a fantastic mother, Sophie," I tell her.

She flushes, uncomfortable with the praise. "Oh, pish. Get on with you, now. Go look in my closet in the box on the shelf. That's where the summer clothes are. You can find my bathing suit. It's yellow."

I've embarrassed her, and I didn't mean to.

"Thanks, Sophie," I tell her.

I leave Lane at the table and Sophie by the fireplace as I head upstairs.

I pass Albert and William playing checkers on the landing.

"How was the hot spring?" I ask them.

"I can't swear to it, but I think my lame hip feels better," Albert tells me.

"That's amazing!"

"My ma always said there's something magic about hot springs," Will mentions. "She'd have plumb died if she knew we had one right under our noses here on this mountain. Pap took her to the one on Baranof Island. She swears it healed her lumbago."

I don't want to know what lumbago is.

"I can't wait to try it," I tell them.

They go back to their checkers game, and I continue up to the second landing, where I pad down the hall to Dale and Sophie's bedroom.

It's rustic with wooden beams crisscrossing overhead, yet warm and inviting too. And incredibly neat. The bed is perfectly made, the cushions are perfectly aligned. Everything on the dresser is lined up just so.

Knowing Sophie as I do now, I wouldn't have expected anything less.

I open the closet doors, and the interior is just as neat as the bedroom.

There aren't many clothes, but that is normal for this time period. They don't have the overindulgence issue that we do in the present day. They have what they need and not much more.

On the shelf above my head, there are two hatboxes and two larger boxes. One is marked *Summer*.

I stretch up on my tiptoes to reach it.

My fingers are just touching the edge when I lose my balance and fall directly into the closet. I manage to knock the boxes off and they tumble down on me as I fall face-first through the hanging clothes.

I have a Sunday dress draped over my head when I sit up.

And that is when I notice the tiny door hidden behind the clothes at the back of the closet.

CHAPTER FIFTEEN

I stare at the small wooden door curiously.

I've never seen it, and I've lived in this house my entire life. To be fair, though, this was always Gran's room, and I never poked around inside. After she died, I just didn't have the heart to go inside and explore. I still need to do that . . . and to sort through her things. *If I ever get home.*

I swallow hard and stare at the secret door again.

I feel a slight bit of trepidation as I reach for the doorknob, then turn it.

It's unlocked, and the door opens easily, with nary a squeak.

I glance over my shoulder to make sure the coast is clear, and then I duck into the secret room.

It's a windowless, small room, but it's cozy. It's immediately clear that it's Dale's room. There's a desk, with a stack of drawings on top, and a journal with bold writing scrawled within. There are World War I uniforms hanging in the corners, and old photos of Dale and his soldier buddies.

There is a stack of letters tied with twine on the desk, and from one glance, I can see that they're from Sophie. She wrote him while he was off fighting, I imagine.

I feel as though I'm intruding in something intimate and private.

The air in here feels reverent, dignified, and, somehow, weighty.

This is Dale's sanctuary.

It is just as neat and tidy as the bedroom, and has not one speck of dust. He uses this room, and from the looks of it, he sits here among his memories.

"War does something to a man," a voice says quietly.

I spin around to find Dale in the doorway. He doesn't seem bothered that I've invaded his space. If anything, he seems embarrassed.

"It does," I agree quickly. "I'm so sorry. I literally fell into the closet and landed in front of this door. Curiosity got the better of me. I apologize."

"No need," he says easily, his hand in his pocket. He's not meeting my gaze. "Anyone would be curious."

"But not everyone would've looked," I point out.

"You don't need to be quite so honest," Dale tells me. I chuckle.

"Do you think about it a lot?" I ask him, gesturing at the war memorabilia. "You have them tucked in here, so I assume you don't like to talk about it."

"Yet here we are." He sighs.

"I'm sorry," I say quickly. "I pry too much. It's a character flaw."

"You just care about people," he decides. "I haven't decided yet if it's annoying or thoughtful."

"I like to think it's thoughtful," I offer.

"I'm sure you do."

He steps inside and crosses to the small desk, pulling out the chair and sitting.

"When I first came back, I couldn't sleep," he tells me. "I'd lie awake, night after night, wondering why I couldn't. But when I did, my dreams . . . nightmares, really, would be filled with memories. Bloody ones. I guess I just didn't want to face that. So I didn't sleep much."

"That sounds terrible."

He nods. "I felt like I wasn't fit to marry Soph. But I'd promised her before I left. And she held me to it. She said her mother had already made the dress, and we were *not* going to waste it."

"She loved you," I tell him. "She didn't care about your battle scars."

"No, she didn't." He pauses, then looks at me. "I'm not the only one who came back scarred."

He stares me in the eye, and I know he's talking about Lane now. I swallow.

"I know."

"He's not diminished," Dale says firmly. "Some folks think we're damaged goods, but what do they expect? We lived a nightmare. We're going to remember it."

I reach over and pat his hand. "Of course you are. Anyone who doesn't understand that is ignorant."

"Do *you* understand?" he asks gently.

Do I understand . . . Lane.

That's what he means.

I nod slowly. "I do."

"He's a good man," he tells me. "I've known him since he was in short pants. They don't get much better than Lane Hughes."

"I don't imagine they do," I agree.

"You know, Sophie frets that you might have a husband back home and you just don't remember him," Dale says. "But I don't believe it. When you love someone that deep, the deep kind of love that you give to a spouse, you can't just forget it."

"No, I'm sure not."

"It's what brought me home from the war," he adds. "We weren't married yet, but her picture in my pocket kept me going. She saved my life."

"I think Lane might have someone like that," I say before I can think better of it. "Her name is Cecile. He said her name in his sleep."

Dale's head snaps up and he meets my gaze again.

How do you know what he says in his sleep?

His eyes ask the question, but his mouth doesn't speak the words.

"I don't know a Cecile," Dale says instead.

"I think she might be French," I say. "And he was in France, so . . ."

"I know the kind of man Lane is," Dale tells me. "If there's a woman, he wouldn't rest until he was with her. So, either she wasn't who you think she was, or she's . . ."

"Dead," I finish for him.

"Yes." He clears his throat.

"I overheard him at Essie and Fred's," I tell him. "Lane was on the couch, having a nightmare. He shouted in his sleep. He was talking about how she's dead."

"I see the way he looks at you," Dale tells me, and he seems utterly uncomfortable now. "I don't know who Cecile was. But I can tell you that whenever he thinks you're not looking, he's watching you, like he's trying to memorize you."

My stomach clenches, both at the words and the fact that my great-grandfather would notice something like that.

"You're a very surprising person, Dale," I tell him, changing the subject. "You're very insightful."

"I'm not your typical country bumpkin," he says wryly.

"That's not what I meant," I backpedal, but he's chuckling.

"I know. And thank you. I like being able to surprise folks now and again."

I glance around the small sanctuary once more, at the war relics, the sentimental photos, and the drawings of the Alaskan wilderness on the desk.

"You're a surprise," I assure him. I turn to smile at him, but my eye catches something. I bend and examine the drawing. My fingers touch the edge.

"Is that . . ."

I pick it up, studying the delicate lines of my own face. I'm laughing with Marina in the kitchen. We look absolutely joyful, like two best friends sharing a secret.

"It's you and Marina," he says needlessly. "You both looked so happy. I couldn't resist. The past few years have been dark. It's nice to see that joy is coming back."

"The war is almost over," I tell him. He nods.

"We can hope. But until then, we can still take our happiness where we find it. You're doing our family good, Piper."

It's truly a family, boarders and all, and it's more *ours* than he realizes.

"Thanks, Dale," I tell him softly. "You're doing me good too. You all are."

That's no lie.

He nods and pats my shoulder.

"I can find you Sophie's bathing suit," he tells me, and he ducks back through the door. The moment is over, but it was beautiful and I'll never forget it. Who else in the entire world can say that their great-grandfather paid them a compliment?

He paws through the contents of the spilled box, hands me the matronly yellow suit, and then neatly folds everything back into the box before he tucks it on the top shelf, then latches the door after I step through.

"You girls will like the hot spring," he tells me as we walk toward the hall. "Just make sure to take protection. I don't want you going up there after dark."

"Yes, sir," I agree.

I trot with the suit in my hands toward my room, then I remember that it's not my room anymore. Not here. I turn around and trot in the other direction. Dale eyes me curiously but doesn't say anything.

"Amnesia." I shrug.

I disappear into the room Marina and I share without looking back at Dale.

Marina is on the bed, on her belly, her legs crossed behind her.

"What in the world took you so long?" she demands. "It's gonna be dark soon, and then there's no way my father will let us use the hot spring."

"I'll just be thirty seconds," I promise her. I yank my clothes off, pull the suit on, and stare at myself in the tiny mirror on the dresser.

"Oh, boy." I sigh, poking at the folds in the suit. "This isn't flattering."

"Who cares?" Marina demands. "No one will see you but me."

I think of Lane, and the way he'd gazed at me while he showed me how to clean the shotgun. The way his eyes had crinkled when he'd smiled. The way my heart had tumbled through my chest when he did.

"Lane said he'd accompany us with the shotgun," I tell her casually, trying not to make a big deal out of it. Her eyes immediately narrow.

"Lane? Out of everyone in the house?"

I shrug. "He offered."

She stares at me. "Fine. But don't for one second think I won't figure out a way to ask about the girl."

"Cecile," I murmur.

"Yes, her," she answers impatiently, and in this moment, she's so much like Shelly that it almost takes my breath away. Why hadn't I seen it before? Gran had hired Shelly because Shelly reminded her of herself at this age.

Shelly had been in a hard spot. She'd really needed the job. Gran truly did have a soft heart beneath the bluster. And that had always been the case.

Marina's cheeks are flushed now.

"Get moving, sis," she tells me. "We've got an investigation to conduct."

She tosses a flannel shirt at me, which I quickly put on, along with the pair of work slacks she tosses next.

We're walking down the steps with towels in our hands two minutes later.

Marina pauses and raps on Lane's door.

He answers immediately. "Yes?"

"You ready for protection detail?" she asks with a grin.

He grins back. "I'll meet you in the foyer."

We're pulling our boots on when he joins us.

"Are you ready in case we meet ol' Tiny?" he asks.

"That bear is hardly tiny," Marina answers. "And I can take care of myself. It's Piper I'm worried about."

"Hey!" I yelp. She laughs and pulls her hood up.

We crunch down the snowy front steps, then start up the trail for the hot spring. Walking behind us, Lane keeps a sharp eye out.

It's when we approach the shed that he steps ahead of us, to make sure that the bear hasn't figured out a way inside.

"They're ridiculously resourceful," he says over his shoulder as he looks at the latch.

"They're apex predators, for sure," I agree as we step past him and inside.

"They're what?" Marina asks.

"Nothing," I answer.

The fire inside is still going, and Lane stokes it for us.

"You can sit over there," Marina tells him. "With your back to us, of course."

"Of course," he agrees, and he promptly turns around.

"Ever the gentleman," I say as I take off my boots, then strip my clothes off. Impishly, I toss my clothes by his feet. He practically flinches. I smile.

Marina tosses her clothes after mine, and Lane sighs.

"Behave, ladies."

Marina laughs.

She steps into the hot pool of water. Steam rises around us, and I breathe it in.

"Oh land, this is nice," she says as she slides down in water up to her chin. "Piper, get in here. You'll just die."

She's not wrong. It's amazingly nice. I slide in across from her, enjoying the heat that envelops my body, instantly relaxing my tight shoulders.

"Oh boy," I murmur.

"I told you," Marina says. Her eyes are closed.

"Rub it in." Lane groans, without turning around.

"Sorry, ol' chum." She laughs. "You'll have your turn."

"Eventually," I add with a grin.

"Keep rubbing it in," Lane mutters again, not unkindly. I laugh.

"I'm sure Boyfriend would much rather be here waiting for the hot spring than overseas, right, Marina?"

As soon as the words are out of my mouth, I see Lane's shoulders tighten, and Marina's leg goes rigid in response, and I hate myself. I feel just awful.

"I didn't mean it like that," I tell Lane. "Of course you would rather be overseas and not here. I wasn't thinking when I said it that way. Please forgive me for being so thoughtless."

Marina exhales, and Lane's shoulders relax.

"No offense taken," he says softly. I can't tell if he means it.

"Boyfriend is too manly for stuff like this anyway," Marina announces, in an obvious attempt to lighten the mood. "He combs his hair with a Brillo pad. He drinks turpentine for breakfast, he—"

"Is this the same boyfriend I'm thinking of?" Lane interrupts. "Your current fiancé? The one who used a security blanket until he was ten? That boyfriend?"

"Don't you dare say a word, Lane Patrick Hughes," Marina demands. "Just because you've known him since we were children doesn't mean you know who he is now. Not like I know him, anyway."

Lane turns his head ever so slightly as he speaks.

"I'm sure that's true, Marina. It doesn't matter that he wet the bed until he was twelve too."

"That's a bald-faced lie, Lane," she sputters. When he laughs, she realizes he was joking.

"That had better be a joke," she grumbles. "He's the bravest man I've ever known."

"All of our boys are brave," Lane agrees. "*Boyfriend* is no exception. Even if he *was* afraid of the dark until he was ten."

Marina sits up in such a huff that water splashes over the makeshift rock rim of the spring. Lane cackles loudly enough that everyone in the house probably hears.

I can't help but laugh too. There's such joy in his voice—he's forgotten the war, just for this one moment.

"I'm kidding, Rina. He is brave."

"And so are you," I tell him. "You all are."

"What was the last you heard from him?" Lane asks her, after a few minutes.

"He was stationed in the Philippines. He had just eaten frog legs, and he didn't like them." Her voice is soft now, reflective and gentle. "He wasn't able to sleep much, but only because his bunkmates either snore or talk in their sleep. He said he couldn't wait to come home. That he wants to marry me as soon as he steps foot on Alaskan soil."

"If he's in the Philippines, he's probably safe," Lane says. "Roosevelt swore we'd protect the Filipino people. He's just on protection duty, Marina."

"Uh-huh. Until someone actually invades the Philippines," she answers, unconvinced. "Besides, he mentioned that he was waiting for further orders. He might have to move."

"Doubtful," Lane says. "But who knows. I'm sure he's fine. Don't worry. Just say a prayer for his safety every night. I know I do."

"Thank you," Marina answers softly, biting her lip. Her fears aren't allayed. "I just, I don't know why. I've been feeling scared for him. Like, I just have a bad feeling. I can't explain it."

I wish I could tell her that he lives, that he grows old with her, and that together, they live through things they could never have imagined.

But I can't. All I can do is reach over and hold her hand and murmur that everything will be okay.

She nods at me and hides her watery eyes.

I pretend not to notice.

"This hot spring feels like manna from heaven," I announce. "I can't believe no one knew it was here."

I stretch my leg out and flex my toes. My skin is getting wrinkled from the moisture.

"Your legs are so long," Marina remarks. "I'm jealous."

"Your legs are long too," I tell her. "You have no reason to be."

"Your complexion is perfect, though, and I've got freckles."

"Lord, is this pick-yourself-apart day?" I roll my eyes. "You're gorgeous and you know it."

"You honestly look enough alike to be related," Lane pipes up. "I noticed that the other day. If I didn't know better, I'd think you were sisters. So stop bickering about who is prettier. You both are."

"I'm not bickering," I tell him. "I was just responding to her ridiculousness."

But wait.

He thinks we're pretty.

I'm afraid my feminist card might get revoked if anyone found out how happy that realization makes me.

I glance at the silhouette of his face on the wall, flickering in the shadows.

What is it about him that makes me tongue-tied?

"Okay, Lane. We talked about Boyfriend," Marina says. "Let's talk about your special girl."

My head snaps up, and Lane's shoulders stiffen.

"I don't have one," Lane mutters. "You know that."

"You don't have one that I know of," Marina corrects. "But I hear stories of boys who find girls overseas."

"Are you talking about houses of ill repute?" Lane asks. "Because that's not an appropriate conversation, Marina."

"No, I'm talking about sweethearts that you boys meet overseas. It can happen, can't it? What if Boyfriend meets someone over there and decides he doesn't want me anymore? That's possible, isn't it?"

She manages a tone of great anxiety in her voice that is worthy of an Oscar-winning actress. I eye her appreciatively, and she winks.

"I-I mean . . ." Lane sputters, trying to answer a girl who he thinks might be despondent.

"How easy is it for a soldier to meet a good girl over there?" I chip in. "I mean, it's not like the atmosphere is ripe for romance. It's war, right?"

"That's true," Lane says, and he seems relieved. "It's war. It's not an ice cream social, Marina."

"Are you saying there's never an incident where one of our boys might meet a nice girl?"

"It could happen," he says carefully. "But it's unlikely. Not when he's got you here waiting for him, Rina."

"Did it ever happen to you?" she asks boldly. "Did you meet anyone I don't know about, Lane Hughes?" She uses a lilting voice, to make it a joke, but it's clear she wants an answer.

"There's tons of people outside of Wander, Alaska," Lane tells her, avoiding the question. "It's highly possible."

"You know what I'm saying," she replies firmly.

"We should probably get back to the house before your mom frets herself to death," I tell Marina, feeling sorry for Lane. He doesn't want to talk about Cecile. So he shouldn't have to. "She's convinced we're going to get pneumonia."

"And the sun is going down," Lane says. He sounds deeply relieved.

"Good point—that settles it. I'm going to get out, and you're definitely not going to turn around," I tell Lane.

"Agreed," he says cheerfully.

As I step out, he reaches his arm backward, holding out a towel. I reach for it, and my wet skin brushes his wrist.

Electricity crackles at the touch, at least for me.

"Thank you."

"You're welcome," he answers. "Don't slip. I'm too far away to catch you."

"Not every princess needs saving," I announce.

"Probably true. But some do. We found you in a snowbank, Pip."

The laughter in his voice makes me grin.

"*You* didn't. Dale and the guys did. You came later."

"Okay. So the princess was saved by a group of men," he amends. "My apologies, milady. I would've rescued you had I been there."

"Why is she the only princess here?" Marina interjects. "I quite like the idea of being waited on hand and foot, and rescued when necessary."

"I said nothing about waiting on you hand and foot," Lane corrects her. "Only that I'd rescue you if necessary."

"Tomato, tomahto," Marina answers as she climbs out of the spring. I laugh.

"She's got you there," I decide.

Marina and I dry off quickly, pulling our clothes on as fast as we can. It might lock in the moist heat, but this is still just a small shack in the middle of the Alaskan wilderness in winter.

"White Knight, if you would be so kind as to check for bears, I think we're ready to travel now," I say.

Assured that it's safe to look now, Lane turns around.

"Let me check outdoors," he tells us, stepping past.

He opens the door, steps outside, and looks around.

"All clear," he says, motioning for us to follow.

I step on a twig, and it snaps in the dusky light. The cold is penetratingly harsh after we exit the warm little room, and it rests on our damp skin.

"I hope Mama isn't right," Marina remarks as we walk down the slope toward the house.

"Pneumonia isn't caused by cold air," I tell her. "It's caused by a virus. A bug in the air. You have to breathe in the bacteria to get it."

"Tell that to Molly Andrews," Marina says over her shoulder. "She was locked outside her cabin for two hours last winter and she caught pneumonia and died."

"Yikes. I'm sorry. That's tragic. But bugs stay alive longer in the cold weather. Someone carried the germs to her. She didn't die from the cold."

"Neither of you are dying tonight from the cold or otherwise," Lane announces, bringing up the rear. "So let's talk about something more cheerful."

"Okay, back to whether you ever met a girl overseas," Marina answers obligingly.

Lane groans. "You're incorrigible."

"Agreed," she shoots back.

I laugh, then skid on a piece of ice.

Lane's arm darts out and grabs my elbow, holding me upright.

"You have ninja instincts," I tell him.

He lifts an eyebrow, and I suddenly realize I don't know when the term *ninja* became well-known.

"You're lightning fast," I say, just in case.

"That is true," he acknowledges.

He promptly slips and falls into the snow, proving God has a great sense of humor.

Marina and I burst out laughing, and Lane spits snow into the air.

"I stand corrected," he says limply. We laugh again.

"Pride goeth before a fall, big boy," Marina tells him, bending to offer him a hand. He takes it and, with a sharp tug, yanks her into the snow. She sprawls in the powder, arms and legs flying.

She's the one sputtering snow now, and I laugh.

When I do, when I draw attention to myself, they both look at me in unison, their eyes gleaming with the same exact expression.

I take a step back.

"Don't you dare," I shriek over my shoulder, as I take off running as fast as I can through the snow, trying not to slip and slide.

I can hear Marina and Lane get to their feet and chase me.

A snowball hits me between the shoulder blades when I'm fifty paces from the back door.

I power on with long steps. I'm thirty paces away.

The stairs come into focus. I slip but stay upright.

Twenty paces.

Fifteen.

Someone tackles me when I'm ten paces away.

I eat snow as the weight of two human bodies pile on top of me.

Marina laughs in my ear, then groans. "Lane, you're heavy."

A huge weight lifts, and I'm able to breathe.

"Marina, you get off too," I growl.

The lighter weight lifts.

"I'm so glad we warmed up in the hot spring," I mutter, my hands stinging from the cold snow. I sit up, and a strong hand grabs mine to help me up.

"Thanks," I tell Lane, wiping my wet mouth.

We look at each other, our cheeks pink, our eyes sparkling, our faces wet from snow, and we burst out laughing.

When Sophie comes to the back door and chides us for catching our deaths, it just sends us pealing with fresh laughter.

As we climb the steps to the back door, which Lane opens and holds for us, I know I'll remember this moment forever.

No matter what.

CHAPTER SIXTEEN

I need to think of something to make for dinner that doesn't involve meat," Sophie says to Marina and me as we help with breakfast the next morning. "We had beans and cornbread last night."

"Those were navy beans," Marina says. "We could do brown beans tonight. We have bacon grease to flavor them."

"And I could eat cornbread every night and not get tired of it," I add.

"You girls are being sweet," Sophie says appreciatively. "Coming up with meal ideas during the winter in Alaska is challenging in the best of times. When we're almost out of meat, well, it's a whole different animal."

"I'm glad that you haven't even considered butchering a reindeer," I say as I mix biscuits. Both Sophie and Marina's heads snap around. Marina's eyes are wide.

"You ghoul," she gasps. "How could you even think such a thing?"

Sophie's mouth twitches at her daughter, but she still shakes her head.

"We'd never," she assures me. "They're our pets. The men are trying their darndest to scare us up some game, but we'll have to be patient. It could be today, it could be next week. In the meantime . . ."

She pulls a bag of brown beans from the cabinet and, with a sigh, she pours them in a bowl to soak all day.

"What I wouldn't give for a goose for Christmas Eve dinner," she says, a frown creasing her forehead. "I don't mind making do, I really don't. But I'd like a decent Christmas Eve dinner for everyone."

"We'll get something," Marina assures her.

"Christmas Eve is Sunday," Sophie replies. "The chances are dwindling."

"That's still three days away," I point out. "Anything can happen in three days, Sophie."

"I have a few things to wrap today," Marina mentions. "Do you have any paper, Mama?"

"I have a bit," Sophie answers. "In my room. I'll get it for you after breakfast. Or Piper, you can get it if you want. You were in my closet the other day. You know the lay of the land. It's in . . . Dale's area."

My eyes meet hers, and I realize she knows I was in Dale's sanctuary. I'm embarrassed all over again for getting caught being nosy, but Sophie doesn't react.

"Sure. I can go look," I tell them. "I feel terrible, though. I don't have any gifts to give."

"Are you crazy?" Marina demands. "You being here is a gift. Santa brought me a sister this year, and early, to boot!"

She nudges me, and I smile.

"You *are* like a sister," I tell her.

"I feel like I've known you for a hundred years," she tells me. "It's the craziest thing."

"I feel the same way," I answer.

Sophie pats my arm as I pass by to go fetch the wrapping paper.

I'm in Dale's sanctuary when Sophie steps inside. She points to the top of a chest of drawers, where a neat square of wrapping tissue rests, tied together with twine.

"Don't mention this room to Marina, okay?" she asks. "Dale doesn't talk about the war. He doesn't want his daughter knowing that it took a toll on him."

"It's nothing to be ashamed of," I say slowly, as I retrieve the paper.

"I know," she says limply. "But men will be men. Even though he's more sensitive than many, he's still got his pride."

"Well, his secret is safe with me," I promise. "And even though he's sensitive and thoughtful . . . actually, because of that, I think he's more manly than most."

I smile, and she smiles back. It reaches her eyes, which shine warmly at me.

"You're doing Marina a world of good," she says as we climb through the door, back into her bedroom.

"Am I?"

"Oh, yes. She's wanted a sister for so long, she doesn't know what to do with herself at this point."

"I'm sure she'll think of something," I mutter. Sophie laughs again.

"You've really got her number," she says approvingly.

"She's an open book," I reply.

"Don't tell her that," Sophie advises. "She likes to think she's mysterious."

I snort and Sophie chuckles.

"Exactly." She nods. "Anyway. I have just the thing if you want to give Marina a little something for Christmas."

"You do?"

She nods. "I've been holding on to it, thinking that the right time to give it to her will present itself. And here we are."

"I'm intrigued," I tell her, my eyes wide.

She leads me to her dresser and reaches into a wooden jewelry box on top, pulling out a simple gold locket.

She opens it and hands it to me.

"I had Dale draw it in lieu of a photo," she says. A tiny intricate portrait of Marina and me is displayed inside. Though small, it's highly detailed. He even somehow managed to capture the mischief in Marina's eyes.

"It's lovely," I breathe. "The locket too."

"My mother gave it to me," she says. "I think she'll love it."

"You should give this to her from you," I say, trying to hand it back. "It's too lovely to come from me."

"Pish," she says, waving her hands and pushing it back my way. "As long as she gets it, that's all that matters."

"You're a very kind woman, Sophie McCauley," I tell her.

Her cheeks flush and she waves me away again. "We'll have a happy Christmas," she tells me. "Even if we *don't* have a goose."

Honestly, eating a goose doesn't sound good at all, with or without the plum sauce she and Marina have gushed about.

I don't voice that opinion but instead just smile as we return downstairs.

I wrap the locket and tuck it into my pocket so that Marina doesn't find it before Christmas. I also squeeze Dale's arm and murmur, "Thank you."

He nods, knowing exactly what I'm thanking him for.

Marina is oblivious, singing Christmas carols in the kitchen.

"Do you think they could use beans?" she calls in to us. I lift an eyebrow.

"We're thinking we'll see if we can trade with Fred and Ess for some meat, if they have some to spare," Dale explains. "Lane needs to head up there today to check in, so Marina is putting together a package."

"I'll help." I join Marina and eye the sizable food pile she's gotten started, which includes two fresh loaves of bread.

"I think this is plenty," I tell her. "There's just two of them."

"Do you want to go with us?" she asks. "Lane's taking care of the herd, and then we'll head out."

"Sure!" I say, trying to sound casual, but she laughs knowingly.

"I'll try not to be a third wheel." She winks.

I feel the color rise in my cheeks, which only makes her laugh harder.

"You might want to go comb your hair," she suggests. "It appears a nest of rats slept in it last night."

My hand flutters to my bangs, and sure enough, it's not a good situation.

I've made it to the staircase when Lane bursts in through

the front doors. Snow swirls in around him, but even in the cold, he assesses me and his eyes twinkle.

"Did a tornado roll through here while I was outdoors?" he teases, pulling off a glove.

I roll my eyes. "Some people just haven't had a chance to get fixed up yet."

"Some people do it before they ever leave their bedroom, but it's a personal choice, I guess." He shrugs off his coat and laughs at the indignation on my face. "No offense, Pip. It's cute."

I huff and stomp upstairs, where I examine myself in the mirror.

Lord.

He's right. I should've addressed . . . *this* . . . before leaving this room.

Piper, get it together. This isn't the twenty-first century, where some people go to the bank or Walmart in pajamas.

I yank a brush through my hair and French braid it in a plait down my back. Simple, functional, classic . . . and it shows that there aren't any rodents taking up residence in my hair.

When I rejoin Lane and Marina, they're pulling on dry coats. Marina tosses me Dale's big overcoat and a pair of gloves.

"It's frigid," she tells me. "The coat you borrowed from me won't cut it."

I pull the gloves on, followed by the coat. How I miss the tiny hand warmers from back home that I can tuck into my gloves.

Marina shoves a stocking cap onto my head and pulls it down over my ears.

"Welp, I'm officially the Stay Puft Man," I announce.

"Who?" Marina asks.

Will I ever learn?

"No one," I mutter.

Sophie emerges from the kitchen with the knapsack of food.

"I put the makings for a chest poultice in there," she tells us. "Marina, you know how to mix it up. If she still sounds bad, make her use it."

"Make Essie Klein do something?" Marina's face wrinkles. "I don't know if it's possible."

"I'll take care of it," Lane assures Soph. "Let's go, ladies."

Edward and Joe wave at us from the side of the barn, where they appear to be fixing the wooden shutter on the window.

"Watch yourselves," Joe calls. "There's bear tracks all around."

"That's a persistent bear," I remark as we hit the trail.

"Hunger is a powerful motivator," Lane answers.

I can't argue. The sheer lengths I've gone to for a plate of nachos is proof of that motivation.

I stay on high alert as we crunch through snow, rock, and ice toward the Kleins' home. Every time a twig crunches, I spin around to look.

Lane and Marina chuckle at me, which makes me start wondering . . . how wonderful it must be to not have your childhood scarred by movies. *Jaws, Final Destination, Carrie . . .* all movies that made me lie awake at night as a kid, watching my closet door intently for danger.

No one here has ever experienced the fear of things they have never actually experienced in person. Horror movies don't exist here. The internet, filled to the brim with stories about wildlife attacks, serial killers, home invasions . . . doesn't exist. The constant barrage of information and notifications and news stories . . . *doesn't exist*.

On the one hand, it's peaceful.

On the other, I wonder what's happening in the world that we don't know about. Without my phone in my pocket, dinging with notifications, I feel disconnected, vulnerable. We're living during World War II, for goodness' sake, and I don't have the benefit of the internet to keep me informed.

All I have are my fading memories from history classes to remind me of what happens.

Even still, as the days go by, I do feel more and more at peace. Less and less on edge.

Until this bear.

Now I'm hyperalert.

Here, in this rugged place, there's no one to help us. It's us versus the bear.

I pick up my pace and join Lane in the front.

"Catch a second wind?" he asks with a grin.

"I just can't wait to get to Essie and threaten to hog-tie her if she doesn't behave with this poultice," I answer.

"I'll take her feet," Marina offers. "You can have her head."

"Gee, thanks."

"Hey, I called it." She shrugs. "You'll have to learn to be quicker."

"Noted."

Thirty minutes later, as we're chatting among ourselves as we hike through the snow, a figure emerges from the ice-covered landscape ahead, bundled up and small.

I cock my head, trying to focus.

Lane sucks in a breath. "Essie?" he calls.

"No way," I breathe.

"Help!" she calls, waving her arms. "It's Fred!"

We rush to meet her, finding her worried and frantic.

"Fred broke his foot a couple days ago," she tells us. "The bone is poking through the side of his foot. We thought we'd just wait until Lane came back to check on us to set it but we can't wait. He's got an infection and it's bad. He needs help, or I think . . ."

"Oh, no," Marina murmurs. "We don't have any antibiotics at the lodge. There weren't any to be had when we stocked up for winter. Do you have any, Essie?"

She shakes her head, and her distress grows. "Not anymore. I had to take them when I got pneumonia. We need to hurry. He's delirious at this point. He could die."

The magnitude of that hits us all, the fact that things can turn so terribly bad so quickly here.

Lane and I rush ahead, while Marina continues at a slightly slower pace to help Essie. The woman is tough, but she's still a few decades older than us.

When Lane and I arrive at the house, Fred is on the sofa, his black and purple foot propped on cushions. It's hugely swollen, and Fred is sweating.

"Fever," I say unnecessarily, eyeing his wispy hair plastered to his head. Lane nods.

"Fred," he says. "I see you've managed to bang yourself up good. There's better ways to get Essie doing the chores than this, my friend."

Fred opens his eyes but his usual mirth is gone.

"I know," he croaks. "I've gone and done it this time." He flinches when he accidentally moves his foot, which is swollen to roughly the size of a football. A wound on the side is angry and red, and appears to have a piece of bone sticking through it.

He peers at Lane. "Aren't you supposed to be overseas?"

Lane and I exchange a glance.

"I'm home now, Fred," Lane tells him. "And I'm here to help you. We need to splint your foot, and you need antibiotics."

"Splint it? There's bone poking through," I point out.

"There is," he agrees. "I've seen worse. It's a side bone—we can immobilize it and it should heal fine."

"Should? He needs to be able to walk on that thing in the future, Lane."

Lane pauses from examining Fred's wound and looks at me. "Piper, sometimes here in Alaska, we have to make things work as best we can."

"I know, but . . ."

He's right.

"We need to get the swelling down before we try and set it," I say instead of arguing. "But before we do anything, we need to get him some meds."

Lane nods. "Agreed."

"Do you think anyone else around has any antibiotics? We could send the guys out to search."

Marina and Essie burst through the door now, and Lane turns to them.

"Ess, do you have a dogsled?"

"You know we do," she answers.

"Marina, go out and get it arranged," he directs. "We'll load Fred up and pull him back to the lodge, and we'll send a group out to locate some antibiotics. Essie, can you gather some pelts and blankets? We need to make him as comfortable on the sled as we can, so we don't jostle him. It's going to be painful no matter how careful we are."

Essie nods, her face solemn. "Yes. I'll find the whiskey too."

"He'll need it," Lane answers.

Fred moans at just this moment, a harsh groan that startles us all. His eyes are glassy as he asks for Essie.

"I'm here, Fred," she tells him, grasping his hand.

"You're not my wife," he announces. "You're old."

Essie flushes ever so slightly. "So are you. You're not yourself right now, Fred. Just hold on. You hear?"

She turns to Lane with a vulnerable, pleading look. "We've got to fix him up, Lane."

Lane nods. "We need to hurry."

Marina heads for the door. "I'll get the sled."

"I'll help you," I tell her. "I'm sure it's heavy."

As we walk to the barn, I turn to her.

"This isn't good."

"No, it's not."

She pulls open the heavy barn door, and we scan the area for a dogsled. There's machinery, stalls, hay, shadows, a loft.

"I don't see it."

"It's probably toward the back," Marina answers. "They have a sliding door at the back to store big things . . . like the tractor, the plane, probably the sled."

"The *plane?*"

All of a sudden, I remember that Fred has a prop plane.

I take off for the back of the barn, leaving Marina standing in bewilderment.

"How did I forget this?" I mutter, and as I round the corner at the back, there it is.

Dusty and faded, an old propeller plane sits.

I eye it.

The wings look sound, but very old. Normally, I'd never in my life fly in something so rickety. But Fred's life might actually depend on it.

It's partially covered by a tarp, and I'm pulling it off when Marina joins me. I hop up on the side and open the door to the cockpit, looking inside. The instruments appear intact.

"I can fly," I tell Marina in a rush.

"What? How in the world do you know that?"

"I don't know," I lie. "I just suddenly know that I know how."

"That's crazy, Piper," she says slowly, shaking her head. "There's no way."

"My dad was a pilot, remember?" I stare at her. "He must've taught me, because I know how to fly, Marina. You're going to have to trust me here."

She examines my face, looking into my eyes, and after a scant moment, she decides.

She's trusting me.

"What do you need?" she asks quickly, helping me pull the canvas tarp to the side.

"Do you know how often this is used?" I ask, swinging into the pilot's seat.

"A couple times a year," she answers. "Until Fred's eyesight got so bad that he couldn't see to fly it."

"Did he maintain it after he stopped using it?" I ask, flipping switches and checking the fuel.

"I don't know," she answers honestly. "Piper, are you sure you can do this? One mistake and you could die."

"I can do it," I tell her. "I promise. Fred needs me. That's not a simple infection. It's gone past his foot. I think it's in his blood. If we don't get him medication, he'll die."

She nods and rushes to push back the heavy barn door.

I take a deep breath and turn the key.

The engine roars to life and the propellors sputter, then spin, blowing dust and hay all around me. I idle out of the barn. Lane has arrived by the time I emerge through the double doors in the plane. I kill the engine.

I'll never forget the look on his face—the horror, the surprise, the shock . . . the fear.

The fear.

He masks it quickly and rushes to the side of the plane, pulling open the door.

"Piper, get out of there before you hurt yourself," he demands, reaching for my arm. He's as white as a ghost.

"I'll be fine. I can fly, Lane. I can go get medicine for Fred."

Lane freezes, and his first reaction is disbelief. "There's no way you know how to fly."

"My father taught me," I lie. "I don't know why, all I know is he did. And I can fly, and because of that, I can save Fred. Surely you see that he'll die without antibiotics."

"I know that," he answers. "But you don't need to kill your-self trying to save him."

The concern on his face is riveting. Was the fear I saw a few minutes ago . . . was that for me? For my safety?

My heart flutters, just in case.

"I'm not going to kill myself."

"Even if you do know how, what if you get in the air and you realize you don't remember all of it? Landing is the hardest part! That's what they say, anyway. You have to land the plane, Piper."

"I can land the plane."

"But you don't know where to go, you don't know this area. You wouldn't know where to refuel, and you don't even have any money. I'll go with you."

He clenches his jaw, and my mouth opens.

"You're scared of airplanes," I remind him. "And you have to stay . . . you need to drag Fred down to the lodge. Marina can't do it alone."

Lane turns to Marina. "Hike back to the lodge and get Joe and Ed. Have them come get Fred and Essie. Dale can set the bone while we're gone. We'll bring Fred the medicine he needs. Go now, Marina."

He doesn't wait for her to agree, he just rounds the plane, opens the door, and climbs in.

His face is ashen. His knuckles are white. But he does not hesitate to do this anyway.

"Buckle up."

Lane looks at me. "What?"

I glance at the seat. There's no seat belt.

"Nineteen forty-four is trying to kill me," I say limply. I turn the key, the engine fires up, and I steer the plane toward a flat area behind the barn.

Lane's fingers tighten on his knee.

I push the throttle.

"I'm trusting you," Lane says, his mouth drawn and his eyes gleaming.

"I know," I say softly. I push the throttle farther. "We have a short runway, so don't be alarmed."

Lane nods once, his eyes fixed straight ahead.

This plane might be rickety, and it might be old, but its equipment is simple and easy to use. I launch us toward takeoff and lift the nose of the aircraft up. We barely clear the trees at the perimeter of the clearing.

Lane flinches but otherwise doesn't react.

"You *do* know how to fly," he shouts above the din.

"Apparently," I yell back.

He doesn't relax and in fact, doesn't open his eyes.

It's cold up here, but I expected that. I turn the wheel toward Fairbanks. Lane doesn't know it, but I know exactly how to get there. What I don't know are landmarks . . . buildings . . the airport. Not in 1944. I'm guessing, though, that a landing strip won't be too terribly hard to find.

"You can relax," I tell him. "Look at the gauges. All is well."

I point at the individual gauges, all within normal ranges.

"We're safe," I tell him. He glances at me.

"You must think poorly of me," he says now. My head snaps around.

"What on earth for?"

"Because I'm so upset right now."

"You're a man who is scared of airplanes and flying in an old farm plane with a girl who has amnesia," I answer. "I'm pretty sure anyone would be upset. *Not* everyone would have the courage to do it anyway. On top of all that, the man who is basically your surrogate father is on the brink of death. You're actually quite calm, considering."

His gaze flits to me before he looks out the window.

"Don't lean too hard on that door," I caution. "I don't want to trust it."

He immediately pulls away from it and peers out from the safety of the seat.

We're soaring now, just above the tree line.

"It's beautiful from here," he admits, although his knuckles are still white as he grips his knee.

"It is," I answer. We still have to shout over the noise of the wind and the engine. "Fred is not going to die, Lane. We'll make sure of it."

He locks eyes with me for a moment, his searching mine. Finally, he nods curtly. "I trust you."

Those words and the sincerity behind them are exhilarating, but now is not the time to focus on that. Instead, I focus on the clouds, and the tailwind urging us forward.

"I love it up here," I finally say, my eyes fixed on the horizon.

"You're not afraid . . . even a little?" he asks, his eyebrow lifted.

I shake my head.

"No."

It's a lie. For the first time since I can remember, I *do* feel afraid. My parents died in a plane crash in Alaska. Right before Christmas. In a plane that didn't have adequate deicers.

I'd go out on a limb and say this aircraft doesn't either. At all. But I can't point that out to Lane. That would just be cruel.

I swallow hard and picture Fred's face, plastered in sweat from his infection. We've got to set our fear aside and push forward.

Everything will be okay.

"I feel comfortable up here," I tell him, forming words that aren't a lie. "At home."

"You might not be aware of this, but women don't usually know how to fly," he says seriously, his hands still gripping his thighs. I grin to lighten the mood and to distract myself from my own trepidation.

"What about Amelia Earhart?"

"It didn't end well for her," Lane points out.

I suck in a breath. "Not because of her gender," I answer.

"Dead is dead, Pip."

"We're not going to die," I tell him. "Not today."

"And certainly not because of your gender," he tosses back.

"Certainly not," I agree.

We drift into silence as we fly above the silent Alaskan landscape, frozen and glistening. Eventually, Lane relaxes, his fingers loosening their grip, his shoulders releasing their tension.

We fly over the lodge. Dale and Sophie are outdoors. They look up and wave, and Lane shakes his head.

"This will be fun to explain."

"It is what it is." I shrug.

"You're pretty impressive, Pip."

Lane is looking at me. I feel it, I see it from my periphery. I'm just not brave enough to look into his eyes. I keep my eyes fixed in front of us, watching the nose of our aircraft break through the sky toward town.

CHAPTER SEVENTEEN

s there a doctor's office in town?" I ask. "Or do we need to fly to Fairbanks?"

"There's a drugstore in Wander. Charlie Benson will give us the penicillin if I tell him why."

I assume Charlie Benson is the pharmacist, then find myself wondering if a person needed a degree to dispense medication in 1944. Lord, I miss my phone and Google.

My teeth are chattering when we approach Wander. My fingers are icicles inside my gloves as I throttle down. We circle the area, and I get the lay of the land, eyeing any place that might allow me space to touch the plane down.

Lane points to a quiet stretch of road that is cleared of powdery snow. It's icy, packed snow now, very slick-looking, but it fits our needs. I nod.

His hands clench again, and I say a silent prayer as we descend for a landing.

We would've been fine.

Had it not been for a sudden gust of tailwind as our wheels touch the ground.

The plane lurches forward, propelled into high velocity by the wind. The end of the road comes up on us fast, with a line of buildings all along it, all waiting to break our impact with bricks and concrete.

I brake hard, but the wind is blowing harder from behind.

The scenery around us turns into a blur, and my heart pounds.

I'm going to die like my parents did, in an Alaskan winter.

Next to me, Lane sucks in a breath.

I brake harder, and the wheels skid on ice.

The buildings get closer and closer. I'm standing on the brake, to no avail.

We're going to crash. Hard.

"Brace yourself," I tell Lane.

And then, just like that, when we're one breath away from impact, we're spared.

One wheel gains traction, and as soon as I feel it catch, I yank hard on the wheel to the left.

In the nick of time, we plow into powdery snow instead of hitting the row of buildings head-on. It's a hard stop, to be sure, but we're okay.

Lane and I stare at each other for a moment once we're still, then he grins.

"You were right. We're not going to die today."

I exhale, long and loud, and Lane makes the sign of the cross.

"Are you Catholic?" I ask, as I open the plane's door and swing my leg out.

"No. It just seemed the appropriate thing to do."

I roll my eyes, but in truth, I haven't been this happy to have my feet on the ground in a long, long time.

Lane joins me and we look around.

We're in a residential area on the edge of town, but with a row of shops on the other end.

"There's the drugstore." Lane points. It's a small shop on the opposite end of the street we just landed on. Er, in the snowbank *beside*.

We start walking. Lane holds out his arm, ever the gentleman, and I take his elbow. His warmth is nice, his arm is strong, and being linked with him right now just feels . . . right. It feels comforting.

"We're alive." I smile up at him happily.

He narrows his eyes. "Why do you sound so surprised?"

"I'm not surprised," I clarify, although that's also a bit of a lie. "I'm *happy*."

Lane appears unconvinced, but he doesn't press the subject. Instead, we quickly walk toward the pharmacy. We pass streetlights wound in garlands for Christmas and don't encounter one single person as we walk.

Lane opens the door to the drugstore, and bells tinkle overhead.

Stepping inside, the counter and booths are all made of dark wood, and there's a soda shop counter on the wall opposite the pharmacy.

"Charlie?" Lane calls. A moment later, a small man with thinning dark hair and wearing a white jacket comes out of the back room.

"Lane!" he exclaims. "How are ya, friend? You recovering okay?"

"I'm fine, Charlie," Lane assures him. "It's Fred Klein we're here about. He hurt his foot real bad—his bone is poking through, and he's caught the devil of an infection. If we don't get him some penicillin, and fast, I'm afraid it could get fatal."

"It *will* get fatal," I chime in. "His fever is v*ery* high and he's delirious. I think the infection is in his blood."

"Oh, dear," Charlie murmurs, already rushing to the medicine dispensary area. "Poor ol' Fred. He's so hardheaded, this doesn't surprise me any. I reckon he was messing around outside on the ice when this happened?"

"Probably," Lane agrees. Charlie clucks his tongue.

"He and Essie need to move to town. These long winters will be too hard on them now at their age," he says. "Fred's gettin' to the point that he can barely see a lick."

"I can't argue with that," Lane tells him, leaning on the counter. "But try telling either of them that."

"No, thank you." Charlie chuckles. "I'll leave that to you." He glances at me. "I haven't seen you around these parts," he says curiously.

Lane looks at me and then at Charlie.

"So you haven't seen this girl before?" Lane asks.

Charlie looks at him. "Are you funnin' me? Of course not. I'd remember that. I've watched every young person in an eighty-mile radius grow up, Lane Hughes. I'd remember."

"She showed up on our mountain last week," Lane tells him. "She hit her head and doesn't remember a thing."

"You don't say," Charlie exclaims, interested now, as he measures out penicillin into a jar.

"I thought for sure you'd know something," Lane adds.

"You know pretty much everything that happens around here, Charlie."

"That I do," the older man agrees. He studies me. "You don't remember a thing, darlin'?"

"She remembered today that she can fly a plane." Lane laughs. "You haven't asked how we're even here. You're slipping, Chuck."

"Well, you distracted me with all of this and I didn't think about the practicalities. So you can't remember a thing *and* you can fly a plane?"

"Apparently," I answer.

"You're a mighty pretty thing," he says. "You reckon you're married?"

My eyes fly to his hand, where there is a gold band around his ring finger. He notices and chuckles.

"Not for me, dear. But lovely young ladies are few and far between here. If you stay around here, you'll need a stick to fight all of the men off, when our boys all come back from the war."

I smile. "Thank you, Charlie. I'll take that into consideration and find myself a good-sized club."

He smiles back. "You've got gumption," he says in admiration. "You'll need it here."

He puts the bottle into a small paper sack, which he folds over at the top and hands to Lane.

Lane pulls out his wallet and tries to hand him some bills, but Charlie shakes his head.

"I'll just put it on Fred's tab," he says. "Don't worry about it today. You just hurry up and get that to Fred."

"You're too kind," Lane says, putting his wallet back in his pocket.

"I do have some bandages and a splint if you need them?" Charlie lifts an eyebrow.

"I'm sure Sophie will have that covered. Now, if you had a Christmas goose, that would be a Christmas miracle," Lane says wryly. "They've got more boarders than they planned on, myself included, and they're running out of meat. We haven't been lucky enough to get any game yet, and Mrs. McC has her heart set on a goose for Christmas."

Charlie's eyes widen.

"No way," I breathe.

"I don't have a goose," he clarifies quickly. "But I was paid with two turkeys last week. If they'd help, I'm happy to give them to you."

"You are an amazing, kind, wonderful man," I tell him. "Thank you! But you must let us pay you for them."

"I wouldn't hear of it. The wife can't bring herself to eat them, and so you'd actually be doing me a favor. I don't have any place to put them."

"Oh! Well, then. We accept! Sophie will be beside herself," I tell him. "Thank you so, so much."

Charlie beams. "I'm happy to help, miss," he answers. "We do our best to take care of each other here in Wander."

Lane tucks the medicine in his coat.

"Do you reckon the post office is open?" he asks Charlie. "We need to get this medicine back to Fred, but we're right here, and I know Marina is waiting to hear news of her beau."

My heart constricts at his thoughtfulness. He knows what

it's like to wait for news. He'd surely learned that firsthand when he was overseas, waiting on his own orders.

"I'm afraid not," Charlie says regretfully. "Angus has been in bed sick all week."

"Well, it'll have to keep until after the spring breakup, then," Lane answers. "Thank you for everything, Charlie."

"We don't have the time anyway," I remind him. "We really need to hurry."

"Meet me around back for the turkeys," Charlie says, heading for the back, picking up his pace.

"Is his freezer outside or something?" I ask Lane as we step out the front and walk around the side of the building to the back.

"I don't know," Lane answers. "Must be."

We are so wrong.

Two turkeys scuttle around the fenced area behind the shop, fat bellied and very, very much alive.

"Um." I stare with wide eyes, and now I understand what Charlie meant when he said his wife couldn't bring herself to eat them. "Oh, boy."

Lane blinks. "Charlie, this is far too generous," he tries, but Charlie won't hear of it.

"You take these to Great Expectations and feed everyone," he insists. "They'll fit in Fred's plane. If you keep your arms around 'em."

Oh, boy.

I can't help the grin that stretches from ear to ear at the thought.

"Yes, Lane. Make sure you keep your arms around them. *The whole way home.*"

I wink, and Lane sighs, then joins Charlie in catching the turkeys. They each wrangle one into the plane a few minutes later. First Lane, then when he's perched on the seat, Charlie shoves the second very disgruntled bird up onto Lane's lap.

I hop in and close my door before the turkeys fly out through my side.

Lane clamps his arms around them tight, and we wave to Charlie. He shoves us out of the snowbank, and I fire up the engine.

This time, Lane is distracted by the live fowl occupying his space and isn't so bothered by takeoff.

"Do we have enough fuel?" he asks, once we're in the air.

"Yes. I wouldn't have taken off otherwise."

"Aye-aye, Captain."

A pang runs through me. That's something Shelly always said.

"You don't think it's . . . too late, do you?" I ask Lane.

He shakes his head. "No. Fred is strong as an ox."

I'm still nervous. Lane reaches over and lays one hand over mine.

"He'll be okay, Piper. Have faith. We're moving heaven and earth to get him what he needs. It'll be enough. It has to be enough."

I look at him, at the sincere expression, the strong jaw, the gentle yet haunted eyes.

"You're right," I agree. "Fred will be okay, Lane."

I change the subject.

"It was really sweet of you to try and get the mail," I tell him.

He glances away. "Everyone talks about how hard it is for *us*," he says gruffly. "No one talks about what it's like for those who love us."

"What an insightful thing to say," I answer. His cheeks flush and he looks away. "Marina shoulders it amazingly well. She hides behind joking about it. But I know she's worried. And it was very kind of you to notice that too."

He doesn't say anything, and I change my focus to watching for a place to land.

"I don't want to have to land back at Fred's," I tell him. "I don't want us to have to hike to the lodge with two turkeys."

Lane laughs now, and I join him, because the situation is ridiculous. He's wedged into place with two clucking, disgruntled, giant turkeys while we race to save a man's life.

"This will be a good story later," I tell him.

He agrees, and one of the turkeys pecks at his face. He swats it away and looks at me.

"Land this plane before I kill them both right now."

I giggle and scan the horizon.

"You'll have to land back at Fred's," Lane tells me. "There's nowhere to land by the lodge."

Of course not. Because Great Expectations doesn't have a plane yet.

I nod and nudge the plane toward Fred's.

"We can put these birds in their barn and figure out what to do with them later."

"Hopefully you know how to . . ." I glance at the birds, both of which are staring at me. "Er, take care of them for Christmas."

"I do," he confirms.

He's promptly pecked again.

I giggle.

The landing strip shows up on the horizon, and I guide us toward it.

"Hold on," I tell Lane.

He grips the turkeys, and we descend.

This time, all goes well.

We glide to a stop behind the barn with barely more than a bump upon initial landing.

I'm surprised to find Marina here, running around the corner to greet us.

She skids to a stop when she sees the live turkeys.

"What in the world?" she breathes.

Lane and I chuckle.

"It's a long story," I tell her. "How's Fred?"

"He's okay. We got him to the lodge and Dad set his foot." She grimaces. "That was ugly, but it's done."

"We've got the medicine," I tell her.

"That's why I came back," she tells us. "To grab it from you and run back. He needs it. Badly."

Her face is solemn, and Lane doesn't take time to ask questions. He pulls out the drugstore sack and hands it to her.

"I'll be at the lodge," she says, already heading back toward the house at a sprint.

"We'll take care of the plane and the turkeys and then head your way," I call after her. She waves over her shoulder. "Be careful!" I shout. She waves again, without looking back.

Lane is already wrangling the turkeys into the barn by himself, and I check the gauges on the plane. It needs fuel now, but otherwise, it's intact.

"I'm going to pull it in," I call to Lane.

"Let me get them cooped up, and I'll open the doors."

I climb back into the pilot's seat and wait.

A few minutes later, the barn doors open, and I start the engine, then pull it inside.

I kill the engine, and Lane closes the doors behind me.

"Well, this has been a good day's work," he says as he helps me climb down.

"And it's not over yet," I remind him, gesturing toward the turkeys, who are now clucking and walking in circles in the round pen on the other side of the barn.

"Let's get inside, get warmed up, and then tackle this," he says. "I'm cold, you're cold, and I don't know about you, but I'm hungry."

"But Fred . . ."

"We've sent the medicine, Pip. There's nothing we can do there that they aren't able to do."

He's got a point, and my stomach growls, as if on cue.

"I can't feel my fingers," I admit.

"Me either. Let's get inside, Ace."

It's not until we're inside the warm house, and Lane has stoked the fire, that I realize what a luxury being warm is.

Back home, I took it for granted. We had electricity to spare, mounds of wood that Dan always kept in abundance for the large great room fireplace, and every other fireplace in the lodge had been converted to gas. I could turn them on with the flip of a switch. Everything in 1944 is simpler, yet harder.

But they don't know the difference. This is all they know.

"I feel bad using their food," I tell Lane as I hunt for something to cook.

"They won't mind," he says confidently. "I know that. And we're two people. We're not an army. Sophie will make sure they're fed at the lodge."

"We can use the bread that we brought this morning," I muse, eyeing their cabinets. "And we did bring navy beans."

"Let's toast the bread, heat the beans, and have it on toast," Lane suggests. "Then we won't be eating anything of theirs. We'll just eat what we brought ourselves."

"Look at us, being self-sufficient," I say, as I pull a loaf of bread toward me to slice it.

Lane takes the slices and toasts them while I heat the beans. The stove takes longer than a microwave, but the heat is definitely better distributed.

We curl up in front of the fire to eat, rather than sit at the table.

"Lord, the fire feels good," I breathe, as I take a big bite. "But we should get down to the lodge. What if someone needs us?"

"We have to take care of the turkeys, and I need to take care of the livestock here first," Lane reminds me. "They won't need us. It will be dark very soon, and I don't want to trek back to the lodge in the dark with that bear around. I'm afraid we'll be staying here for the night, Piper."

I stare at him, my eyes wide.

"Unchaperoned?" I ask, without thinking.

"Everyone will understand," he rushes to say. "And I'll be a perfect gentleman, I assure you."

"God, I hope not," I answer. Then my cheeks flare hot, and so do his. "You must think I'm . . ."

"A sharecropper?" he asks, his brow lifted. "No, I'd never think that of you, Pip. You're a good girl."

Sharecropper must mean a woman who gets around. *Noted.*

"So you've mentioned before," I answer.

"Because that's what I know," he says. "I know people, Pip. I can read people like a book."

"Can you?" I answer. "Tell me what you see. About me, I mean."

Lane sets his plate down and studies me. He looks into my eyes, his gaze washing over my face. It's intense, and I have to fight to look away.

"I see a very kind girl, someone who tries hard in everything she does. I see someone who is adrift—she can't make heads or tails out of anything, she's out of her element—but she's a good sport. Someone who tries to help, someone who is loyal and true. Someone who has a bit of a sharp tongue, but in a funny way, never hurtful. I see someone who is highly capable and very, very unexpected."

I'm stunned.

"Wow. That's . . . detailed. Do you have a halo to hand out with that description? I sound like a saint."

He laughs and picks up his plate, taking another bite of toast.

"No one is a saint, Ace."

"Except for *actual* saints."

"I've never met one, so to me, they don't exist," he answers, and I can't fault his logic.

"Well, you can't be canonized while still being alive, so I guess we'll never meet one. Unless we bump into a ghost."

And now our conversation has trod into nonsensical waters.

"Speaking of ghosts, we should do something with the turkeys."

Lane lifts his eyebrows now.

"Do you plan to help?"

I think of their faces, so indignant, yet so innocent.

"No," I say honestly. "I can't. I can help carry them afterward, but I can't actually do the—"

"It's fine," he interrupts. "You don't have to. I can."

"I'm sorry. I'm not a vegetarian—I eat meat. But I hate hunting for sport, and I only want to hunt what we need. I can harden myself to the knowledge that it must be done, I just don't want to see it. Is that bad?"

"Nah. I think that's normal," he answers. "Most people don't want to see it."

"How about this . . . I'll clean up the kitchen, and then I'll come join you in the barn. That should give you time to . . . do the deed, and I can help load them up."

Lane holds out his plate. "It's a deal."

I take the empty plate, knowing full well I got the better end of that deal.

He bundles back up and heads outside, while I run dishwater in the sink and put away food.

I keep an eye on the barn door from the window above the

sink, and to my chagrin, I can't dawdle long enough for him to finish and return to the house.

With a sigh, I pull my coat and boots on a few minutes later.

I keep hoping he'll appear in the doorway and say it's all been done, but he doesn't. So eventually, I crunch across the snow to the barn to join him.

CHAPTER EIGHTEEN

'm nervous about what I might find, so I take my time pulling the barn door closed behind me. I definitely don't anticipate what I see when I turn back around.

Lane is sitting on a hay bale, feeding the two turkeys from his hand.

"Lane Patrick Hughes," I exclaim. "You're supposed to be . . . well, you know what you're *supposed* to be doing."

The turkeys turn their heads to me in unison, annoyed that I've disturbed their meal.

"I know." He sighs. "It's the damndest thing. If you repeat this to anyone, I'll deny it. But after coming back from France, I just don't have the heart to take a life. Any life. Even a turkey's."

He sighs again and doesn't look at me.

"What have they done to deserve to be someone's meal?" he asks. "Not a thing. They just eat and cluck and occasionally peck. They haven't done a thing."

"I know," I agree. "I hate it too. I don't know how y'all do it. Butcher meat to eat."

"Well, it's a necessity. I didn't think too much of it before, but now . . . well, everything is different. Maybe that will fade with time."

"The appreciation for life?" I ask. "I hope not."

"It doesn't come in handy when I'm trying to help feed the lodge," he points out.

"Dale will definitely understand. I think he feels much the same way. After the first war, I mean."

"I know he does," Lane agrees. "I've seen it."

"There's nothing wrong with it," I tell him. "It doesn't signal that you're weak or less than. To me, it feels enlightened. You've realized that you aren't owed anything by this world, that you don't necessarily deserve to kill something just because you want to."

I think of the hunters who pay me to shepherd them out into the wilderness to shoot their prized bucks, and I shudder. How could we have ever made a business out of that? How did I ever think it was okay?

"I think Marina sees it too," I tell Lane. "And she doesn't understand. About her father, I mean. Here, it seems that men must be so . . . hardened to be respected. But you and Dale are two of the best men I've ever met and you're not hard and cruel."

"It's not cruel to butcher for meat," Lane tells me. "I just don't have the stomach for it anymore."

"And that's okay. That's all I'm trying to say," I tell him. "I want to help Marina understand that it's okay. She gets very defensive of her father when she thinks anyone might dare disrespect him for that. But it's not a weakness. Appreciating life is a *strength*."

"I agree, Ace," Lane says quietly. His fingers are long and slender as he allows the turkeys to peck grain from his palms. He tosses it out onto the barn floor, where it scatters. The birds chase it, making sure to eat each piece of grain.

I watch them cluck and peck and stamp at the ground with their scaly feet.

I'm mindlessly trying to think of what to do with them, when they pause, then start fluttering about, clearly upset.

I look at Lane, and he looks at me.

And then we hear it.

The huffs and heavy steps of the bear.

"Son of a . . ." Lane jumps to his feet and runs for the barn door. He pulls the chain on the outside through to this side and padlocks it closed.

I do the same on the back sliding doors behind the plane.

We stare at each other and listen.

"Well, here we are again," I say, trying to break the tension. "Another barn, another bear. Well, same bear."

Lane rolls his eyes.

"He heard the turkeys. He knows there's food in here."

"What should we do?"

"There's really nothing we can do . . . but wait it out."

I pad to the front door and peek through a crack in the hinge.

The bear is clearly out front, lounging in the snow, flat on his back, pulling at one of his hind feet.

He looks ridiculous.

"He's there." I sigh. "What's more, he doesn't look like he's moving any time soon. He's blocking our path to the house."

"Well, first things first," Lane decides. "I'm going to start a fire."

"In here?" I'm startled. "There's so much hay, and we could suffocate."

"Pip, the floor is concrete. We can light it over here, far from the hay, and the roof is so far up, it won't catch fire. There's a window in the loft we can open to vent. We won't suffocate, and we won't freeze to death."

"So, win-win."

"Exactly."

Lane sets about finding things for the fire. He drags over cement blocks that he positions in a circle, then twists hay into starter sticks. There is a stack of firewood along one wall, and before long, he does have a fire going.

"Thank goodness for the matches on the workbench," Lane says as we watch the fire leap to life. "I'll have to remember to thank Fred for that."

"I hope he's doing okay," I say. "I hate that we're here instead of there. They're going to think we didn't want to help. Or worse. I can't imagine what they'll think."

"They'll think we didn't want to hike in the dark, and then we'll explain about the bear when we see them. Don't borrow trouble, Ace."

"At least we had dinner," I say, as I crouch on my heels next to the warmth.

"True. Way to look at the bright side," Lane commends. He pulls two bales of hay over to us, one by one, arranging them as seats far enough away from the flames so they don't catch fire, but close enough for us to still feel the warmth.

"Thank you," I tell him as I sit on one. "That's much better."

"See? Where there's a will, there's a way," he says. "You were hell-bent on getting Fred help, and we did. I'm hell-bent on making sure we don't freeze to death. I want you to consider the possibility that we might be in here all night, Piper. He can easily wait us out, or try his best anyway."

"We can wait him out too," I decide. "Oh, no. I just thought of something. What if Marina comes to check on us in the morning and stumbles upon the bear alone?"

"Stop borrowing trouble," Lane tells me again. "It's more likely that Joe or Albert or Ed will come with her for that very reason—because of the bear. They'll have the shotgun with them. So don't worry."

He easily swings onto the ladder to the loft and opens the wooden shutter that covers the window, then climbs back down.

"There we go. Now we won't asphyxiate."

"Thanks."

He sits down on a hay bale next to me, and together, we stare into the crackling fire.

"I didn't think this would be the way we spent our first night together," I tell him honestly. He looks at me, mirth in his eyes.

"Oh? And how, pray tell, did you envision it, Saint Piper?"

"I thought we already established I'm not a saint?"

He laughs.

We fall into silence. The only sounds are the infrequent huffs from the bear outdoors, the cackles of the turkeys, and the crackles of the flames.

"Do you ever wonder if you're married?" Lane finally asks.

His voice is quiet, concerned. It feels like something he's been worrying over and is afraid to bring up. It's almost as though he's afraid that by saying the words, he's breathing life into the possibility.

"I don't think that's possible," I answer limply, wishing with all of my heart that I could just tell him the truth. "I'm not wearing a ring, for one thing."

"Some people don't," he answers. "Maybe you're one."

"That doesn't seem like me," I reply. "I like a nice piece of jewelry as much as the next girl."

He chuckles but doesn't look entirely convinced.

"I can't be married," I finally say quietly. "Because if I were, I wouldn't feel the way I do about you."

My heart skips a beat as I admit to him what I feel.

I feel like I can't breathe, like I can't focus, like I can't exist . . . until he answers.

His lips stretch into a smile.

"I'm glad to hear you say that, Ace."

"Because?" My voice is embarrassingly tremulous.

"Because I feel the same way."

We both exhale at the same time, a release of pent-up emotions and silent attraction and allayed fear.

"How do *you* feel?" I ask, needing to hear the words.

He considers that. "I feel . . . consumed by thoughts of you. It doesn't matter what I'm doing or where I am. I'm thinking about you. I watch for you in every room, I listen for your voice. I'm acutely aware of where you are in relation to me at all moments of every day."

I'm stunned. I wasn't expecting *that*.

"And I'm afraid," he adds. "I'm afraid that you might belong to someone else, and it will break me."

Oh, boy.

I'm utterly silent, utterly stunned at the depth of this admission. The eloquence of it. The bravery in the words, the sincerity. This man plays no games. He just lays himself out there and waits to see what I'll do with it . . . with *him*.

"I don't belong to anyone," I say softly. I reach up with one finger, tracing the edge of his stubble-covered jaw. "But for the first time in my life, I want to."

He groans and reaches for me, wrapping me in his strong arms and pulling me to him in a crush against his solid chest.

I bury my head in his neck and inhale, smelling the manliness, the outdoors, his skin.

"Piper." He sighs.

I stretch my arms around his back, pulling him closer to me, and he moans again, helplessly now.

"We shouldn't," he says.

I kiss him, effectively silencing him. His lips are firm, yet soft. He tastes like alpine wood and he feels like heaven.

When I finally pull away, I stare into his eyes. "That's more along the lines of what I envisioned our first night alone together to be like."

He growls and pulls me back for another kiss, this one more frantic, more desperate.

"We really shouldn't," he finally says against my lips, pulling back again. "How is it that you taste like peaches?"

I smile, my lips curving against his, and lean my forehead against his.

"You smell good."

He curls his hand over mine and rubs my thumb with his own.

I decide it's now or never.

"Lane, can we talk about Cecile?"

He tenses, his gaze darkening.

He swallows hard and grips my hand, and I'm suddenly so very sorry that I asked.

"You don't need to tell me," I say quickly.

"It's okay," he says. "Cecile was a girl in France. You were correct about that."

Was.

I wait.

"She wasn't *my* girl, if that's what you were thinking. She was lovely and bright, and eager to help the American soldiers. Me. My buddies. She took chances she shouldn't have. And she paid for that."

"Did you love her?" My voice is soft and scared.

"I think we all did, just a bit. She was charming and feisty and very sure of herself. *Too* sure."

"Did the Germans capture her?"

"They killed her," he says simply. "She was feeding starving village children, and they gunned her down with a howitzer as an example. There was nothing left of her. Nothing at all."

"Lane," I whisper, a tear squeezing from the corner of my eye. "I'm so sorry."

"The kids . . . I'll never forget their faces. We couldn't help her quickly enough. We couldn't stop it. All she did was try to help us all. She tried to make the world less ugly. They killed her for it."

"I'm so, so sorry."

I don't know what else to say. I'm relieved that she wasn't his girl but crushed that she suffered, crushed that he'd seen it, crushed that the children had seen it.

"War is cruel," I decide. "I hate that it touched you like it did."

"It's in the past now."

"But it's not. Not for you. You dream of it, you're tortured by it."

"*Tortured* is a strong word," he protests. "I can handle it. We all have to. I'm not the only one. Everyone over there has to carry some sort of burden from it. Not a one of us escaped unscathed."

I think of Dale and his sketches and his tiny sanctuary hidden from the rest of the world.

"You're right. No one escapes unscathed."

I pull him to me, my hand cradling the back of his head, and he rests his cheek on my shoulder. In this moment, I feel I would lay my life down to protect him. In this moment, I also know that I can't possibly hurt this precious man any more than he already has been.

If I somehow can go home, what will happen to him?

It would break him.

But realistically, what are the chances that I can leave here? In all likelihood, I'll live out the rest of my days here.

With my gran. With my great-grandparents. With Lane.

That's not a bad future, even when it's technically the *past*.

From outside, the wind howls and the bear bellows.

I startle, then jump up to peer through the door.

He's on his feet now, lumbering around the perimeter, trying to find a way into the barn.

"He wants in," I tell Lane.

"He's not getting in," he assures me. "The walls are thick. The doors are chained."

I sit back down on a hay bale, and this time, I don't lean into Lane. I'm very, very cognizant, though, of where his leg is in relation to mine. I can tell that he is too.

He reaches out and takes my hand.

"Piper, I don't know who you are or what your last name is or where you come from. But I do know that I'm falling in love with you. I don't want to pressure you, but I hope you'll consider me as someone you might want to live your life with."

Is he proposing?

Did he just propose?

"Lane," I say slowly. "What are you saying?"

"I'm saying I want to spend my life with you," he says simply.

"But . . . we've only known each other for a week," I answer. "I feel it too, I do. But what if we're wrong? A week isn't enough time to base anything on."

"A week is plenty of time," he answers. "Hearts know things that our brains do not. I know this might sound arrogant, but I think you were meant for me, Piper. You were born for me."

"Do you think everyone has only one match? One soul mate?"

"I wouldn't presume to try to figure that out," he answers. "All I know is that you feel right for me. You feel like the other half of me. When you're with me, I feel whole. I hope I'm not making you feel uncomfortable. I just . . . I want you to know how I feel."

"Thank you," I whisper quickly. "I . . . feel the same way, Lane Hughes."

"You do?" He seems so incredulous, that it is so inconceivable I would return the feelings. I nod.

"I do."

"You're supposed to wait until the wedding to say that," he says with a small smile.

The wedding.

He's asking me to marry him.

"I wonder what people would say if you got engaged to a girl with amnesia?" I wonder. "They'll think we're foolish."

"No, they won't," he assures me. "Anyone who has met you will understand why I need to marry you."

Marry me.

This beautiful man wants to marry me.

In 1944.

A week ago, I was in the twenty-first century, trying to decide what to do with my life, trying to decide where I wanted to go, what I wanted to accomplish. Now, all I want to do is be with the man in front of me.

In this place . . . the very place I wanted to escape from.

"Life is strange," I say out loud.

"It is." He pauses. "But you haven't answered yet, Pip."

"I . . ."

His eyes meet mine.

"I . . ."

He watches my lips, waits for the words.

"I . . . Yes."

His eyes light up.

"Yes?"

I nod, quickly, before I can change my mind.

"Yes. I don't want to be without you. Ever."

He hugs me tight, and I soak him in, and as the night passes, I can't help but worry . . . Will I be yanked away from here . . . breaking both my heart and his?

"Let's not tell anyone yet," I say, at some point in the middle of the night. Neither of us is asleep; we drift in and out, leaning together, listening for the bear, listening to the wind, listening to each other's heartbeat. "I don't want anyone to judge us."

"They won't. But we can wait. It's enough that *we* know."

"I don't want anyone thinking that anything inappropriate happened here," I go on, trying to explain so I don't hurt his feelings.

He nods. "I get it. You're right. We'll tell them later. It's enough that I know, Ace."

As we nestle together, guilt pulses through my veins.

I'm not who he thinks I am. I'm lying to him. But in this situation, if I tell the truth, everyone will think I'm crazy.

I don't know what I'm supposed to do with that.

We fall asleep finally, with Lane's arm tucked behind my head and my cheek resting against his heart.

CHAPTER NINETEEN

When we wake, the sun is up. I know this from the thin sliver of light that floods under the barn doors and from above us in the loft. The fire is reduced to dying embers, and my back is tight from slumping over onto Lane all night.

I sit up straight, rubbing my back, and Lane rouses.

"It's morning," he says quickly and gets up to look outside. "No sign of Tiny," he tells me.

I stand up and join him by the door.

"Did I dream last night?" I ask.

"Lord, I hope not," he answers. "Because to my recollection, we're engaged."

My heart flips and flops, and I smile. "Okay. Good."

"No takebacks?" he asks.

I shake my head. "None."

He grins, a smile that lights up the entire barn.

"But with Marina waiting for word on Boyfriend, and with just . . . everything, I want to wait to tell everyone."

"I understand," he says. "Truly."

I smile at him, and he presses his lips to my forehead.

"Sophie has eagle eyes," he tells me. "So if you truly don't want them to know, you'll need to control yourself around me. I know it's hard, but try."

I grin. "Oh, it's hard. You're irresistible."

"I'm aware. For instance, you swooned the first time you met me."

"You know what word people don't use enough? *Swoon*," I confirm.

"You kid, but I apparently have magical powers." He pauses. "But truly, Sophie notices every glance, every shift in energy or mood. It's uncanny. So don't treat me any differently, or she will notice."

"What do you think they'll say when we tell them?" I ask, as Lane cleans up the fire debris.

"They'll be happy," he answers. "Very happy. They like us both. They treat us like family."

"They're pretty amazing," I answer. "Is everyone around here like them?"

He considers that. "Mostly, I guess. Although Soph and Dale are at the top. Everyone relies on each other. We're a whole other breed here, and we know it. We've got some that are different, but heck. You saw Charlie in town. People are kind here, Pip. I don't know where you're from, but I do think you'll like it here."

"Does it bother you that I don't know where I'm from?" I ask.

"Why would it? My only concern is that you don't have a husband," he answers. "Wherever you're from . . . it must be a wonderful place. It brought you into the world."

I think of the lodge, of this place. I don't even know our neighbors anymore at home. I don't know when the lodge changed, or when Gran changed . . . from someone who was surrounded by family all of the time to someone who just focused on me.

Yes, she kept a few loyal staff members but nothing like what it is here. With the boarders as extended family and neighbors from all around.

Was it when my parents died?

That notion hits me hard and fast, almost knocking the air out of me.

Lane notices. "Are you okay?"

I nod, but my face is pale. I know it, because I'd felt the blood rush away. I reach for the hay bale to sit down.

My gran had started shielding her heart when my parents died. She'd stopped letting people get close to her so that her heart wouldn't break if she lost them.

It makes perfect sense, and I don't know why I'd never realized it before.

I guess because I didn't know her like I do now, as someone who is her peer. I saw her from the viewpoint of a child, a grieving child, and she took charge of the situation, and life changed after that.

I focus, and I can see my parents' faces . . . laughing as groups of friends played cards at the table, just as the men do here. I think about how my mother used to swing me around outside, and we'd spin until we were dizzy and fell onto the grass. My mother was like Gran, and I'm like them both.

If I can, I need to somehow impart the importance to Gran

that no matter what life throws at her in the future, she should never forget the importance of loving others. And of letting them love her back. I don't know if I can change my parents' deaths, but surely I can change the way my grandmother reacted to it. And if I'm creative, maybe I actually *can* change things.

"Piper?" Lane asks, and I can sense that it's not for the first time.

"I'm sorry." I shake my head. "I was lost in a few memories."

"You remembered something?" He's so excited, so hopeful, that I nod.

"Yes. I remember how my parents died. It was a plane crash a few years ago."

"Oh, no. God, I'm sorry, Piper." He sits next to me, rubbing my shoulder. "Do you remember anything about it?"

"Their wings iced over," I say honestly. "We could've died the same way yesterday, Lane. We could've. And so could anyone who flies in the wrong flight conditions. We've got to make sure everyone knows—don't fly when there are no deicers."

"It's okay," he tells me soothingly. "We'll tell them. Don't worry, Ace. I'm so sorry. Do you remember anything else about your family?"

Now I have to lie. *Again.* This gets harder and harder, and I just . . . don't want to do it anymore. At this point, I'm purposely deceiving him. It's not okay, yet I don't know what to do about it.

I shake my head.

"No, not yet."

"I'm sorry," he says. "I know you want to remember."

"I do," I tell him. "And I know I will. Things are coming back to me a piece at a time. Someday, all the pieces will fit."

"That's the perfect way to look at it, Ace."

"Thanks." I smile weakly at him, and he hugs me.

"Are you ready to head to the lodge?"

I nod. "But what will we do about the turkeys?"

"I'll tell Sophie they're here. If she wants me to butcher them, I will."

"You're a good man, Lane Hughes."

"Go ahead, get the flattery out of your system. I'm telling you, Sophie will notice if you talk like that at the lodge."

"She's not actually magic," I tell him.

"She's pretty darn close. She can figure out anything."

I hadn't noticed that, and I'm ashamed to admit it. But as I think on it, I remember observing her quietly patting someone's shoulder after she noticed they were upset, or turning around like she had eyes in the back of her head, catching Marina and me wisecracking behind her.

"She's very perceptive," I agree. In modern times, she'd be known as highly sensitive, or an empath. Back here, they'd probably think that is witchcraft. I smile at my own silent humor.

"What?" Lane asks, catching my grin.

"I was just thinking how funny I am," I tell him honestly. He cocks his head.

"Are you? I hadn't noticed."

"Oh, you." I swat at his arm. He grins.

"I'm practicing. For when we're at the lodge. I'll need to be a scamp. Just fair warning."

"Good thing I like scamps," I tell him with a wink.

He chuckles, and I stand up. "Okay. I'm ready. Let's go check on Fred."

We venture outside, then lock the barn in case the bear returns tonight. Then we head for the lodge, for home.

It is home, I realize, as we track through the snow.

No matter when, or who lives in it, the lodge is home. It's the energy that is steeped in the walls, the memories that fill the air, the love that built the foundation.

It's home, now and forever. For me, for my children, for their children.

"Lane?"

He turns to me without stopping.

"Yes?"

"How many children do you want?"

A man from my time would swallow his teeth. But Lane doesn't blink.

"Two boys and a girl who looks just like you."

"I've decided something, Lane Hughes."

"What's that?"

"I love you."

He smiles, slow and sexy.

"What a coincidence! I love you too."

My ovaries explode, and I reach for his hand. Our fingers stay interwoven until we come upon the lodge, and I release him.

"Thanks for the adventure, Ace," he tells me, and I picture him in the cockpit with the turkeys.

"My pleasure," I reply. "Truly."

When we stomp off our boots on the back porch, Marina comes rushing outside.

"Good golly, where have you been?"

"The bear penned us in the barn," I tell her. "But he was gone this morning. Is Fred . . . all right?"

She nods. "His fever is already coming down now. He's on his second dose."

"Thank God," I breathe.

"And thank *you*, I hear," Dale says, stepping outside. "You're full of surprises, Piper."

"I'm surprising *myself*," I tell him. "Trust me."

I mean, I'm engaged.

"Well, we thank you both," he says. "You saved a life here."

"I'm just glad to help. You all have been so kind to me and treated me like one of your own. I'm just glad I could somehow start to return the favor."

"It's our pleasure," he says, before he turns to head inside. "And it'll be nice to have someone able to fly for supplies, now that Fred can't see well enough to do it."

"Nice, Dad," Marina says as he disappears into the house. "So sentimental." She's being sarcastic, but I ignore it.

"He is sometimes," I tell her. "And that's okay. It's awesome, actually."

She studies me curiously.

"It's okay to be in touch with your feelings, Marina. Your dad deserves it, and so do you."

"Did you hit your head again?" she asks me loudly and slowly, enunciating each word.

"No," I say, enunciating just as clearly. "I'm fine."

She grabs me by the arm and pulls me into the house. "Tell me about the bear," she says.

I start telling her about it, and Lane follows us as we enter the kitchen. Sophie stops what she's doing and comes to me.

She looks at me, then Lane. "Something's off," she announces. "Something happened."

No. Way.

"Nothing happened," I stammer. "We flew to get Fred his medicine. The bear hemmed us in the barn all night."

She squints her eyes. "Something else . . ."

"Oh! Lane. Tell her about the turkeys. That's probably what you're sensing."

"Turkeys?" she asks.

"Charlie Benson gave us a couple turkeys," Lane tells her quickly.

Her face lights up. "Oh! What a wonderful man."

"Tell her the catch," I instruct Lane.

"They're *alive.*"

Sophie's face falls, but she steels it. "Well, no matter. We'll just have to butcher some birds. We'll have ourselves a nice Christmas yet!"

Apparently satisfied that she'd sniffed out whatever was "off," she returns back to the counter to pull out her recipe books.

"What do we have that we can make with turkey?" she asks Marina, although she's clearly envisioning it in her head.

"They're alive," I tell her again, just for good measure. "Lane brought them here on his lap in the plane."

Sophie's head swivels around. "I didn't think about that . . .

about how you'd gotten them home." She laughs. "Boy, Lane. I bet they gave you a run for your money."

"One pecked my eye," he says solemnly.

She peers at it. "Well, it looks like you still have it. So you're fine."

She's hardening herself to the situation, knowing that the birds will have to die. I see right now where Marina gets it from.

"We don't have to eat them," I suggest. "We can make something else."

"And waste two perfectly good turkeys?" Sophie asks dubiously, yet hopefully. She waits for my suggestion.

"Well, we could make a nice quiche," I suggest.

She narrows her eyes. "A what?"

"A quiche. It's a baked egg dish, inside of a crust."

"Like an egg pie?" She wrinkles her nose.

"Well, if you put it that way, it doesn't sound good," I admit. "But it's actually very delicious. We could even have Christmas brunch instead of Christmas dinner. We could make heaping stacks of pancakes, a quiche, biscuits and gravy . . ."

"That sounds nice," she answers. "But not as nice as a candlelit Christmas dinner with a fancy turkey and all the trimmings. It's tradition."

"Traditions can always change," I say lightly. "I could be wrong, but I sense things sometimes too. Like you. And I sense that you don't really want to butcher the turkeys. But you can be the judge of that."

I continue through the house to the great room, where Fred is resting by the fire, his foot propped up on a stool. His foot is bound in leather straps and clean flour sacks. Even from all the way over here, I can see that the fever has subsided.

"Fred, it's good to see you," I tell him as I approach.

He smiles, his eyes crinkling.

"I hear tell that I have you to thank for that," he says. "For the fact that I'm here to see at all."

"It was nothing," I tell him, fully aware that a female pilot is unheard-of here. "I'm just happy to help."

It's Essie, who joins us when she comes downstairs, who pushes the issue.

"Girlie, it's not normal to know how to fly. Not for most people, and certainly not for a woman. You know that, right?" She peers at me. "Can you think of any reason at all that you'd know how to fly?"

"My dad taught me to fly. I don't remember much, but I do remember that."

"Are you certain of that?" she asks, bolder now.

"She remembered something just today. Don't push her, Essie," Lane tells her. "It'll take time."

"What did you remember?" Essie asks bluntly.

"That my parents died in a plane crash a few years ago."

Instead of any kind of sympathy, Essie snorts. "That seems convenient."

"Essie," Marina gasps as she joins the group. "Why in the world would you say that?"

"Does no one else think it's very strange that a young woman shows up out of nowhere in the middle of Alaska? That just doesn't happen. And now, we learn that she knows how to fly?"

She looks at me, her eyes hard and glistening. "Missy, hear this. I'm very grateful that you saved my husband's life, but if you turn out to be a spy, I won't hesitate to turn you in."

There's a collective gasp from everyone in the room.

It hadn't even occurred to me that someone might think that, but of course they would. Why wouldn't they? It's wartime, and I remember from history lessons that World War II was a wake-up call to everyone about spy activity. Essie is completely correct.

"It's unheard-of for a young woman to fall from the sky in the middle of the winter freeze," she continues. "If you crashed a plane here, girlie, it'll turn up after the spring thaw. And we'll all know who you are."

"I don't know who I am," I reply steadily "But I can assure you, I'm not a spy."

Her mouth flattens into a line, and she walks out of the room without another word.

I lock eyes with Marina.

Fred speaks up. "I'm sorry, Piper. If it means anything, I don't think you're a spy."

"The idea seems so outlandish to me," I tell them. "It never occurred to me that you might think that. I'm not nearly brave enough to do something so dangerous as espionage."

"Flying a beat-up old plane into a snowstorm to get an old man medicine seems pretty brave," Fred says. "So I don't think you're lacking in that department. But I don't think you're a spy."

I turn around, to the face I most want to see.

Lane's.

But when I see his eyes and see the questions there—the confusion, the doubt—I feel like I've gotten kicked in the stomach.

In this split second, I understand why Marina closes herself off to avoid pain. It's because of looks like the one on Lane's face right now.

"You don't believe that, do you?" I ask Lane.

It takes him a second too long to shake his head.

I rush from the room before anyone sees the tears that have leapt into my eyes.

would never do something like that," I wail to Marina after she follows me to the bedroom. I flop onto the bed, and she sits next to me.

"I know," she assures me. "We all know."

"Not Lane. Did you see his face?" I demand. "He thinks it might be true."

"He won't," she answers. "Not after he thinks it through." She turns to me. "Piper, he just came back from the war. He's not thinking altogether clearly about things like this. He knows you would never. But he's been trained to examine every aspect of something like this. He just needs to think it through."

I sit up. "You might be right."

"I am," she agrees. "Anyone with half a brain can see that he's head over heels for you."

I can't help the smile that stretches across my lips.

"What happened up there?" Marina asks me. "Or do I want to know?"

"Marina!" I exclaim. "I'm a lady. He hugged me. And kissed my forehead."

I leave out the passionate kiss and the way his lips were perfect. A girl has a right to a couple secrets.

Her eyes widen. "Oh, my," she declares. "Whoever Cecile is, she can eat your dust."

"I know who she is," I admit. I tell her the sad story that Lane had shared with me, and when I'm finished, her eyes are wet and her hand is pressed to her heart.

"That's so tragic," she whispers.

"I know. It hurts my heart. And to hear him talk about it . . . It was awful."

"I can't imagine," she says. She wipes at her eyes. "Well, we've never needed a Friday night like we need this one, girl."

"It's Friday," I realize aloud. "Bath night."

"Bath night," she acknowledges. "And I'm guessing that you want to look extra pretty tonight. So I'll let you use my lipstick again."

She hugs me and pats my back. "We love you, Piper. I don't want you to worry. None of us think anything untoward about you. Essie is just suspicious. She always has been, and she always will be."

"Thanks, Marina. I love you too. All of you. I'm so lucky to find myself here. I don't know how, and I don't know why, but I know I'm thankful."

That part is completely true. I don't know how or why I'm here, but I *am* thankful. I'll always be thankful, no matter how it all turns out.

"You can take your bath first," she offers. "You've had a hard couple of days. Did a turkey really peck Lane in the eye?"

I giggle and nod. "I'll tell you all about it," I promise. "You've never seen anything so funny in all your life."

She follows me to the bathroom and perches on the toilet while I bathe and tell her the stories. She laughs when I tell her about us realizing the turkeys were alive, and laughs harder when I describe Lane in the cockpit with the birds.

"How much do they weigh?" she asks, still laughing.

"I'd say over twenty pounds each. Maybe thirty. They've been well taken care of."

We laugh together, and I tell her how Lane had tried to get the mail for her. "It was so sweet," I muse.

"Oh, boy. You've got it bad, Pippie."

"I know," I admit. "I never would've thought this would happen."

"I knew it the first time he looked at you," Marina says. "I happened to be looking at him when he saw you. His face was priceless. Like he'd just seen the Sistine Chapel."

"Really?" Just when I thought my heart couldn't swell any more, it does.

She nods. "So don't worry. He'll be fine."

She grabs my towel and hands it to me when I stand up. I towel my hair and my body and she hands me a robe. I put it on and comb my hair.

"I washed the hair clips," she tells me. "Earlier. Would you mind running down to get them while I bathe? They're on a towel by the kitchen sink. We'll need them to set our hair."

"Sure," I agree.

I pad downstairs in my bare feet and wet hair and manage to avoid bumping into anyone. The record player is already going in the great room, and I can hear chattering coming from the dining room.

I gather up the metal clips and tuck them into my robe pocket. It's when I turn around that I realize I'm not alone, and that I hadn't managed to avoid bumping into *every*one.

Lane leans against the doorframe.

His face is troubled, his eyes dark.

"I don't want you to think I doubt you," he says quietly. "Because I don't."

"You don't think I'm a spy and that I'm working to hurt American soldiers . . . soldiers just like yourself?"

"No."

The weight of the world seems to slip off my shoulders and I can breathe again.

"That's good. Because I would never."

"Essie doesn't mean any harm," he offers. "She just doesn't trust people. Fred likes you."

"I know."

I want to go to him, to lean into him, to touch his face and promise him that I'd never do anything to jeopardize his safety or anyone else's.

But anyone could see.

I force myself to remain still.

"You like me too, right?" I ask, hating that I need the reassurance. But after the look on his face when Essie was speaking . . . I do need it.

"Of course I do," he assures me. "Everything is just like it was in the barn, Ace. Essie's suspicions took me off guard because I hadn't even considered that as an option. And once I took a minute to consider it, I knew it still wasn't an option. You are definitely surrounded in mystery, Piper. But you're not a spy."

"Thank God you see that," I tell him, relief flooding my heart. But also . . . there's the guilt again.

He deserves to know.

No matter how he reacts, even if they put me in an asylum, they deserve to hear the truth.

"This is harder than I thought it would be," I tell him, and my meaning encompasses several things.

"Hiding things from Sophie, you mean? Are you feeling the urge to swoon again?"

I roll my eyes.

"Not just yet. You might want to try harder."

He grins. "Challenge accepted."

I get the distinct impression that I just messed up. Big-time.

His eyes twinkle merrily as I scoot past him. "I'll see you soon, Ace," he says, but he says it like a promise.

I scurry upstairs with the hair clips, just in time for Marina to snatch them from my hands as she emerges from the bathroom. She practically sits on me on the bed so she can set my hair with the pins, and then I do hers.

We pull on stockings, mark the lines up the backs, like good 1940s girls, and apply our bright red lipstick.

"Lane won't know what hit him tonight," Marina finally decides as she fluffs my hair and does the final touches to my face. "You look stunning."

"Thanks, M." I turn to look at her. "You do too. I wish Boy-friend could see you."

"He will," she tells me. "Soon enough." She kisses her fingers and holds them up to the sky. "From my lips to God's ear!"

Her face in this moment is so sweet, so young, so innocent. It's not the face I grew up loving, but it's the face that I've grown to love here.

It's the face of a friend.

"You're the sister I never had," I tell her.

"You don't know that you don't have sisters." She giggles.

"I think I'd remember that," I tell her. "But it doesn't matter. You're my sister now, M."

She studies me. "You get sentimental after you've saved a life, Pippie."

I laugh, and she wraps her slender arms around my shoulders and squeezes.

"Everything's okay," she murmurs. "You know that, right?"

I nod. "Yes."

"Good." She stands up and straightens her dress. "Then let's go have some fun."

We link arms and stroll downstairs to the great room, where Friday-night festivities are already in full swing.

Dale and Fred are sitting by the fire. Fred has his foot up, a whiskey in his hand. Dale leans forward, speaking earnestly, and I smile at the ever-so-thoughtful look on his face.

Sophie bustles out from the kitchen with a tray of honey cake, sliced thick and sprinkled with powdered sugar.

Essie stands by the windows, looking out at the snow, and when she turns and sees me, she stares at me unabashed for long minutes. I finally break the stare and whisper into Marina's ear.

"If looks could kill, I'd be dead."

Even Marina can't deny it.

"I don't really know what's gotten into her," she says uncertainly. "She's a suspicious person, yes. But this is a new level, even for her."

The men, including Lane, are sitting around the table, playing cards and drinking punch. Their hair is damp, carefully combed, and their shirts are clean and buttoned to the top.

"Friday nights here are truly my favorite," I tell Marina.

"Aren't they fun?" she asks, her eyes sparkling.

"I hope we never stop doing this," I tell her, hoping she remembers as she gets older. "We all deserve a day of the week when we can dress up, chat, relax, and just enjoy each other's company."

"I couldn't agree more," Marina answers. "It's the best night of the week."

"Hands down," I agree.

Lane looks up at me, and his face lights up like the sun. He smiles, and that smile is so crooked, so handsome . . . it turns my insides to jelly. I smile back, and he stands, laying his cards down on the table.

"I'm out, boys," he says.

He makes a beeline straight for me and bows slightly in front of me. Marina giggles.

"May I have this dance?" he asks solemnly.

"No one is dancing," I point out.

"But we have music, and we have a wide-open space," he says, gesturing to the gleaming wooden floor. "It's almost Christmas, and I feel the need to dance."

"Then by all means, let's dance," I say. "Far be it from me to prevent you from stepping on my feet." I grin, and he shakes his head, offering his elbow. "Let's do this."

We glide in a circle around the room, Lane deftly guiding me. He doesn't step on my feet even one time, something that he makes sure to point out.

Sophie watches us, and I murmur to Lane, "I don't think we're being subtle enough."

"Pip, I'm pretty sure even the most obtuse person in the world would pick up how I feel about you right now."

"Right now?" I tease. "Do you anticipate your feelings changing?"

"I do," he says. "I anticipate that they'll get stronger every year."

"Good Lord," I tell him. "Just when I thought I couldn't be any more attracted to you."

"You are a very blunt woman," he announces. "Has anyone ever told you that?"

I laugh. I can't tell him that I'm a product of my environment and era.

"It must run in my family," I say instead.

"I can't wait to meet them someday," he answers.

I think about that. He already has, he just doesn't know it. It's mind-boggling.

"Piper!" Joe calls from the front door. Lane spins me, and I find Joe and Marina leading in Nugget. He's wearing a diaper and a red bow around his neck.

"He's gussied up for Christmas," Joe tells me. "We figured you were missing him."

"I've only been gone a day, but . . . yes." I laugh as Nugget comes flying toward me. His leg doesn't bend, but he doesn't let it slow him down.

He nuzzles my hip, hunting for a treat.

"You little rascal," I tell him, rubbing his fuzzy nose. "You look very handsome."

"Don't tell Mama," Marina croons to him while she feeds him a small piece of honey cake. Nugget scarfs it down and roots around for more. "That's it, you little beggar," she tells him. "That's all I have."

He doesn't believe her and tries to stare her down. He doesn't flinch, and she laughs.

"You're something else," she tells him, patting his neck. "You're spoiled rotten. Look what you've done, Pippie."

"Me?" I demand. "I'm not the one who fetched him from the barn tonight and got him dressed up for Christmas."

Everyone laughs, because it's true.

"The gig is up, M," I tell her. "We all know that you're a softie. You can't deny it."

"I can." She nods. "And I will."

"But that doesn't mean it's not true," Albie pipes up. "You *do* make sure to take them all treats every day."

"She does?" Sophie asks, her eyes narrowing.

"Not every day, Mama," Marina placates her mother. "Only when I have a little something extra."

"And you do try to bring us towels straight from the dryer," Edward interjects. "That seems a bit soft-hearted, Marina."

"That's just being considerate," she argues. "Really, Edward.

That's just plain mean to try and turn that around on me. I'm going to leave yours out in the snow next week."

Edward laughs, and not a one of us is fooled.

"Listen, people," Marina announces. "I am not soft-hearted. I am a strong-willed, thick-skinned Alaskan woman. I am not soft."

"You're not soft at all," Lane tells her. "But your heart is just a bit mushy."

She hmmphs and flounces off to fill her cup with punch. Her parents laugh, clearly pleased with their efforts in her upbringing.

I watch her take a sip of punch and promptly wrinkle her nose, sniffing at her cup.

"Edward spiked the punch again," I tell Lane.

"Oh? Remind me that I deserve a refreshment later," he answers.

"You and me both," I mutter.

"Why, Pip, how scandalous," he drawls. "Would you like a refreshment *now*?"

"Why not?" I answer. "It's Friday night. Anything can happen on a Friday night. The possibilities are endless."

He winks and steers me to the side of the room, where he leaves me to retrieve our drinks.

Essie stands with Sophie, chatting, and I ponder whether I should approach her. Dale appears at my elbow.

"Give her some time," he says, apparently reading my mind. "I think she's being a bit of a mother hen to Lane right now. Anyone with eyes can see that he's sweet on you, and she's not sure of your intentions."

"Has she said something to you?" I ask in surprise. "That

didn't occur to me. Of course she's protective of him. But I'm not going to hurt him, Dale. I . . . quite like him."

"I know," he says wryly. "You're not a very good actress, Pippie. If you two are trying to hide it, you might want to try harder." He chuckles, and I stare up at him.

"Oh, boy. Do you think anyone else has noticed?"

"Oh Lord, child." He sighs. "You must think we were all born yesterday. It's as plain as the nose on my face."

"It might look bad that we were together all night," I tell him hesitantly. "But nothing happened, Dale. I would never . . ."

He blushes. "Of course not. No one would think that, Piper."

"Thank goodness," I mumble. Back home, in my time, it wouldn't be a big deal. But here, it's a very different scenario.

For just a moment, as I watch Lane chat with Edward by the punch bowl, I wonder what Shelly would say if she saw him.

She'd call dibs, first of all.

She'd cry when she heard that she was too late.

She'd drool unabashedly and say, *That's a* man, *Piper*.

I smile at the thought and find myself missing her. Will I ever see her again? What will they think happened to me? Will I be featured on an episode of *Unsolved Mysteries*?

Lane returns with two cups of punch.

"Careful of that," Dale warns me with a wink. "Edward has a heavy hand."

He joins his wife, and I sip at the punch.

"Lord, he wasn't kidding," I sputter. Across the room, Edward laughs and tips his proverbial cap.

I take another sip, to prove I can. He laughs again.

"Careful, Pip," Lane cautions. "I don't want to have to carry you to bed tonight. Not for *that* reason anyway."

He flushes, and I laugh. "Why, Lane Hughes. Are you flirting with me?"

"How'd you know?"

I smile and watch Sophie lighting candles.

"I thought she was saving those for Christmas Eve," I muse.

"It's such a nice evening tonight, she must've decided to splurge," Lane answers. The candles flicker, creating another layer of cozy ambience in this room filled with friends, family, and laughter. Behind it all, the giant fireplace roars, and Christmas music crackles on the record player. Lane takes my hand, and we sway together to the soft music.

"It is a nice evening," I agree. "It's hard to believe that Christmas Eve is in two nights."

"I hope your family isn't missing you too much," Lane says. "They must be worried sick, and it's the holiday too. I feel badly about that. I wish we could reach them and let them know."

"Me too," I say. "But for now, they'll just have to trust that I'm safe."

"The second you remember, we can fly to them," he points out. "Now that you know you can fly."

"That's a good point," I tell him. He nods.

"I make them. Sometimes." He winks, and I wonder if I'll always feel this way when I look at him.

"Will you always make my knees weak?" I wonder out loud. He cocks his head.

"I'll always *try*," he promises.

My hand tightens on his back, feeling the muscle ripple. He's slender yet strong. I notice Essie staring at me yet again, and I sigh.

"That woman is going to stare a hole in me," I say. "I've got to talk to her and smooth things over."

"Good luck," he tells me wryly.

"This is your fault," I tell him.

"How is it my fault?"

"Because she loves you and is protective of you. Otherwise, she wouldn't even care."

He looks dumbfounded. "Huh. That didn't occur to me."

"She's afraid I'll hurt you," I say quietly. He lifts his gaze to mine.

"And will you?"

My breath hitches.

"I'll always try very hard not to," I promise. "For now, I'm the one to be concerned about. Essie might hurt *me*."

I step away from him, hand him my empty punch glass, and walk toward the older woman.

She watches me approach and doesn't let her expression waver. I don't know what she's thinking, but she definitely takes my measure. She examines me, looks into my eyes, and I have to hand it to her.

I *do* have something to hide.

I'm *not* who I say I am.

And she's the only one who's noticed.

She's just wrong about my intentions. Very, very wrong.

I sidle up beside her and meet her gaze. She doesn't look away. Her faded eyes are cloudy, but they still see every single thing in this room.

"I won't hurt Lane," I promise her, direct and to the point.

She doesn't react.

"I know you must be worried about that. And I know it must seem odd . . . A stranger shows up out of nowhere. I get it. I wish I knew what happened. I wish I knew why I'm here, or how it happened. But I don't. I'm as clueless as everyone else. But what I do know is this . . . I'm not a spy. I'm not anything nefarious. I'm just a girl who is lost."

Essie remains quiet for a few moments.

"I don't think you're lost," she finally answers. "Not anymore. Lane has found you. And you're a lucky woman for that. He's not the same man as the one who went to war, Piper. I hope you know that, and I hope you respect it. He's a good, good man. And there's not a thing about him that doesn't command respect."

"I agree," I say quickly and firmly. "He's worthy of everyone's respect. He might be the best man I've ever met."

She seems satisfied by that.

"You've heard the night terrors, I assume," I say.

She nods.

"It would be hard not to," she answers.

"Yes. They're a bit startling. It worries me that he's so troubled. I don't know how to help him."

"You're helping him already. I just want to make sure you're sincere," she says, not unkindly. "That you won't leave him high and dry whenever your memories return. He's worth more than that, Piper. He's not the kind of man for a fling. He's the kind of man you stay with forever."

"I know," I answer softly. "I swear, that's my intention. He's so lucky to have you looking out for him, Mrs. Klein."

"His ma is gone," she answers. "I do my best for him."

"Your best is better than most people's," I tell her. "He's very lucky to have you on his side."

"I'll go toe-to-toe with anyone for that boy," she confirms. "Including you, if need be."

She's less severe now than she was but still direct.

"I know, Mrs. Klein," I assure her. "And I respect that. But you won't need to. I'll protect him in every way as much as I can."

She actually smiles now. Not a broad smile, by any means, but I'll take what I can get at this point.

"You might be good for him," she finally decides. "You're strong-willed and smart. He could do worse."

"So you don't believe that I'm a spy now?" I ask, just to confirm.

She shakes her head. "That was a bit far-fetched," she admits. "But you have to admit, the situation is unique."

"It is," I agree. *More than she knows.*

"But if your intentions toward him are true, then I have no quarrel with you."

Her tone is still a bit threatening, because she still wants to drive home her point.

"Point taken." I chuckle. "My intentions are true."

"Then you won't have a problem."

I sigh, ever so slightly. Because while we do have a truce, she doesn't trust me just yet. But that's okay. She'll come around.

"I'll prove myself to you, Mrs. K," I promise. She almost smiles, and then I walk away.

"How'd it go?" Lane asks when I return to his side. He's

tossing the ball for Nugget and watching the baby reindeer scamper to chase it.

"As well as can be expected," I answer.

Nugget scoops the ball into his mouth and trots back. He drops it at my feet and nudges it toward me.

I laugh and toss it for him again.

It bounces into Dale's leg, and so does Nugget.

"Sorry!" I call. Dale waves me off and bends to scratch Nugget's chin.

"I wonder how many treats he's gotten tonight?" I ponder aloud.

"Plenty."

"Would you like to dance again?" Lane asks me. The candles flicker around us, casting us all in a lovely glow. Tonight almost feels magical.

"I'd love to."

He twirls me around the room, and Edward and Marina join us. Fred taps the side of his leg to keep time, and Essie hums beside him. Sophie and Dale take to the dance floor next, and before I know it, it feels like a ballroom.

I laugh until my lips hurt.

It's almost midnight when one by one, the tapered candles burn down to nubs and flicker out.

Marina and Edward take Nugget back to the barn, and Essie and Albert get Fred settled onto the sofa for the night.

I help Sophie clean up the kitchen. The grandfather clock is chiming midnight when we emerge.

When we do, Fred is snoring lightly on the sofa, Dale is

asleep in a wing-back chair by the fire, and Lane sits on the bottom step of the stairway.

Waiting to walk me to my room, I realize.

He smiles at me gently, and I turn to Sophie.

She's covering Dale with a blanket.

"He'll wake up in the night and stumble to bed," she says with a gentle smile. "He made those chairs himself, and he's determined to prove they're comfortable."

"He looks pretty comfortable," I point out, observing the way his feet are propped, he's covered cozily, and his head is leaning against the chair back.

"He does, doesn't he?" Sophie says softly. She bends and presses a kiss to the top of her husband's head before she moves toward the stairs. "Good night, Piper."

She steps around Lane.

"Good night, Lane." She pats his shoulder. "If you need anything, you know where to find me," she tells us. "I'm a light sleeper," she adds pointedly.

I giggle. "We're coming to bed, Soph."

She nods, a small, satisfied smile on her lips, and continues up the stairs.

Lane waits for me, and I take his arm.

"She doesn't miss a single thing," I confirm to him.

"I told you," he answers.

We stroll to my room and stop outside. I look up at him, at his sparkling eyes and sure smile.

"There's a lot of things I don't know right now," I tell him. "But I do know one thing. I'm meant to be here right now. With you."

"Ace." He half sighs, half groans, and he reaches for me, pulling me close. He kisses me softly, his lips pressing ever so lightly into mine.

"Ahem." Sophie clears her throat, her head poked out her bedroom door. I yank away from Lane.

"Sorry, Sophie. We were just saying good night."

"Use your words, not your lips," she advises, before she closes her door again.

"I mean, technically, you need your lips to speak," I say quietly. Lane smiles.

"Don't tempt me, Pip," he murmurs. I nod.

"Good night, Lane."

"Good night, Ace."

I step inside the bedroom, close the door, and then lean on it, with my hand on my heart and my back to the wood.

From the bed, Marina watches me and laughs.

"You've got it bad, girl."

"I know. It hit me suddenly, like someone took a baseball bat to my head."

"Land, what a charming comparison." She shudders.

"I mean, there was chemistry there from the first moment, obviously," I say, moving to the bed. "But yesterday, it just hit me hard. I knew I was falling, and then it just happened. I fell."

I sigh and collapse on the bed, and Marina laughs again.

"I'm happy for you both, Pippie."

I do a snow angel on the bed, and we collapse into giggles when I almost knock her off by accident.

"You're a mess," she tells me.

"I know."

We get ready for bed and cuddle together for warmth. She slips into sleep almost immediately, but I'm too wound up.

I replay the night in my head, Lane's every smile, every wink. I feel pathetic, to fall so hard, but if this is what love is, then I can honestly say this is the first time I've fallen into it.

I feel like I'm floating from it.

It's in the middle of the night when I hear a scratching, spinning noise.

I quietly get up and poke around, the light from the moon illuminating the room just enough for me to see. It takes a few minutes to locate the sound.

It's the compass, which I'd tucked under the mattress.

It spins wildly now, as I hold it in the palm of my hand.

Moonlight makes it almost glow, and it wildly spins with abandon, not stopping, not resting.

A sense of foreboding fills me. It had done this the day I'd come here.

All I know is, I'm suddenly quite aware of the fact that while love can lift us high, high up, it can crush us equally low when something goes wrong.

There is something unearthly about this compass, and I can't let it ruin everything.

I wrap the still-moving compass in a scarf, but it doesn't stop the arrow hand from spinning. I tuck it firmly back beneath the mattress, wedging it so it can't move, but I can still hear it throughout the night, attempting to spin.

I don't know how long it continues. All I know is, when I wake up in the morning, the sound is gone.

CHAPTER TWENTY-ONE

et's go sit in the hot spring," Marina says, bouncing on the bed to wake me up. The sun hasn't even come up. It's pitch black outside.

"I do not negotiate with terrorists," I mumble. Marina giggles.

"Come on. My neck and back hurt from all the dancing. Edward isn't as light on his feet as Lane is."

"He does his best," I defend him groggily.

"Oh, he does. But the more of his punch he drinks, the less his *best* is enough." She giggles again. "Let's just go relax before it's time to help Mama with breakfast. We're having eggs in a nest this morning, so it's not much work anyway. She probably won't even need us but to set the table."

"Oh, fine." I sigh, sitting up. "How do I let you talk me into things?"

"You love me, that's how," Marina announces.

"That's true. But still. If I go with you, then you have to wash after breakfast, and I get to dry."

"It's a deal," she says, and I silently wonder when the first dishwasher will be invented, and how long I'll need to wait for that convenience to reach Alaska. "Just get your skinny caboose out of bed, and let's go soak our aches and pains away."

I grumble as I get dressed, and Marina cheerfully ignores me.

She's already bounded out of the room when I realize that the compass has stopped spinning. I pull it out and, sure enough, the arrow hand is still. It points north, and I would wonder if I'd dreamt it, but it's wrapped in the same scarf that I'd used to subdue it in the night.

So it happened.

I wrap it back up and put it beneath the mattress.

Marina is impatiently waiting for me by the door, already wearing her coat and boots.

"Here's your stomper," she says, tossing me a boot. It narrowly misses my face.

"Hey," I yelp. "I don't need a black eye."

"Lane would love you with a black eye," she says, as she opens the back door. "Or even if you lost an eye."

"Let's not get too crazy. I like my eyes where they are."

I pull on my second boot and follow her out, the frigid air freezing my nose instantly. I wrap a scarf tightly around my face.

"We're insane," I tell her as we hike to the shed.

"Yes," she calls over her shoulder. "We are."

The morning is calm and still as we tread silently through the powdery wonderland. I keep an eye out for Tiny, but there's nary a sound except for our footsteps in the snow.

I'm out of breath when we reach the shed, and Marina pulls the door open.

The steam instantly flows over us, a comforting moist blanket.

"Oh, man, that's nice." Marina sighs, setting down the towels. "Close the door, Pip. Don't let the hot air out."

I slam it behind me and pull the wooden crossbar down, latching it into place.

"It's unlikely anyone is going to be out this early," I clarify for Marina. "But just in case."

She strips off her clothes and steps into the spring.

"Hello? I'm right here," I tell her. "Has modesty gone out of style?"

She rolls her eyes. "I was in such a hurry that I forgot my swimsuit." She sniffs, daring me to give her a hard time.

I choose not to, but only because it's early, and I don't have the energy yet.

I strip off my clothes to reveal Sophie's yellow swimsuit.

"Some of us have modesty," I sniff back at her.

She rolls her eyes and lays her head back, enjoying the hot water.

I have no idea where my grandmother is in the naked young woman in front of me, but it's clear she's nowhere in this shed. And for today, that's okay.

It's nice to see Gran before she becomes set in her ways.

It's nice to see her before she judges herself for every little thing and questions every little decision she's ever made.

It's nice to see her . . . free.

Free of guilt, free of grief.

I know I have a very rare opportunity to try to help her. To help her adjust the way she sees certain things as weaknesses, and to not be so hard on herself for things that are out of her control.

If I can do that now, maybe she won't punish herself for the rest of her life after her daughter dies.

Maybe she won't punish herself by isolating herself from those she loves.

I take a deep breath, step into the pool opposite her, and think about how to start that conversation.

No pressure, Piper. It's not like you can change the course of this woman's life for decades to come. Oh, wait, it's exactly like that.

"M, I can't help but notice that you're kind of hard on your dad."

"What?" Her eyes pop open, and she stares at me. "What do you mean?"

I decide to just bite the bullet.

"It feels like you're embarrassed when he shows compassion for others. Or animals."

"You mean, the reindeer?" she demands. "They don't have a use, Piper."

"They make him happy," I tell her. "He thinks they make the guys happy, and you know what, M? They do. They make everyone happy. That's a good use, right there."

"It might be a good use, but that doesn't pay for their grain," she says curtly. "My father needs to think about that."

"I'm sure he does," I answer. "How do you know that he doesn't make his own private sacrifices in order to pay for their food? Maybe it's just that important to him."

She blinks, clearly considering that.

"You know, I don't think I told you this, but Lane didn't

want to butcher the turkeys. I went to the barn to help him, and he was just sitting there, watching them. He said that ever since he's come back, he doesn't have the stomach for it."

"That's understandable," she says.

"Don't you see? Your dad deserves the same understanding. He's just as manly as he ever was. Maybe even more so. He's confident enough to be compassionate and kind."

Marina blinks back tears. "Does it seem like I disapprove of him?" she asks. "Because that's not true. I just don't want any-one to judge him. Men are hard on each other, Piper."

"I know," I tell her. "Just try not to play into that toxicity, M. Say it aloud—to anyone—'It's okay to be kind.'"

"That seems like such a simple principle." She sighs. "I don't know why we have to have this conversation at all."

"Because men *are* hard on each other. And women come to expect it, and anything less is considered weak. We need to stop it," I say. "We all deserve to be flawed, and accepted any-way."

She nods. "It sounds so sensible when you say it. I think folks just . . . well, they don't like to discuss things like this."

No, they don't. They won't start that for another few de-cades.

"It's okay," I tell her. "We can start that dialogue right now. With everyone around us. We control that."

If nothing else.

"I've also noticed that while you're hard on your dad, you're also hard on yourself," I say carefully. "You expect perfection, M. Both out of him and out of yourself. Have you ever noticed that?"

She shakes her head. "No."

"When things go wrong in life, they aren't always your fault," I tell her. "You don't bear the responsibility of everything that goes wrong in the world."

"I know that," she says patiently. "Where is all of this coming from, Piper?"

"I don't know. You're just such a kind person. I want to make sure you never change. Always give people the benefit of the doubt. Love is always worth it, M. Even if it can eventually cause pain."

She laughs a bit now, although she's clearly confused by my serious tone.

"Did you have a bad dream?" she asks. "I've had those too. Where something seems horrible and so real. But Piper, I'm fine. I don't know what you dreamt, but we're all fine."

"I didn't dream." I sigh. "I just had a moment of reflection. And I want the best for you always."

"Ohhhh," she says suddenly. "I know what this is. You're worried about what will happen if you marry Lane and move away. Piper, we'll always be friends. You can't get rid of me that easily. So don't feel you need to cram all of your advice into this very moment. We'll have years for you to stretch it all out."

She chuckles, then smiles at me.

"I do love you, though. For caring."

"I love you too," I answer. "That's why I wanted to say something. Just promise me you'll remember. Okay?"

She sighs, long and loud. "Okay. I promise to remember."

She pauses.

"If you'll promise to remember that you're stuck with me. No matter where you end up or who you marry."

She eyes me sternly.

"I promise."

"Good." She lies back. "Now that we've gotten *that* settled, I'd say that's enough serious stuff for one morning. A girl needs coffee first, Pip."

I settle back into the hot water until it reaches my chin and close my eyes.

The steam moisturizes my face, and I feel it nourishing every cell.

"I like that Dale loves the reindeer," I tell her, circling back to that. "As humans, we don't need to crush every existence around us just because we can." I vow to myself that if I get home, I'll change the way Great Expectations does business.

Marina sighs without opening her eyes.

"Why are you like this?" she asks. "Seriously. Why?"

I dangle my fingers in the hot water, watching the drips fall to the surface.

"Because my brain never stops. Because I'm always wondering how I can make things better for everyone else or how I can be better. I think you're the same way."

Of course she is. I inherited that trait from her.

"You think entirely too much for it not even being eight A.M.," she decides.

"It's not even seven A.M.," I tell her.

"Even worse."

She opens her eyes and levels her gaze at me. "Listen, Pip. I know that everything is confusing to you right now. I know that you must spend a lot of time thinking about the situation and trying to remember your past, and, honestly, just trying to figure yourself out. I get it. I really do. But don't wear yourself out. All of these things . . . the answers you're trying to figure out . . . they'll just reveal themselves. You'll just figure it out. When the time is right, though, and not a moment before."

"Sometimes, though, we'll never figure out why something happens," I tell her. "No matter how long we ponder it. Sometimes, there's just no answer. And we have to be okay with that too."

When your daughter and son-in-law die in a plane crash, it won't be your fault, Gran.

"You're starting to scare me," she decides. "I'm serious. There isn't any reason to talk like this, Pip. Everything is fine!"

She stands up and reaches for her towel, and as she does, water sloshes onto the rock rim of the pool. And I hear a slight huff.

I freeze, my finger to my lips.

Marina and I listen, and there it is again.

A slight huff along the back wall of the shed.

I focus and can see a large shadow moving along the crack at the bottom of the wall.

My eyes widen at the same time as Mariana's, as we both realize at that exact moment we're not alone here.

Heavy paws sound outside the wall, and the huffs get louder.

"Oh, no," Marina mutters. "We didn't bring the shotgun. How could we be so stupid?"

She wraps the towel around her and pulls her coat and boots on while she tosses me a towel.

I get up as quietly as I can, but the bear hears me and pauses.

The huffs startle me as they echo next to my foot.

The twelve-hundred-pound bear is right on the other side of this thin wooden wall.

I exhale silently.

Marina's eyes widen. And then, there's a loud thud, and the shed shudders.

"Holy crow, he's ramming it," Marina shouts needlessly, because I'm quite aware of what's happening. I yank at my boots and pull on my coat, like Marina, foregoing the rest of my clothing for the coat.

"We're going to die," I wail.

"We are not," Marina snaps. "Pull yourself together, Piper."

The bear launches himself at the shed again at just this moment, and this time, the wall smashes into smithereens, and the remainder of the shed topples to the ground around us.

The next few moments are blurry at best.

Marina and I run.

Fast.

Hard.

Quicker than we've ever run before. I'm in a swimsuit, coat, and boots, and Marina in a towel, coat, and boots. We slip and slide, ducking the wreckage of the shed.

The bear whirls around on his muscular haunches, pivoting to chase us.

"You're never supposed to run from a bear," I scream to Marina, who is two paces ahead of me.

"I'm not playing dead," she shouts back. "Or we'll *be* dead."

"Help!" we shriek, as we skid down the trail, ducking

behind this tree or that to thwart the bear, now hot on our heels. His massive size aside, he's quite fast and probably quite hungry.

He roars, and he means business.

I hurdle over a skinny felled tree, and Marina shrieks for help again.

It suddenly occurs to me that if we stay on the path, in this straight line, he'll get us for sure. He can easily outrun us. I shove Marina into the copse of trees, and then signal her to start zigzagging toward the house. It's a trick I learned while picking up survival skills on television as a kid.

I can almost feel the hot pant of the bear's breath on my neck when a shotgun rings out.

The bear skids to a halt, sliding in the snow.

Marina and I keep running.

Tiny realizes after a minute that he isn't hit and can't seem to figure where the noise came from, so he lumbers to his feet and once again starts chasing us.

We're twenty paces from the barn when the shotgun rings out again, from the back porch.

Edward stands there, firing the gun into the sky, trying to scare the bear away.

"Shoot it," Marina screeches.

"You're in the way," he shouts back.

We're ten paces away now.

The bear somehow trips and goes flying toward us like a massive woolly-mammoth bowling ball, taking Marina and me down along with everything else in his path. He slams hard into the back of the barn, sprawls out, and goes still.

Marina and I spring back up and bolt for the house, lunging up the stairs and behind Edward.

The bear lumbers to its feet, faster than I'd anticipated, and looks us dead in the eye before it gallops away into the trees.

"You should've killed it," Marina tells Edward. "It chased us all the way from the shed."

We're shivering, both from shock and from the cold, and Edward pretends to not notice the state of our clothing. Or lack thereof.

"What in the blazes?" Sophie rushes to the porch, and in one glance takes in our appearance, the shotgun in Edward's hands, and the cause of the issue.

"Did you get it?" she asks him.

He shakes his head. "No."

"It's okay," she tells him. "Next time. At least the girls are safe. That's the important thing." She turns to us. "And why were you up there so early? You could've died."

"My back hurt. I wanted to soak," Marina says, and it seems so trivial now.

"And you?" Sophie demands, looking at me.

"I wasn't awake enough to make good decisions."

Sophie stares at us. "You've both got more sense than this. Use your heads, girls."

"Yes, Mama," Marina says contritely. "We're sorry. It was silly."

"Don't lead Piper astray again," Sophie adds sternly. "I'm responsible for her."

"Okay, Mama," Marina says meekly.

Sophie grabs us each into the crooks of her elbows, squeezing our necks tightly. "Do not ever scare me like that again," she says, quietly and seriously. "I mean it."

"Yes, ma'am," we say in unison.

"Go get warmed up and dressed before you catch your death."

We rush away. We bump into Lane and Albie on the staircase, both of whom stare at us in astonishment.

"Oh, what? Have you never seen a half-naked girl before?" Marina growls as she stomps up the steps.

The men's eyes widen, and I trail behind Marina.

"The bear almost got us," I tell them, as an apology for Marina's gruffness.

"What?" Lane asks, his jaw instantly tight.

"It's okay, we're fine. Let us get dressed and we'll tell you all about it."

Marina and I rush past, and I'm honestly looking forward to gathering myself a bit before we have to discuss what just happened.

We enter our bedroom and sit on the bed at the same time.

"Did we just almost die?" Marina asks aloud.

"Yes, I believe we did."

Marina throws herself back onto the bed. "I'm too pretty to die by mauling," she decides. "I'm sorry, Pip. I put us in danger."

"I agreed to it," I point out. "I could've said no."

"If you believe that, I've got some oceanfront property to sell to you. Right here in Wander."

"I don't believe that's how the saying goes," I say as I fall backward onto the bed beside her.

"Not everyone is vulnerable to your charms," I tell her. "I'm not."

She sniffs. "We'll see."

"We're still recovering from your last grand plan."

We lie side by side, until our breathing regulates and we calm. We finally roll to our sides and face each other.

"I'm sorry," Marina says.

"Me too," I answer. "I got hysterical there for a second."

"But then you started running in that crazy way. If it hadn't been for that, for slowing him down in the trees, he'd have gotten us both. Where did you learn to do that?"

From a million television shows growing up. I mean, I think it's intended to keep someone from getting hit by a bullet, but it was pretty effective helping us elude the bear.

"I don't know. It was just instinct." I shrug.

Marina stares at me, then lets it go. "Have you ever just felt weird?" she asks me, as she stares out the window.

"Every day," I confirm. She smiles lightly.

"I'm sure," she agrees. "But I'm talking about feeling weird beyond our own personalities. Like . . . something isn't right."

This gets my attention.

"What do you mean?"

"I can't explain it. For a few days now, I feel like something is terribly wrong. I can't put my finger on what. After we fixed Fred up, I thought the feeling might go away. It didn't. Then the bear incident. I was thinking that should clear it up. But it hasn't. I still feel . . . weird."

"You mean, your intuition is trying to speak to you?"

"Maybe," she says. "I honestly don't know. I have this strange feeling that the other shoe is going to drop soon."

"But maybe there's not another shoe," I answer slowly. "We're all a bit on edge. That's probably all it is, Marina."

I think of the spinning compass wedged under our mattress, and I know she's right. Something is off.

It's possible that something is going to happen, and I have every reason to believe it involves *me*.

"We're going to have to face the music sometime." Marina sighs as she sits up. "We might as well get it over with."

"Besides, I'm hungry," I answer, trying to put the troubling thoughts away for now.

"I swear, you'll be eating at your own funeral," she mutters, and I freeze. It's something Gran said to me my entire life. She looks at me. "What? No offense, but you will be."

I roll my eyes, pull a dress on, and tidy my hair.

When Marina and I join everyone at the table for breakfast, the conversation stops.

Lane stands up, pulls my chair out, and waits for me to sit in it so he can push it in for me.

Marina stands by her seat, and eventually Albie does the same for her. She sits primly.

"Were you waiting for us?" she asks innocently.

Dale stares at her. "You owe me an explanation, young lady."

"I already spoke with them," Sophie tells him. "I was stern."

"She was," I confirm. "I was scared."

"Oh, pish," Sophie says, waving her hand. She passes around a platter of eggs in a nest, and the men load up their plates.

"I've been thinking," Sophie says after a few minutes. "I *will* try a new tradition for Christmas, Piper. If you can write down the recipe for quiche, I think we'll try Christmas brunch."

"Do you mean . . . the turkeys have been pardoned?" I ask. She nods.

"For now."

I laugh. Because of course that means *forever.*

As I gaze at every face surrounding this table, I know they'll all hold a place in my heart. They're family. Not all by blood, but all by love.

CHAPTER TWENTY-TWO

The next day passes uneventfully, regardless of both mine and Marina's misgivings. By early evening on Christmas Eve, Fred and Essie work on an old puzzle at the dining room table, Sophie and Marina are planning out Christmas brunch in the kitchen, and Lane and I sit in front of the fire.

"Are you warm enough now?" Lane asks me, still clearly worried after the bear attack. He's tried to make sure I've been warm enough all day long.

"I'm fine, Lane. I'm warm. See?" I lay my palm on his face. He nods.

"Let's keep you by the fire just in case."

"I did not catch my death," I insist. "Cold doesn't cause sickness, Lane."

"It doesn't hurt to be on the safe side," he says.

I gaze past him to the Christmas tree, standing so tall and full. The strings of brass bells hang from it, the ones Gran always loved. The ones I had forgotten to put on the tree back home.

"We're having lentil pot pie," Marina tells us as she joins us from the kitchen. "For dinner tonight. Just when I thought our stock of lentils had run out, *wait, there's more.*"

"Be grateful for the lentils," Essie says from the table. "Without meat, we need the protein."

"I know, Mrs. Klein." Marina sighs. "I'm just tired of them. But I'm gratefully tired!"

We exchange a grin.

"It's okay to be grateful for something but still not like it," I murmur to her.

"I'm going to start calling you my moral compass," she tells me. "My divining rod."

"Girls, can you set the table?" Sophie calls from the kitchen.

"Coming, Mama," Marina calls back.

"Duty calls," I tell Lane. "Save my spot."

Marina and I set the table, folding a napkin for each place. Sophie brings out the pot pies, and they look delicious, their buttery crusts delicate and piped.

"These look delish, Mama," Marina says, echoing my thoughts, and she actually sounds like she means it.

"They do," I agree. The men wait for us to sit and quickly follow suit. Dale says a prayer, and then the food starts getting passed.

It feels as though we've shared a million mealtimes here, when it's really only been a little more than a week.

How is that possible, when it feels I've been here forever?

Because I have, I decide. I've lived here forever. My entire life. The year doesn't matter. It's home.

I take a bite of the hot lentils, and they're so savory, so filling, so warm, that I sigh in contentment. I never would've thought I'd love lentil pie.

But here I am, shoveling it in my mouth like it's a Big Mac.

I'm getting ready to take a second bite when we hear footsteps on the porch, followed by a pounding on the door.

"What in the world?" Sophie asks, as Dale gets to his feet.

Dale opens the door to find two figures standing there, one short, one tall. They're wearing army uniforms and army overcoats. They're clearly exhausted, and they're covered in snow.

"How in the world . . ." Sophie breathes, her hand to her heart.

"Ma'am," one of the snow-covered figures says. "Does a Marina McCauley live here?"

Oh, no. No.

Marina steps forward hesitantly, her hand pressed to her heart in an identical fashion to her mother.

"I do," she tells them. "I'm Marina McCauley."

"Miss, we've been hiking against all odds to reach you," the taller man says. "I'm—"

"Short Stuff," she says tearfully. He startles, then nods. "And you must be Danny Boy," she says to the shorter one. Her voice is breathy and weak.

My heart is in my throat, because I know there's only one reason these two men would be here, risking their lives in these elements.

"I'm here to give you this," Short Stuff says, handing her a small bundle. "And to tell you, regretfully, miss, that Cedric has been killed in action. I'm so sorry."

Cedric.

What?

My head comes up in bewilderment.

Cedric is not my grandfather's name.

Marina slumps into her father, her hand over her mouth. I rush to her, patting her back, stroking her hair, and Sophie ushers the men inside and closes the door.

Marina moves by the fire, the men at her side and Sophie at her feet. Marina opens the package.

It's the compass, gleaming in the firelight.

"I knew something was wrong," she's murmuring. "I've felt it for days."

"He made us promise that if something happened to him, we'd get this compass back to you, come hell or high water," Danny tells her solemnly.

Danny.

I stare at him more intently. At his face and his familiar eyes.

Dan.

A much younger Dan O'Connell. The Dan who has worked at the lodge my entire life.

Oh my gosh.

Marina holds the compass tight and thanks the men profusely, through tears and through whimpers.

"He can't be gone, Mama," she says. "He just can't. He was in the Philippines."

"He was," Short Stuff says. "I mean, we were. But we got orders to move out, and they pulled us to France."

"Oh, no," Sophie says, covering her mouth.

"My name is Oliver Riley, ma'am," Short Stuff says. "That's my real name, anyway."

Oliver Riley is my grandfather's name.

He kneels to murmur to my grandmother and I realize in this moment that this is how they met. They met right here, when Oliver had come to do his duty to a fallen soldier.

My grandfather trekked through an Alaskan winter to stick to his word and return the compass to my gran.

In all my life, I don't think I've ever been so moved.

And Dan.

Dan accompanied him. Because they'd given their brother-in-arms their word.

I'll never think of Dan the same way again.

I leave Marina with the men and hang back by the kitchen door, not really sure what to do with myself. Essie makes herself useful and brings Marina a snifter of whiskey. Marina knocks it back and holds the empty glass out to be refilled.

Essie fills it without a word.

"I don't know what to do," I tell Lane. "I can't help."

"Of course you can," he tells me. "Tonight, when it's just you and her in the dark, tell her that everything will be okay. That she's strong enough to get through this."

"I will . . . and she is."

"Let her talk about it as much as she wants or as little as she wants," he advises. "Let her decide."

I nod. "Okay."

"Piper?" I hear Marina's soft voice call.

I rush to her. "I'm here, M."

"I can't believe it," she tells me. Her eyes are watery and red. Oliver makes room for me, and I sit by Marina's knee.

"I'm so sorry, M. Tell me what I can do."

"There's nothing," she whispers. "I can't think of a thing that will help."

"Time will," her mother tells her. "Just try to survive each day."

Marina nods. "Yes, Mama."

"Marina, let's get you to bed," I suggest. "Let's get you in your nightgown and settle you down in our room."

Where it's private and dark, and she can cry in peace.

She nods quietly and gets to her feet. She leans into me, and I help her to the bedroom.

She sits numbly on the bed and lets me undress her. I pull her nightgown over her head. Her face is pale as a ghost, and her eyes are sunken.

"I can't believe it," she tells me woodenly.

"I know," I say simply. I pull back the covers and help her into bed. Then I curl up behind her. I'm fully clothed, but I wrap my arm around her and pull her close.

She rests back against my chest, her breathing soft and light as she cries.

"He was so young," she whimpers.

"I know."

I rub her back and let her cry here, in the privacy of the dark.

"It doesn't feel like it now, but you'll be okay," I tell her. "Life will move on, and you'll move on with it. But for now, grieve the boy you knew."

"The boy I loved," she answers.

"Yes."

I keep rubbing her back and stroking her hair, and after a while, I hum a nameless, wordless lullaby that my gran used to hum to me . . . back when I was small, and she'd rock me to sleep after my parents died.

"Will I ever see them again?" I'd asked her one night. She'd looked down at me, her eyes so tender and wet.

"You will," she had told me. *"I promise. Someday."*

"You'll see him again," I promise Marina now. "Someday."

Marina cries, and I wrap her more tightly in the blankets, holding her until she falls asleep. I let her rest for at least thirty minutes more before I slip from the bed, careful not to wake her.

Carefully, I open the top drawer of the dresser and pull out the locket, wrapped in its tissue. I lay it on the nightstand. Maybe, when she wakes up in the morning, she can open it, and it might bring her just a tiny bit of happiness.

When I emerge into the hallway, Lane, Danny, and Oliver are sitting there.

"Is she okay?" Lane asks me.

I shake my head. "No."

"He loved her," Ollie tells us. "He talked about her every day. I feel like I know her myself. He told us how she's clumsy, and how she exaggerates, how she sometimes gets too big for her britches."

"She loved him too," I tell them. "She's finally asleep. I want her to sleep as long as possible. When she's sleeping, she can't feel the pain."

It's something I remember from when my parents died.

Quietly, we walk downstairs. The men are solemn. I'm silent.

"I'm glad you're both safe," I tell the two men when we reach the bottom. "You were so brave, and so loyal, to come here in person."

Oliver, my future grandfather, looks at me in surprise. "We promised Rick, miss. He was our brother."

My eyes well up, a lump forms in my throat, and Lane wraps his arm around my shoulders, squeezing gently.

When we enter the dining room, everyone looks up.

"How is she?" Sophie asks. "I wanted to come up but thought she could use some privacy."

"She's sleeping now," I tell her. "She's taking it hard."

"I just can't believe it," Sophie says, shaking her head. "I've known that boy his entire life. I wasn't supposed to outlive him." A tear slips down her cheek.

"War is cruel," I say.

Essie pours whiskey for the men. And then one for herself.

"To Cedric," she says, holding up her glass.

"To Cedric," they say in unison, before they knock the whiskey back.

I walk past them, my heart in my throat, and sit in a wingback by the fire. The compass lies on the hearth, gleaming in the firelight. I pick it up and turn it over and over in my hand.

It's battered now, by war and the elements. The journey it has taken to get back to where it began has taken a toll on its metallic sheen.

I think about it, how this compass has brought my grandfather to my grandmother, in one of the most painful moments of her life. How he met her, and how they'll eventually get married.

The compass guided my grandfather home.

Something so small has played such a huge part in the story of Marina and Ollie.

In this moment, I know that I can't attempt to change history. I can't leave a note warning my parents not to fly. Things happen the way they are meant to . . . in intricate, detailed, and sometimes very small ways.

Small ways that eventually have giant outcomes.

I slide the compass in my pocket so I can give it to Dale, and stare into the fire, watching it lick and lap at the stones. I think I'm grieving too, not like Marina, but because I know now that I can't save my parents.

"Are you okay?" Lane appears beside me, his voice low.

I stare up at him, at the face that I just want to reach out and touch.

"I'm just thinking about life," I tell him honestly. "It can be filled with such tragedy and sadness, yet also with such love."

He sits next to me and considers that.

"That's true," he finally says. "But I have to believe that everything is worth it, Piper. Cedric died knowing he was loved. That had to have made a difference."

"I know," I agree. "Surely love makes all the difference. Even on the hardest days of heartbreak, I wouldn't trade it. Not for anything."

Lane pulls me to him in a soft hug, and not one person in the room says a word about it.

We all sit in silence, and the seconds turn to minutes.

Finally, Sophie takes Dan and Oliver upstairs to settle them into a room, and Dale helps Fred recline more comfortably on the sofa for the night. Essie puts away the liquor bottle and retires for the evening.

The emotions from this day weigh heavily on me, and somehow I know that I have to talk to Lane. I can't continue on with this lie . . . It's not fair. Not to anyone.

"Can we get some air?" I ask him quietly.

"Of course," he answers, quickly getting to his feet. We pull coats over our shoulders and step onto the back porch. He looks down at me. "What's wrong?"

I take a long, shaky breath.

"I haven't been honest with you. And tonight, with all the raw and honest emotion, I feel like I just have to tell you everything. Even if it means you won't want me anymore."

He's startled now, his mouth tight. "What do you mean? I'll always want you, Piper."

"You might not. Not once you hear this. And if that's the case, I'll have to be okay with it," I decide.

"Just tell me what you want me to hear," Lane finally says. "Don't borrow trouble, Piper. Let *me* decide what I can handle and what I can't."

I take a deep breath.

"I'm not from here," I say bluntly.

"That much is fairly obvious," he says dryly.

"I mean, I'm not from *here*. From 1944."

"And now I don't understand."

"I know. It's going to sound outlandish. I'm fully aware of

how crazy it will sound, which is why I haven't told you before now."

Lane waits without a word. I shiver from the cold, and he takes his coat off, draping it on top of the coat I'm already wearing.

He doesn't flinch from the cold air. He just waits.

"My last memory from home was a week ago. I was out in a snowstorm hunting for a group of hunters who pay me to let them stay here at the lodge."

Lane's face is blank now.

"In 2022."

Lane doesn't react.

"In 2022, what?"

"In the *year* 2022."

Lane is completely still now.

"You're telling me that you're from the future," he says stiffly.

"Essentially. Yes."

"You're telling me that you live in a time seventy-eight years past this one."

His face is impassive, and I can't gauge his thoughts.

"Yes."

There's more silence.

"There's more. Marina is . . . my grandmother. I'm a McCauley."

Now there's a reaction. Lane's mouth drops open.

"Is it possible that you were out in a snowstorm, and you hit your head and this is just what you believe?" he asks slowly, and I can't blame him. That's the reasonable and logical thing to assume.

"I have proof," I tell him. "It's upstairs now, so I can show you tomorrow. But back home—"

"In 2022," he interjects.

"Yes. In 2022, Gran—Marina—died a couple weeks ago. She left me a compass. The very compass that Dan and Short Stuff just brought to Marina. I have the original upstairs, tucked under the mattress. I think it's how I came here. It was spinning like crazy that day, and then the next thing I knew, Dale was pulling me out of a snowbank."

Lane is silent. Processing. Absorbing.

I rush to continue. "Think about it, Lane. There's no logical explanation why a girl like me should be plunked down in the middle of Alaska in the middle of winter. It's impossible."

"That much is true." He nods.

"And the compass was spinning again yesterday. And then today, this happens. Cedric is gone. It's like the compass knew. Gran told me in a letter that she left for me that the compass would always guide me home. I felt so lost after she died. I didn't know if I wanted to stay at the lodge or if I wanted to sell it—"

"Sell Great Expectations?" Lane's head snaps up.

"I know. It sounds outrageous now. If I ever get home, I'll never sell. I swear it."

"If you get home," Lane repeats, and his eyes are guarded. "You think you'll somehow get home?"

"I have no idea. I live in fear of it now. Because you're my life. I can't leave you. Back home, Gran is gone. But here, Marina is alive and well. But this isn't where I belong. It's not the natural order of things. I don't know if I'll be allowed to stay."

"This is a lot to absorb," Lane says, and his hand is on my back. "It's late, and we've had a lot to handle today. I think maybe we should go to bed. We'll wake tomorrow, on Christmas, and we'll think about this more. It'll all work out, Piper."

"Do you think I'm crazy?" I look directly into his eyes, without flinching.

"No," he says. "I don't know what to think about any of this, but I don't think you're crazy."

"I don't want to leave you. Ever," I tell him.

"I believe you," he says. "I do."

"You believe all of this?" I ask pointedly. He shrugs.

"I don't know. I believe *you* believe it."

"You trusted me once," I remind him. "Remember? You climbed into that plane with me and trusted me not to kill you. I know how to fly because I'm not from 1944. I'm a pilot in 2022. You can trust me, Lane. I know I haven't told you the truth about this, but that's only because it sounds so crazy, and I didn't want you to think less of me . . . or stop loving me."

He exhales. "I'm not going to stop loving you."

"But can you trust me?"

"I'll try, Ace. That's all I can promise right now."

My shoulders fall. I guess I can't expect more than that. I just handed him a lot to think about. I nod.

"I understand." I turn for the door. "We should try and sleep. I have a feeling tomorrow will be a long day."

We walk to the stairs, and once there, Lane pauses.

"I can't say what tomorrow will bring," he tells me. "But I can tell you that I love you. Is that enough?"

"It has to be," I say limply. I lean up on my tiptoes, kiss his cheek, and then walk woodenly to bed.

CHAPTER TWENTY-THREE

I don't sleep.

Instead, I curl up behind Marina, trying to shield her from pain with my arms. I hold her close and listen to her breathing evenly and deeply as she sleeps.

I know when she wakes up in the morning before she even opens her eyes.

She turns to me.

"Was it a nightmare?"

I shake my head.

"No. I'm sorry."

Her eyelashes flutter closed onto her pale cheeks. She drops her head to my chest and stays there, hiding from the world.

"We can stay in here as long as you want to," I tell her.

"It's Christmas," she reminds me. "We need to get up."

"Everyone will understand."

We don't move.

"I just can't believe he's gone," she says. "I can't believe it. I can't make my mind grasp a world without him in it."

Lord, I understand that more than she knows.

Her shoulders shake as she silently cries, her grief expelling onto her cheeks in wet streaks.

In this moment, I realize that I can help her. I can tell her of a world that goes on without him, a world where she exists and is happy. If I dare take the risk to tell her.

And as I stroke her skinny back as she cries, I know I have to take the risk.

"Marina, there's something I need to tell you."

She doesn't lift her head.

"What is it?" she mumbles.

I quickly tell her what I'd told Lane—detailing everything I can recall. By the time I'm finished, she's sitting up in front of me, her eyes wet and her mouth agape.

"You're telling me that I'm your *grandmother*," she says incredulously.

"I know it's hard to believe," I say.

"You're telling me that I marry someone else, and I'm happy."

"Yes."

"And that I don't die from the pain of this," she says out loud. "That's good to know." She glances at me. "It would explain why we look so much alike," she says thoughtfully.

"You don't think I'm nuts?"

"Yes. I do. But maybe not about this."

"I have proof," I tell her. I get up and pull out the two compasses. "One is from the future. You gave it to me and I had it in my pocket when I came here. The second is the original— the one Dan and Short Stuff brought to you yesterday. It's the same compass, and somehow, it's responsible for me being here. I just don't understand how."

"Someone told me once that we can't always know why things happen the way they do," Marina reminds me. "But that we shouldn't blame ourselves for things we can't control."

"You listen to me!" I exclaim. "That's good to know." I pause. "Because listen to me now. There will be things that happen that you can't control and that aren't your fault. You cannot carry the responsibility for those things. You cannot close yourself off from love and family because you're afraid of the risk. Promise me, M."

"Can you give me specifics?" she asks, and her face is tear streaked, her eyes red.

She wouldn't be able to handle the details today.

"Maybe a different day," I answer. "You have a lot to deal with right now."

She nods. "I agree about that." She stands up. "We should go downstairs. I don't want Mama to worry." She glances at me. "I don't think we should tell them, Piper."

"Okay," I agree.

We step toward the door. "And don't start calling me Gran," she instructs as I turn the doorknob.

"That won't happen for years to come," I promise.

"If you're stuck here, will it ever happen?" she asks curiously. "I mean, if you're here, and you age with me now, how can you become my granddaughter in the future? Will everything change?"

"I have no idea," I tell her honestly, as I reach behind me and grab her Christmas gift. "But let's not borrow trouble before it happens."

We're on the staircase when she freezes in place, then turns to me.

"So if this is all true, you know who I end up with."

I swallow. "Yes, I do."

"Don't tell me. I want it to be a surprise."

I smile. "Good. Because I wasn't going to tell you anyway."

"Piper?"

"Yes?"

"Don't take this the wrong way, but my heart still hurts."

"Of course it does." I hug her tight. "But you'll eventually be okay. I promise. Take it one day at a time, and just know that everyone here loves you."

And those who don't yet, *will.* I glance at Oliver, who sits at the table sipping coffee with Dale, Lane, and Dan. Lane meets my gaze, but I can't read anything there. I can't tell what he's thinking.

We join them, and everyone fusses over Marina. I settle into a chair, where Sophie pours me a cup of coffee.

"Merry Christmas, everyone," Marina tells us softly. "I don't want anyone to think we can't celebrate, because we need to more than ever. Cedric would want it. We *need* it."

Sophie brings out heaping platters of toast, two giant quiches, and two platters of pancakes.

She turns the record player on low, allowing Bing Crosby to croon to us while we eat. Afterward, we gather around the Christmas tree.

We exchange small, mostly handmade gifts, and Dale reads from the Bible with his deep voice.

When he's finished, Marina looks at her father. "Dad, I have a gift for you." He turns to her, surprised.

"Piper has inspired me by knowing how to fly. I want to

do something brave too. And for me, that means keeping the McCauley name when I eventually get married. You don't have a son, and this is a name that needs to continue."

The room falls silent. A woman keeping her maiden name isn't a common thing in 1944.

But after a couple of minutes, Dale breaks into a grin.

"Just so," he decides. "And so it shall continue with you, my brave, sweet girl." He hugs her and kisses her forehead. "You are the best Christmas gift a father could ask for," he says. His eyes gleam from unshed tears, and everyone pretends not to notice.

"It's only fitting since you're the best father a girl could have," she answers. "Merry Christmas, Dad."

Everyone chats quietly, and while there is a sad pall over the room in respect to Cedric, the room also feels warm and loving. Albert slips outdoors to take his turn feeding the reindeer, and I take the opportunity to pull Marina over to the fireplace to give her her gift.

She unwraps the tissue and sucks in a breath when she sees the locket.

"Your mom wanted to give this to you," I tell her, "but kept waiting for the right time. Look inside."

She unclasps the locket and reveals the tiny picture of the two of us inside. A tear streaks down her nose.

"They don't even know how appropriate this is, do they?" she asks softly, glancing at her parents.

"No. But it is. Very appropriate. I love you, Marina. I love you now, and I love you in the future. You don't know this, but you end up doing so much for me over the years. I never think to tell you how much I appreciate you, because people always think they have time for that. In reality, sometimes we don't. So we should *always* tell our loved ones how we feel. And I love you. I appreciate you. You've changed my life in so many ways. I wouldn't be who I am without you."

Marina studies me, looking into my eyes.

"You know how I die, don't you?" she asks.

I pause, then nod.

"Don't tell me," she instructs. "I want to be surprised."

I startle, then smile. "Consider it done."

Marina puts on the locket and glances across the room. "I think Lane wants to talk to you," she tells me, gesturing to where he lingers by the kitchen door, keeping an eye on us.

"I'm sure he does," I acknowledge.

"I'll send him over," she tells me as she walks away.

She murmurs in his ear, and then he heads in my direction.

Soon, we stand by the fire together, the flames lapping at the stones, and my hand so very close to Lane's.

"I believe you," he says bluntly.

I raise my gaze to meet his.

"You do?"

"Yes. It's an outlandish story, but it's something that fits you. Of course you came to me in an outlandish story. Of course you did."

"I'm not sure if I should be offended," I say.

He chuckles a bit. "Not at all. You are a unique, interesting person, Piper. Your story, I'm sure, will always be interesting, if a bit outlandish. And if you still want me, I'd like to be there for that story. For all of it."

I squeeze my eyes closed for a moment, grateful for his trust in me.

Grateful for my life. For this life.

"I still want you," I tell him quickly. "Always. I can't imagine my life without you."

"Then you won't have to," he says with a gentle smile. "You'll always have me in it."

"This is a family," I tell him. "And we're part of it. We're so lucky, Lane. So many people never get the chance to have this."

I look across the room to where Marina sits with Dan and Oliver at the table, watching them tell her funny stories about Cedric from the war, things that make her smile. And I know that I'm watching history unfold.

Things are happening right now as they were always meant to happen.

Oliver will become her rock, the person she depends on until the day he dies, many years in the future.

I'm pondering all of this when Albert bursts in the front doors.

"Nugget is gone," he tells us. "When Tiny slammed into the barn yesterday he broke a piece of fence. Nugget slipped out, and I can't find him."

"Oh, no," I cry out. There's no way I can let something happen to that sweet little life. "Tiny is out there. And we literally have been training him to listen for Nugget crying. We were using Nugget as bait. And now . . ."

I trail off. We all know what the situation is.

I don't wait. I don't hesitate. I rush toward the back porch and grab one of Dale's heavy overcoats and my boots, pulling them on.

"Piper, you can't go out there," Sophie says, coming to the porch. "It's a whiteout now. You won't be able to see anything anyway. It'll have to wait until the snow lets up. He'll be okay, Piper."

But she's not confident and neither am I.

And then . . . I hear Nugget crying in the distance.

A faint bleat, carried to us on the wind.

I leap from the porch like a shot, chasing the sound of his little voice. Behind me, I can hear Sophie and Lane calling for me, but I can't stop.

I can't.

I can't let Marina lose Nugget too.

First Cedric, then Nugget. It would crush her.

And I won't let it happen.

I barge into the storm amid the swirling snow.

The wind whips at my face, freezing my nose. I didn't grab a scarf. I didn't take the time.

I fight against the wind, using all of my weight to push on.

Again, I hear Nugget.

"Nugget!" I call. "Nugget!"

I hope that he hears me and comes to the sound of my voice. But I can't see a thing. I can't see more than a foot in front of me, and the snow is closing in.

I've been foolish, I realize with a start. I've let my heart make a bad decision.

It would crush Marina if something happens to Nugget, but if something happens to *me* instead . . .

I swallow hard and push on, face-first, into the black, swirling night.

It's faint at first, the buzzing in my pocket.

It takes me a moment to realize what it is.

It's the compass spinning.

I shove my hand in my pocket and feel the hand moving, fast, faster, faster, until I almost feel that I'm moving at the same speed. The wind howls loud, louder, and I'm rushing into the whiteout, into the snow, and then suddenly . . . all is white and still.

CHAPTER TWENTY-FOUR

I don't know how long I'm in the snowbank.

All I know is that everything is quiet and still, a far cry from the noisy oblivion that I'd just been in.

I lie motionless for a moment, and I put my hand on the compass.

It's not moving.

But my heart is beating.

I'm alive.

I sit up, pushing at the snow that is on me and clawing my way upward. Someone grabs my hand and pulls me through the snow.

"Piper, thank God," a voice says. I expect it to be Lane.

It's not.

It's Dan.

Old Dan.

The Dan from my time, not the young Dan who I'd just left at the lodge.

"Dan?" I ask. His grizzled beard and gray hair curl outside

of his stocking cap, and how is this happening? So sudden, so abrupt?

"Piper, I've been looking for you for hours. I thought you were dead."

I stare at him, my heart sinking.

"I'm not," I say needlessly.

"Let's get you home," he says, pulling me to the snowmobile.

The snowmobile.

I'm home.

And Lane is not.

"Oh, no," I say tearfully, as I climb on behind Dan. His frail body is cold and worn. He's been out for hours searching for me in the cold. And Lane isn't here.

Lane is in 1944.

I hold on woodenly as Dan drives us home, as we fly atop the snow toward Great Expectations.

"Did you find the Nortons?" I ask him as he cuts the engine and we climb off.

He looks at me strangely. "The Nortons?"

"The Norton hunting party. The one I was out searching for in the first place?"

Dan shakes his head. "Piper, why would the Norton women be here hunting? They're here for their yearly girls' trip, though. Mrs. Norton and her daughter-in-law are currently having a massage."

The Norton *women*?

Dan helps me into the lodge, and when we walk inside, my mouth falls open.

It's grand.

The fireplace is the same, huge and rugged. The wing-backs are still there. But the rest is different. It's . . .

"A spa," I say out loud. I inhale the eucalyptus diffusing in the air and absorb the quiet melodic tones being filtered through speakers. "The lodge is a spa."

Dan stares at me, looking increasingly concerned.

"Ellen!" he calls. "Shelly!"

The two women come running and are mothering me before I even know it.

"Piper, oh my God. I don't know what you were thinking, rushing out into the snow, but we've been worried sick," Shelly lectures me.

I look around at the lodge as they guide me upstairs to the master bedroom—Dale and Sophie's bedroom. My gran's bedroom.

I hadn't moved her things yet, so I'm surprised when they usher me in and all of my things are here. It looks as though I've always lived in this room. It's lovely, and it's foreign.

"I don't understand," I say limply, as I sit on the bed.

A scant few moments ago, I'd left this lodge, filled with people I love, and now I'm back and they're gone. They've been gone for decades, and I'll never see them again.

"Piper, calm down," Shelly demands as she strips off my clothes, in much the way I'd done for Marina earlier. "Lay down. Cooperate, woman."

I lie back and she peels off my wet pants.

"What in the world are you wearing?" she grumbles. "A burlap sack?"

"Shelly, I wasn't here. I was there," I babble.

"You're upset," she says. "You were lost in the snow. Of course you're upset. We need to warm you up. Do you think you want to go sit in the spring for a bit? You're chilled to the bone."

That gives me pause.

"You know about the spring?" I stare at her.

She stares back.

"Yes . . ." She studies me. "We all know about the spring, Piper. It's what our business revolves around."

"Not hunting?" I ask.

She wrinkles her brow. "No. Piper, should I call a doctor?"

I shake my head. "No. I'm . . . just . . . disoriented."

"You sure are," she agrees. "Ellen, can you get Piper a hot toddy?"

"No, thank you," I say quickly. "I just want to sit here for a minute, if you don't mind. In fact, maybe I need to rest for a bit. I'll take a hot shower and rest."

Shelly looks at me dubiously. "You sure?"

"I'm sure," I tell her. I can't let her know how upset I am, how confused, how upside down.

I've been ripped through time again.

Or have I? Has all of this been real?

I get up and poke around. Then something occurs to me.

I open the closet, push back the clothing, and there is the door.

My breath freezes on my lips as I turn the knob.

It's just as I left it in 1944.

Dale's desk, his drawings, his chair. Everything is here. I sit and rifle through his things, and find some of my gran's as well. She'd found this room, apparently. And she'd used it as her own.

I'm stunned as I find the beautiful drawings . . . of Marina, of the boarders, of Lane.

In one drawing, his face is so real, so detailed, that it takes my breath away. I trace the lines of his jaw, wishing with everything I am that I could touch him now.

It was real.

It had to be.

But that doesn't help me now. I'm here, and they aren't.

I'm all alone once again.

An orphan.

I see a coral-colored journal poking from the edge of the desk. Curious, I lift it up and flip through the pages.

It's Gran's.

She talks of life after Cedric died, of how Dan and Oliver stayed on, of how she'd eventually married Oliver. How they'd given Dan a job, and he'd stayed.

She talks of her friend Piper, and how she'd disappeared into the snow and had never been seen again.

She doesn't mention Lane.

Not a word.

How could she let me down like that?

Later, she talks of how she'd suggested the name Piper when I was born. How my parents had loved it.

How it suited me like it was made for me all along.

Tears well, the lump forms. My life has changed.

Things from 1944 changed, and changed the course of my life.

I stand up and leave the room, vowing to explore it another day. I can only take so much today.

My heart feels broken as I get dressed in my regular clothes, pulling something from the closet. I make my way downstairs, just in time to see Dan leading a small group of people through the great room.

I pause, curious.

"To your right, you'll see the formidable fireplace," he says. "Eberdale McCauley Senior built that fireplace with his own hands, before he passed this lodge to his son, Eberdale. Eberdale Junior is the visionary behind Great Expectations as we know it today."

He leads them farther into the room.

"If you look up at the photo on the mantel, you'll see Dale, his wife, Sophie, and their daughter, Marina. Marina ran this lodge until her death recently."

I gaze at the photo, and I want to cry from relief at seeing their faces. It's a vintage photo, one of the old-time pictures that make people not seem real . . . but they were real. I was with them this morning.

Dan continues his tour. "Marina's granddaughter, Piper, has taken over now. Dale is the one, however, who discovered the hot spring that runs beneath the ground here. People from all over the world, just like yourselves, come here to soak in the natural mineral water, to sleep in one of the clear glass huts that we have on the property, where you can see the northern lights from your bed. And, of course, don't forget the reindeer herd and the dogsled tours."

He gestures to the sign over the door, GREAT EXPECTATIONS DAY SPA AND LODGE, with a reindeer head as the logo.

I do a double take.

Our logo is a reindeer?

"Now, folks, if you'll follow me, I have a particularly funny story."

I follow with the group, standing in the back, and Dan stops, showing everyone a large bearskin rug spread out on the floor.

"This bear was the last animal ever killed at Great Expectations," he announces. "Marina used to tell this story to all of our visitors, and now it has fallen to me. Because she'd haunt me to my grave if I let the story die."

He pauses for effect, then continues.

"This grizzly came out of hibernation one nasty winter in 1944," he says. "It was near the end of the war, and the McCauley family had taken in boarders to help make ends meet. Meat was getting low that year, and they weren't able to hunt anything for Christmas dinner.

"This bear was hungry and stalked the family for a good week, eyeing the reindeer herd, the family members, anything it could get its paws on. But Marina McCauley wasn't going to stand for that.

"Christmas Day 1944, this beast showed up on their porch, raging and roaring and ready to eat. Marina McCauley, having just found out that her fiancé was killed in the war, wasn't about to let something happen to another of her family members. So the story goes, she picked up a shotgun, went outside, and faced it down.

"As you can see, this bear weighed close to two thousand pounds," he says.

I interject, "It was closer to twelve hundred."

Dan stares at me. "Your gran always said two thousand."

"Yes, but Marina was always one to exaggerate."

Dan glances at me.

"Gran," I amend.

"Either way, this bear was symbolic," Dan says. "Because Eberdale McCauley declared that the only killing henceforth would be for eating or self-protection, never for sport. He saw firsthand that animals, even apex predators, are just trying to survive. He dedicated the rest of his life to showing the Alaskan nature-scape to tourists."

My heart fills to the brim.

Dale did it. *He did it.*

His gentle spirit found peace.

"Do you know what happened to the boarders?" I ask Dan.

He glances at me. "That's an excellent question, Piper. You are looking at one of them. The McCauleys took me in as one of their own, and I've never left. Marina married another boarder. The others all eventually found their own families, although everyone stayed in touch for the rest of their days. Here in Alaska, folks, we know our neighbors, and everyone sticks together."

He ushers the guests through the great room and into the dining room, where trays of champagne are waiting.

"Enjoy the refreshments," he tells them. "As you get a glass of champagne, notice the deep gouges on that table. Eberdale McCauley built that table from the original barn doors . . . after that very bear we were just speaking about hemmed a group of the family and boarders in, and tried to break into the barn. They lived to tell the tale, and he created this table to preserve the memory of how heroic his daughter was that day."

The guests murmur their appreciation as Dan continues, "Shelly will be along momentarily to show you to your rooms. You'll want to freshen up. It is a longtime tradition here at Great Expectations to have a Friday-night festivity. There will be refreshments, music, dancing, and chatting. We'll see you this evening."

Dan joins me a few minutes later.

"How do you feel?" he asks, staring at me in concern. "You don't look right, Piper."

"I'm okay. I'm just confused. Everything feels off."

"You were lost in the snow," he says understandingly. "Sometimes it's hard to tell which way is even up when that happens. You're lucky to be alive, Piper. You gave us a scare."

"If I wasn't hunting for the Nortons, what was I doing outside?"

I look at this man who has known me my entire life and wait for answers.

He shakes his head. "Honestly, we don't know."

I stare at him, not knowing how to explain it.

"Truth be told, Dan, I haven't felt right since my gran died. I think maybe I just need to rest."

"You've been burning the candle at both ends, for sure," he agrees. "Tryin' to prove that you're worthy of running this place. But Piper, we all know you are. Your gran was so proud of you. And your parents would be too."

"Dan, how did my parents die?" I ask him.

He glances at me again.

"Did you hit your head?" he asks.

"I'm just checking," I tell him.

"They died in a plane crash, flying tourists here."

My heart sinks, even though I had a feeling. They still died. Everything happens the way it's meant to happen.

"That's what I thought," I say limply. "Was it because of ice on the wings?"

"Piper, you know better than that. Your gran would've had their hides. You know she lectured everyone not to fly without deicers. They took off and lost radio contact. Faulty equipment. There wasn't a thing to be done."

At least that much changed. Maybe Gran didn't live her life filled with guilt and regret.

"Was Gran happy when she died?" I ask.

"Yes," he says simply. "She'd never been happier. You were going to take the reins from her, and she was going to live out her life wandering the meadows picking wildflowers in the summer."

"Really?"

He nods. "Really. You know, that envelope she left for you is still on her desk."

"It is?"

I think of it, of the letter she'd left me, and the compass.

"Yes. It's waiting for you to open it."

"Maybe I'll do that today," I tell him.

"I think she'd like that."

"Thank you for being such a loyal friend to her, Dan."

"It's nothing she didn't do for me over the years, many times over."

I leave him with the tourists, and I make my way to Gran's study. It's just as I remember it.

The only difference is, the letter on the top hasn't been opened yet.

It has *Pippie* scrawled on the envelope. And it sits with a small box.

I open the letter with shaking fingers.

Dear Pippie,

On a snowy morning, many years ago, a beautiful girl told me a fantastic story.

You know the story, though, don't you?

It was true—every word, including the part where I'd survive the pain. I did survive it. And I built a lovely life, one that involved a beautiful granddaughter who I cherish more than anything in the world.

Everything about you makes me proud, Piper. You're beautiful (you get your looks from me), smart, and strong. I'd like to think that you're my legacy, and everything good in me lives on in you. That's how family works, though, isn't it?

You saved me when my world fell apart. When your parents died, you gave me a reason to live. You showed me that love is always worth it, even when it hurts. You were my moral compass . . . my divining rod, reminding me that love is worth risk.

It's time to return this necklace to you. Wear it, and think of me. Remember the moments when we laughed together, and the moments when we cried, and the moments when we lived through it all.

   And know this . . . you'll see me again. Someday. I promise.

                              Love always,
                              Gran

Tears stream down my face, and my fingers shake so much I can barely open the locket. I know, of course, the picture that waits inside. It's of Marina and me, laughing like two sisters. The very locket I'd given her just this morning, but also, somehow, seventy-eight years ago.

"I didn't get to say goodbye," I murmur.

Shelly comes in and rubs my arm.

"You didn't have to, babe. She knew how you felt. That's one thing about this family. You always make sure everyone knows how you feel. Trust me, she knew."

"Can you fasten this?" I ask her, and she lifts the locket over my head and snaps the fastener. The locket nestles under my shirt, and I know I'll probably never take it off.

"It's lovely," Shelly tells me. I nod.

"It is."

"Can you come get something to eat? You're worrying Ellen, and you know she shows her love with food. She's already got a plate dished up for you."

"I'm not hungry—" I start, but Shelly is already shaking her head.

Obediently, I follow her to the kitchen, where I pull up a

stool and pretend to eat the wild rice, shaved grass-fed beef, and sautéed mushrooms.

"That's a girl," Ellen says encouragingly, watching me take a few bites. "You're peaky."

"I'm just tired," I protest.

Because I just traveled almost eighty years.

I push the food around on my plate, not wanting to waste it, but my grief makes everything taste like wood.

I had a fiancé, and I had to leave him.

No one knows.

I'll have to grieve him alone.

I'm rinsing off my plate and putting it into one of the industrial-sized dishwashers when I hear a ruckus at the door.

Curious, I head out of the kitchen and stop dead in my tracks.

The door is wide open, and Lane is filling it up, with Nugget in his arms.

My mouth falls open, and I shake my head in disbelief, but he's still there.

"Pip?" he says uncertainly. His face is handsome, his eyes are confused, but he's here.

He's here.

Nugget jumps out of his arms and careens toward me, his legs splayed, his nose fuzzy. I rub it for a scant moment before I careen myself . . . right into Lane's arms.

"How is this possible?" I murmur against his lips.

"I followed you to find Nugget in the storm. I found him, and then all of a sudden . . . I'm here." He pauses. "I want to ask where I am," Lane says hesitantly. "But I know where I am. It's just . . . not right."

I step back and remember how I'd felt when I first arrived in 1944. I'd been confused and scared and all alone.

"What in the dickens?" Dan demands, and when I turn, I see his face as he realizes who Lane is. And then he peers more closely at me . . . remembering the night from so many years ago, when he'd come to tell Marina that her fiancé had died.

I was there.

And I'm also here.

His face is stricken.

Lane's is too.

"You were telling the truth," Lane says limply. "It was all true."

I hold out my hand.

"I've got some explaining to do," I say simply, and I sit them down in front of the fire, in the wing-back chairs my great-granddad made by hand, and I tell them the fantastical story of how I found myself by coming home.

EPILOGUE

Two years later

Lane and I lie together in one of the glass-domed rooms that allow our guests to watch the heavens unfold as they rest.

My head rests in the crook of his arm, and I've never felt as comfortable in my life as I do right now.

"Pip?" my husband asks softly, brushing the hair out of my eyes.

"Mm-hmm," I answer without actually answering.

"Thank you for my son."

I smile, thinking of our infant son, sleeping by the fire, while Shelly watches him for a few hours.

"You're welcome."

"Do you think anyone will tease him for his name?"

"McCauley? Why would they? It's a family name."

"I know. But it's a mouthful."

"Lane, you aren't used to this time yet. We have weird things here and weird names. We have freeze-dried ice cream and moving walkways."

"I know. But if anyone ever gives him a hard time, he's allowed to smack them right in the kisser."

"We don't say that here," I tell him. "And violence is frowned upon."

"Defending yourself isn't violence."

"He won't get teased," I tell him. "His parents own this mountain."

"I don't want him to get uppity either, though."

"You worry a lot. Someone told me once not to borrow trouble. You should listen to him."

I snuggle into his chest, where his heart beats strong and true.

"Do you ever wonder why this happened to us?" Lane asks. "I mean, why us? Why do we get to defy nature in order to be happy?"

"I don't know. I don't want to question it. I think maybe my gran somehow arranged it. For me to be happy. And so I'd find the meaning of family."

"If anyone could, it would be Marina," he agrees.

"Did I tell you . . . a new baby reindeer was born today? I named him Dickens," I tell him. "Because Marina and Sophie always said *What in the dickens?* It seemed apropos."

He laughs. "I assume Nugget is showing him the ropes?"

"We can hope."

Nugget had become a fan favorite, and, in fact, we have a reindeer cam streaming live on our website, for the world to watch his antics. He's known far and wide, and has his own merchandise to prove it.

"Well, if Dickens walks in Nugget's hoofprints, we'll have another star on our hands."

"When is Shelly's bachelorette party again?" Lane asks.

"Next weekend. It's all planned out."

"I can't believe the day has finally come." He sighs. "Thank God."

When Lane had first arrived, Shelly had drooled, just as I'd figured she would. Then she'd begged for one of her very own. Since we couldn't figure out how to time travel to make that happen, she'd settled for finding a tourist who puts up with her attitude. And breaking house rules in the process.

"She knew not to date a guest," I grumble.

"Don't begrudge her happiness," Lane says with a chuckle. "She deserves to be happy too."

"Yes, she does," I agree.

"The great room is going to look beautiful for the wedding," I say. "Shelly is going to bankrupt herself buying the flowers. Speaking of Shel, she's probably itching to shower and go to bed. We should get back."

I sit up and straighten my hair.

Looking around at the cozy dome, I almost can't believe how my life has turned out. It's beyond comprehension.

I help Lane to his feet, and together, we stroll down the path to the lodge.

I point at the barn door, one that isn't original to the barn.

"Remember that night?"

"How could I forget it? I single-handedly held that bear off you."

"Oh, geez. Marina isn't the only one in this family prone to exaggeration. You weren't the only one there that night, mister."

"I think that's the night you fell in love with me," he says with a wink.

"Don't let this go to your head, but I fell in love with you the first night I met you. I just didn't know it until later."

"Really? Tell me more," he urges cockily.

I roll my eyes. "I've told you this before. I fell in love with you on first sight just like Dale fell in love with Soph."

We stop at the corral behind the barn, and we watch Dickens wobble around sniffing at everything. I laugh as he careens into our legs, just like Nugget used to.

"There's hope for you yet," I tell him, rubbing his fuzzy nose.

Nugget tugs at my shirt with his teeth. "Oh, you." I pat his neck. "You can share a little attention with the new baby."

He nickers lightly at me, and I rub his nose too.

"I'll bring you a treat tomorrow."

"And break your own rule?" Lane lifts an eyebrow and I look at the sign.

PLEASE DO NOT FEED NUGGET. HE'S VERY WELL-FED, DESPITE WHAT HE MAY TELL YOU.

I giggle.

"We have a really good life," I tell my husband. He nods.

"Yes, we do. I was thinking . . . maybe tomorrow we could take McCauley for his first plane ride."

"Oh?" I lift an eyebrow. Ever since I'd given Lane flying lessons last year, it's all he's wanted to do. He's conquered his fear of heights, and now the world is his oyster. "Well, you never have to ask me twice to go flying."

Lane grabs my hand, and we wander into the lodge, where Shelly is patting our infant son's back, as he sleeps against her shoulder.

"When Judd and I have our first baby, it's going to be as cute as this one, or I'm sending it back," she announces.

"That's not quite how it works, but okay. Let me know how that works out for you."

I reach down and gently take the baby from her arms.

"Thank you for watching him, Shel. Lane and I needed some alone time."

"I don't want to know the details," she says, then pauses. "Well, maybe I do. No, I don't."

"There's no details to tell, weirdo. We just wanted to rest. A newborn is a lot of work."

"Uh-huh, well, I hope you 'rested,'" she says, shaping air quotes with her fingers.

"We did," I assure her. "And now, I'm going to rest again. Sleep while the baby sleeps. That's what they always say."

"I'll take him up," Lane says, and he gently takes the baby from me. He disappears upstairs, and Shelly heads for the door.

"My dress arrives tomorrow," she says. "If I don't fit in it, I'll kill myself."

"You'll fit in it," I promise. "You look fantastic."

"Says the woman who is almost down to her pre-baby weight."

I shrug. "I'm not focusing on it. I'm just focusing on being happy, and heathy, and enjoying the baby."

"You make me sick," Shelly announces. "But I love you."

She hugs me and skips out, closing the door behind her.

I start to head upstairs, but instead, I sit in a wing-back chair for a moment, in front of the fire. They haven't gotten any more comfortable, but by God, I fall asleep in one at least four times a week.

Tonight, I settle in, put my feet up, and close my eyes.

In my mind's eye, I see everyone I love bustling around the table, passing homemade food, and chatting for hours.

Marina, Sophie, Dale, Charlie, Albie, Edward, Joe. Dan. William. Oliver.

Our stories are woven together by ribbons that bind us in love.

That love is our history.

That love is our future.

The warmth from the fire makes me feel cozy, and I think of how many times Dale had fallen asleep in this very chair.

"Good night," I whisper, to no one in particular, yet also everyone. Their spirit is here. Their energy is here. Their love is here. It surrounds me every day as I add to our family in this very home.

A blanket is pulled over me, and Lane kisses my forehead.

"I'll see you when you come up," he whispers. "Take your time."

He leaves me here, to rest and to recharge, in the chair my great-grandfather built, in the house my great-great-grandfather built, in the life that *I* built.

I drift to sleep, confident that tomorrow and all the tomorrows after that will bring love and pain and grief and joy. All the things that make up a life.

I drift to sleep with a smile on my lips, as my great-grandparents and Marina stare down at me from the mantel, with warmth in their eyes and love in their hearts.

This is home.

Now and forever.

ACKNOWLEDGMENTS

My grandparents aren't here any longer for me to thank, but I won't let that tiny obstacle stop me. They shaped a huge part of who I am, and I'll be eternally grateful for it.

They say I'm very like my grandma Helen. I hope it's true—she was a force to be reckoned with. During the war, she worked at the Cessna plant and was a real-life Rosie the Riveter. She once told me a woman good at her job could spit rivets, chew gum, and hold a conversation at the same time.

Once the war ended and my granddad came home, they got married and lived a life filled with helping the community, feeding those in need, and volunteering their time to those who needed it. My grandma showed her love for you by feeding you.

In 1944, cooking was greatly influenced by what was available (and what was not, given wartime rationing). Our grandparents' (or great-grandparents) generation learned to enjoy the simple things in life, and many of us still remember eating these things with them when we were children.

The effects of the war, and of the Depression before that

(a decade earlier), influenced my grandparents' generation in every aspect of their lives.

Many of them never allowed their freezers to go empty, if they could possibly help it, for the rest of their lives.

The things we take for granted, they could never have imagined.

A tiny computer in our pocket, which also takes pictures and connects us to anyone around the world, day or night?

Uber Eats? Meals delivered to our door . . .

Fireplaces that turn on with the flip of a switch . . .

Cars that don't use gas and can park by themselves . . .

Online shopping . . .

FaceTime? Video chatting? Think of the ways they impact our lives. For instance, my son in the Marines . . . I can Face-Time with him when he has a cell signal. They could never have dreamed of such a thing in 1944.

At the same time, while we have made so much progress in many areas of our lives, there are some ways that life in the 1940s was simply better.

People were undistracted by the technology in their pockets. They interacted much more, without the constant, isolating entertainment available on our cell phones. While they didn't have fast food or food on demand, their food was wholesome and eaten together around family dinner tables. They weren't spoiled yet by the instant gratification of the internet. Instead, they made do with what they had, and they were thankful for it.

My grandparents' generation is frequently referred to as the Greatest Generation.

Let's not allow their memories to die with them. Repeat their stories to your children, who will repeat them to theirs.

If we do that, their legacy will live on forever.

We are that legacy.

I'd like to thank them for everything they did to shape who we are.

For this book, I'd also like to thank:

My amazing agent, Kevan. You are the best, and you know it.

My editor, Tessa. Your finesse and eye for great copy astounds me.

My squad. You know who you are. I love you, I appreciate you, I would be nothing without you.

And to YOU. The reader who is reading this now—you've chosen to trust me with your time. I hope you consider it well spent. Thank you for reading this story . . . I hope Wander, Alaska, and the McCauley crew has made your heart feel warm, and your love for Christmas and your heritage swell.

The family we were born with, and the families we create . . . those are our legacies. Our lives eventually pass away, but the love we create and the lives we build . . . those memories last forever.

ALSO BY
COURTNEY COLE

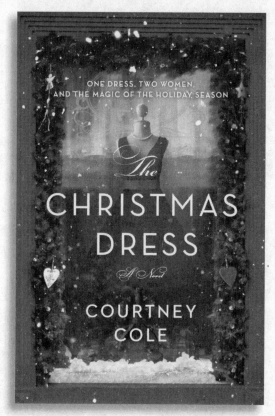

"A very heartwarming, touching story about the magic of true love, family, and friendship."

—HARLEQUIN JUNKIE